For A Glimpse Beyond the Terminus
Jordan R. Anderson

If you like what you read, or even if you hate it, please consider reviewing this book on Goodreads, Amazon or wherever you purchased it from.
Every review counts.

jordanandersonfiction.com
jordan@jordanandersonfiction.com
Twitter: @JAndersFiction

Cover art is "Lonely Sailor" by Sandeep Karunakaran, licensed in 2017 for use by Jordan R. Anderson.
Cover design by ebooklaunch.com

ISBN: 0-9983541-3-9
ISBN-13: 978-0-9983541-3-2

Foreword

A lot can happen in a year's time. Personally, I hate fluffed-up introductions and forewords, so I won't go into too much detail here. You've come for the fiction, so I'm just going to say that this last year, since the release of my first book, has been a hell of a ride for my imagination and my writing. I've read some great books and some not so great books. I've had some good beer and some not so good beer. I've worked on some great story ideas and some not so great story ideas. I've laughed. I've cried. Most importantly, I've continued my creative endeavor of writing stories that (hopefully) will live beyond the inevitable decay of my bones.

As was necessary with the first book, I have some people to thank for their contributions to this second collection of stories, whether through their imaginations, criticisms or general support. As they say, no man is an island.

To my writers group (Lily, Michael, Katie, Val, Quinn, Matt, Nikki, Nate, Lindsey), I'm sorry I was so damned busy this year. I appreciate the critiques in the initial stages of these stories, nonetheless, and I miss you guys. Gratitude goes to my parents for their support in everything I do. To Chris Coleman, Matt Porter, Chris Padin, Corey Stephenson, Brett Dent, Anne O'Malley, Steve Kempf and Scott DeLack, thank you for being my closest friends, for entertaining my talks of conspiracy theories, death metal and my random story ideas.

Thank you, Jennifer, for being a wonderful partner and an excellent editor.

Most importantly, some major thanks go to you, the reader, for your interest in these stories. I don't know if I'll ever actually consider myself a "writer" but I do know that I have plots and characters and scenes that I want to share with the world. I don't pretend to be better than anyone else at this, but I write because I don't know what else to do with the ideas rolling around in my skull. That all being said, I sincerely hope you enjoy these stories.

Jordan R. Anderson

"No, no. Listen, listen. He said that if they dug his father's body up, it would be gone. They planted a seed over his grave. The seed became a tree. Moses said his father became a part of that tree. He grew into the wood, into the bloom. And when a sparrow ate the tree's fruit, his father flew with the birds. He said... Death was his father's road to awe. That's what he called it. The road to awe."

—Izzi, *The Fountain* (2006)

"We have such sights to show you."
—*Hellraiser* (1987)

For A Glimpse Beyond the Terminus

Jordan R. Anderson

For Jennifer
You are so much more than I ever thought I deserved.

As You Wade into the River of Vermin

...Do not falter. Do not hesitate. These pestilent swarms hurtling over the banks of that dried river bed upon which you've decided to tread, they are that which make up His senses. This snaking nervous system, quivering before you, gathers stimuli and speaks in waves, carrying messages between the bars of the drainage grate that sits directly ahead of you like a mouth, down into the sewers to His place of infernal operation. Even now, as you stand so seemingly safe just outside this current of blight, in a cold night of uncertainty, He can taste your odor through the pathways that lead down to His very abode. From deep inside the bowels of those petulant depths, He drinks the very air around himself for traces of data, for information given over so willingly by that stinking fright that emits from you right this moment. It is not only the smell that gives you away. No, He *feels* it, and desires the fear, like an ache in the pit of his boiling stomach, a hunger crying out for a very specific type of sustenance. So, silence your chattering teeth, make still your shaking limbs and whatever you do, do *not* falter.

Once you've slipped between those bars, you'll be welcomed by a wave of putrid warmth, as if the tunnel ahead were the throat of some great beast with a breath of its own. When you've found your footing in that stench, hold your mind from wandering back to the outside world, to that sameness from which you've strayed so far on this curious night, a night that originally seemed like it would play out just as any other but, as is now very apparent, rose from the cradle of dusk with other plans to weave throughout its creeping darkness.

Keep your mind present as the shivering pests cover your feet and shins. They go about deeds unknown to you but not unguided. No, He is the keeper of these things, the One that drives them with an evolved hive-sentience they've never known before. And you will meet this overlord of fur and teeth. Yet, do not let this sway your resolve. Do not turn for fear of these waves of thralls or the impending contact with the Most High. Keep your thoughts on what lay beyond the terror that threatens to unanimate you. Remember, *remember*, the reasons you drifted from that external life, why you brought yourself here to begin with. Try again to hear that cosmic music that hexed and coaxed you into coming to this place.

Do not cast your gaze into the strange things writhing over the sewer walls as you lose sight of the entrance behind you. When your flashlight turns on and illuminates the shifting and biting rodents, the tide of tails, fur and teeth, hold steadfast as if your life depends on it, because now it does.

Make no mistake in understanding the costs of what you seek.

Continue on. Do not glance at the mounds and shapes that birth from the river of blight through which you tremble. Though their shapes seem human in stature as they rise, do not gaze into the bizarre white globules that open and peer out from within those transmorphing heaps. *They* are the eyes of the King. *They* are His all-seeing retina, reporting back through a widespread network of synapses that wiggle through every crevice and crack in this underground necropolis, down further and further, finally falling through the core of His verminous being. Through them, He gazes at you even now. Avoid staring into those alien oculi peering out from the indiscriminate movement, and avoid stumbling into the rats skittering about the raised path leading ahead of you. If you are able to do this, the unlit tunnel ahead may just open up for your flashlight like an orifice, might spread itself out for the luminous beam like a lover willing.

Inside of a wide expansive chamber is where you will then find yourself. In this chamber, even with the flashlight, your vision will be dampened by the stark fiber of that darkness surrounding you, seeming to thickly absorb any light falling upon or into it. The ever-present din of scurrying claws will still be the funereal dirge whispering from behind you, underneath you, above you, the background of your entire reality. Beyond this, though, once your ears have grown accustomed to the multitudes and their gibbering, you may hear other deeds of flesh being done. You may hear decrepit chains swinging and smacking wetly against each other from the dark high above you. If you're lucky, you'll hear what sounds like a kind of corpulent slick churning mixed with the stifled moans of someone else, a follower not unlike yourself, suffering a luscious torture beyond your comprehension, a torture that you may come to know in time.

From here, continue forward, regardless of what your instincts tell you, for, by then, you will have already reached the point of no return. The creeping mass will have closed behind you like a swallowing throat. There will be no going back.

You will come upon, and be compelled to cross, what appears to be a low stone pathway. Murky turd-laden sewer water will lap against the rough concrete to either side of you. Remain staring into that poorly lit black ahead of you, though, and continue on your way. Do not look into the faces that float just under the surface of those wretched gutters at your sides, for the eyes you would see atop those mutated craniums are His eyes and His eyes are the putrid products of the void machine, wretched enough to hypnotize and stop, all together, even the most valiant of hearts.

Waiting at the end of this chamber, open and gaping, will be another tunnel, another of this city's orifices few humans, save for its long-dead architects and the prospective acolytes before you, have ever laid eyes upon. It will appear in your flashlight's uncertain lumens like a giant gaping eye socket, without an eyeball, yet still staring at you with an impossible intent. The arching walls of the tunnel will not be covered in moving things as was the last. Instead, it will seem made of concrete so dark that its insides will almost cease to exist beyond a rough blackness that your light cannot penetrate. You will enter this hole because it will be your only hope of returning home. You will know this as well as any of us did.

The grotesque sludge that drips from between each and every brick around you will appear almost ethereal, transmogrifying the

3

stone it smears, toying with its base materia and making it appear instead like glass, as if waiting just beyond those curved walls was an endless abyss, unknown leagues deep and dark. Perhaps in that darkness will be harbored unspeakable things, beings that have come to watch you, have crowded together to wait for you on the other side.

The deeper you tread, the muggier it will become. You will begin to taste the air more than you thought possible, and the more visceral those spores floating in the beam of your flashlight will taste on your tongue and in your sinuses. It is at this point that you will only just begin to truly fathom the abomination waiting for you a bit further on. His overpowering stench will ride the particulates entering into your nose and you will smell the miasma that radiates from his dripping flesh. I know this, I know *all* of this, because I tasted those very spores when it was my time to experience the revelation that the Lord of these sewers had to offer, when *I* was the one smelling that fungal excretion emitting from the burbling mounds rising around me, the rats shaping themselves into unnatural things as if formed by my God's hands using a clay of rodents, shit and darkness.

There is no other way to describe what will be gained from an exploration of these places beneath the very streets you've walked on your whole adult life. Simply, it is revelation that I did find. It is revelation you will find, too.

So, again… you *must* move forward.

This black tunnel of obscurity will snake to and fro. Follow it further into the sewer's bowels. Heed not the shuffling and slithering sounds that emit from the other side of those window-like walls that encase you. Heed not but, instead, pay close attention as you come eventually to what appears to be a wall in the middle of the tunnel, as if this one tunnel simply failed to fully realize the visions of its original architects and was bricked up in some last effort of rushed masonry. Your flashlight will reveal this strange seemingly misplaced ending and, if you touch the cold stone, you will feel its concreteness and a seemingly dead end to your journey. It is then, while the sensory of that coarseness rides through your fingertips, that you will hear that scuffling and sliding from outside the walls around you, and you will hear these noises move to the inside of the tunnel behind you, something splashing down onto the wet stone. That's right: this newly birthed *it* will know you're there and therefore *He* will know you're there, and both slave and master will be more certain of your mortality than ever prior. You'll sense the thousands of tongues that wait to taste you, and the biting blackness that undulates to swallow. In that moment of terror and anticipation, you must do that which is furthest from your mind:

You must turn your flashlight off.

It is only then that the path out of this madness and into the light ahead will be revealed.

If you follow my instruction and thwart His appendage that follows, if you've prevented it from gnawing and chewing into you while you gaze up at its deformity in the falsely secure beam of your flashlight, if you haven't refused to give in to your basest terror but, instead, switched off the only source of illumination you had, you will notice that the sounds of that pursuing *thing*, no matter how close it came, will dissipate almost instantly. Rather, the only sounds you will hear will be the dripping of water somewhere overhead, perhaps droplets of that goop falling from between a few bricks here and there. Do not search for light in this darkness that envelops you. Instead, close your eyes, find and steel your nerves, for what comes next will be your ultimate trial.

The space of blackness that once seemed so close in front of you, that dead end of sodden brick, will now feel distant, for a slight draft may tug at your jacket or lightly play with the hairs along your nape. When enough time has passed, and you've tempered your frightful heartbeat, you will begin to hear what sounds like a voice humming in the distance ahead. Impossibly clear from beyond the space in which you thought you remembered the wall at the end of the tunnel being, this voice will wash over you like an elegant chant, something one might encounter in a mountaintop monastery, except that this will be more strained, filled with anguish rather than serenity, and it will be just as beautiful as anything sung by the hopeful and the loved. Its source will groan a singular note, and how long that note will last for you I cannot say, but you must continue to listen. Listen, keeping your eyes shut, until a slight lilt occurs in its seemingly perpetual tone. It will shift from that flat A to its gimped 5th, a haunting D sharp. *Only* when that happens may you open your eyes. Even a moment before and you will be devoured whole.

In this black distance ahead of you, after your eyelids have retreated, you may see a glow, hardly visible but still existing. It will be of a red hue, the color of blood backlit by a burning flame. It will warble and flicker in that dark distance ahead and then it will be time for you to continue forward one last time, for your journey will almost be complete. When you're trembling steps have brought you to the end of this straightaway tunnel, when the sanguine color has filled all that you are and all that you know, it is then that you will step into that final chamber.

And there, sitting on His noxious throne in all His glory, will be the King of Rats. His seven arms will have already unfurled like the petals of a flower, anticipating your arrival into its presence with a furious and ravenous ecstasy. His gibbering mouths, wielding fleshy broken jaws and spindly needle teeth, will all cry in accord. They will speak a gravelly choking dialect you've never heard but, for a reason unknown to you, will be words you recognize. The language will slither ghoulishly from those flicking tongues and will produce meaning in your mind as you make sense of their broken talk. Your mental synapses will translate it as if you've heard that blithered yattering your entire life, as if they'd chanted those strange whispers from the states between dreams and reality in which you often rest. The voice of my God surpasses all barriers of speech and understanding, for He speaks using the base elements of consciousness: fear and suffering, anguish and defeat, perseverance and triumph, desire and love. While you are in this state of existential hysteria, you will hear His rotten mouths speak their utterings so clearly of events to come, of the end times, of horrors yet unburied and of deep caverns in the earth in which His kin and thralls alike await their final instructions. Then, you will notice the one separate head, protruding from the top of His lotus of gore and bone, continuing the hum that led you into this sinister light. This singular mouth will sing a melody that commands for the breaking of the planes over which humanity walks, of the world you've grown so comfortable in, the world within which you grind away, slaving at the whim of others while the great maw that is Death moves ever-stoically toward you, *at* you, stretched to swallow all that you've ever been and ever will be.

Lo this chamber of suffering and discovery. From amongst the corpses that line the walls surrounding you, all crucified as their price for the same visions He'll show you too, I will watch you with my death-burnt eyes. I will point to you with my ruined fingers, frostbitten black by the touch of the void, and I will add my voice to that song that welcomes you and curses you in hymns of filth and decay. I will share unto you the droning music that growls through the grey and dreary forests of the underworld and curdles up into those colorless skies that hang above the realm of the dead, where the great cosmic eye watches, so that you may see the end for what it truly is and so that, in some horrid augury, you may just catch sight of what awaits you after that final curtain drop.

Here, in this temple of dust and inevitability, we revel in the impending doom we cannot escape. Rather, we try to understand it.

Here, in the last hours of the last days, we pull back the veil and set our sights upon the machinery already in place, those stalking constructs fueled by the ancient combustion of blending the reality we know with the horrific foresight given to us by our long-forgotten connection to the infinite darkness, a darkness from whence we came and a darkness to which we all will surely return.

Here, we leave the world of the so-called living behind and delve into the abyss beyond the monotony of the flesh.

Here, we use the gifts of God to peer into the unknown that lay beyond Him, for if there is He, if there is one, then there must be the other, the opposite. What *is* must be bed fellows with what *isn't*, and we are here to turn our sights toward that emptiness on the other side of existence.

You've overcome your apathy, dragging it and yourself to this place of mortal cleansing, to be freed of the shackles you were bound into upon your blood-ridden birth. You've overcome what fear you thought you knew in order to now experience a horror much greater, more potent, but also to experience reverie and to experience hope and joy and loss, to see what comes next, to gain the knowledge. You are here for your baptism in pain and emotion, to bathe in the temporary sights into those other worlds offered here, far removed from the safety of your earthly indoctrination.

Remember why you've come all this way.

Stop. Think. *Remember*.

You have come to this den of death and divination for a

glimpse beyond the terminus.

Under and In and So It All Begins

A slit between the rubber seal of the window and the mount for the driver's side mirror, this space being only a couple millimeters wide, made a constant whistling sound of the night air while the car was in full motion. This was the first thing Michael Chamberlain had noticed about the "new" used sedan he'd just picked up this afternoon from Dela Luna Used Cars, and he could still hear that shrieking sound, even with the window rolled all the way up.

Olivia, officially his ex-wife as of four days ago, received the Mercedes in the divorce. He'd still been charged to make the monthly payment for her until it was fully purchased, though he'd no longer be driving it. In the wake of this unfortunate stipulation of the divorce agreement, and rather than give this new compact thing he'd now bought a thorough inspection, or maybe shopping around a bit for a different vehicle, the tension and stress of the last few months had culminated into some kind of unexplainable moment while he stood there on the black concrete of that used car lot, surrounded by gibbering salesmen he had no desire to listen to or understand. It was the first sedan he'd seen as he approached the central office. It wasn't pretty but it was cheap and the odometer only read seventy-thousand miles, which was good for an '02. After reluctantly agreeing to the additional insurance, boosting the total cost of the thing by two grand in the end, some autonomous version of Michael's self provided all the signatures and initials and account numbers required, all just so he get the fuck out of that irritating place. When it was finalized and done, and he was in six grand for a car not worth more than two, it was then that Michael realized he hadn't even taken the fucking thing for a test drive. It was no wonder those motherfuckers had been smiling the entire time. *We just got her day before yesterday*, he remembered one of them saying. *If we didn't absolutely guarantee our inspections, this one'd be too good to be true!*

Their relationship hadn't been the best in the recent past but he'd never expected Olivia to divorce him. It had all happened too quickly—the last few months, the divorce, this bullshit with the car. They'd only been separated three weeks. She'd already found someone else, too, turned out. While the shrieking little rip of rubber sang its terrible song at him through the glass of the driver's side window, the value of those six years they'd had together was dissected by Michael's incessant machinations, pondering why she'd been so eager to fill the gap, no pun intended, as quickly as she had. She hadn't touched him in months. He'd been too chicken-shit after the first dozen rejections to attempt any sort of intimacy with her in the meanwhile, and he'd forgotten already what her skin had felt like. It was strange considering that, so early on in their relationship, it used to be everything that had driven him, those sensations of their connection, of her pumping heartbeat and sweating flesh against his. He'd worshipped it. Memories of those times, of them together, seemed already to be losing their viscosity, slipping from his mental grasp. This slipping, upon reflection, left a heat in his gut and an anxiety in his breath at the thought of this being a symptom of his age finally catching up to him, the thought of some deterministic facet of life latching onto his will and pulling it down into the grime of knowing that he was getting old and the odds of finding someone to deal with his baggage were growing slimmer by the day.

In the rearview mirror, only the crown of the sun was still visible as it fell in the distance, having crept down through the firmament and into the western horizon, far away from the dark clouds hanging bloated directly above. The rain spattered against the windshield and the oncoming dusk opened like a wet salivating mouth.

Yet, the tinge of irritation he felt over how easily she'd

seemed to move on was based out of something like envy, maybe hypocrisy, too. He was willing to admit that about his own anger because, when he was being honest with himself, he knew their marriage had been going downhill for a while, had seen the disinterest in her eyes. He knew that having a flesh and blood body to touch, to taste and be inside of and to forget things with while this whole situation wrung itself out would've been real nice on quite a few of these more recent nights. He'd have taken someone who wasn't his wife if it meant he could feel the warmth of bodily contact again, just to be able to fall asleep with that feeling of someone holding him. Though he still felt spurned by this entire ordeal, he couldn't really blame her.

Life had changed so goddamned quickly…

The car jumped as it hit the pothole Michael usually avoided on the off-ramp for the exit to Twelfth Avenue, causing his attention to return to the present, if only momentarily. After turning left under the overpass onto Twelfth, he came to the crossing of Adams Street. The red stop light burned brightly in the all but black dusk and ropes of rainwater fell onto the hood of the car from the overpass above. A long hauler with a white trailer flew through the intersection with a mist of rainwater from the road billowing behind it, the glow of the few street lamps that had come on flaring orange in the spritz.

Olivia's new guy had accompanied her to the divorce paper signings. Michael had told the dude to fuck himself on the way out after they'd been done and signed what they'd needed to. Olivia'd been pissed, of course. He wasn't sure if it was easier this way, though, a childish attitude to spur a quick severing of all things past and now fading, or if he'd simply made things worse. It seemed weird how life had managed to push him where it had. In the reflecting back on what had transpired, with Olivia, with work, with his life, he didn't remember making many decisions. It had actually felt as if life had moved in a direction, never slowing whether he'd wanted it to or not, and that it had left him treading water amidst the choices of others, left behind in his own personal muted apathy and decay. Perhaps this apathy *was* his decision, the only will exacted upon the world through a surrendering into mundanity.

There was movement beyond the dewy glass of the passenger

side window, Michael's peripheral catching it through the downpour. When he leaned slightly to get a better look, wiping the condensation from the glass, a kid riding a skateboard, no older than fifteen, seemed to manifest out of the rainy evening. The boy rode up to the crosswalk, swerved and almost fell backward when he reached the dark street lamp under which Michael was idling. The kid caught his balance right when it counted but, immediately following, there was a *thud* against some part of the undercarriage of the car. Through the glass, the kid looked to Michael and mouthed *Sorry*, to which Michael responded with a nod and put the car into park.

The skateboard was underneath the car.

Michael fumbled for the passenger window switch, a habit well established from years of driving the Mercedes, but then remembered the second thing he'd noticed about this car only after having purchased it: the windows had to be rolled down manually. *Heathens*, he thought. He reached over and rolled the passenger one down, muttering under his breath. "Go ahead, kid," he called out and took his other hand off the wheel. "It's in park. I'm not goin' anywhere."

The kid nodded and smiled and moved toward the front quarter panel, leaning down out of sight. Michael rolled the window back up. Dark wet spots riddled the right side of the passenger seat from the raindrops that made it in. Though the vehicle was out of gear, he kept his foot on the brake, just to be sure, while he sat back and stared out of the cold glass windshield to the wet streets ahead. The last thing he needed was a flattened teenager on his conscience.

Forty-two... No kids... Divorced...

He let out a sigh.

Fuck it.

Headlights approached from behind. Michael's eyes flicked to the side mirrors, then to the rearview, and then he rolled down the window and waved for the other vehicle to move around while his other hand probed areas under the steering column to find the hazard lights. As the car passed, he found the button and clicked it over. The interior hazard indicators blinked on and off. Another set of headlights approached from behind, steering around Michael's own vehicle as it passed without additional instruction.

He leaned out the driver's window.

"Hey, kid. You get a hold of it, yet? Is it stuck?"

The sounds of distant late evening traffic seared over wet pavement, of cars turning down soaked alleyways and making U-turns in nearby parking lots, clusters of anonymous drivers passing rapidly on the freeway above. The noises of it all were amplified by the underside of the overpass. The infinite patters of rainfall filled the background of the world but there was no response from underneath the car. Michael checked the rearview once more—no headlights in the growing darkness. He clamped the parking brake back, then pulled the door handle and stepped outside.

Sheets of cold water poured down from the overpass and clapped against the pavement in front of him. A light drizzle misted his face. He leaned over to get a partial look under the car.

"Kid, you get it or what?"

Only the rain answered him, saying the same thing it had been for months now. He loved the Pacific Northwest—it was in his blood—but a man could only take so much rain. Spatters of it were getting in his eyes and the drops landing on his nape sent shivers down his spine. The street lamp above came to life, flickering a moment then burning brightly. Michael glanced up to the glare, then moved to the front of the car. The plastic housing of the headlights was dim with mildew—he would need to replace them—though the hazards strobed a luminous yellow. He crouched to look again underneath, this time leaning down on all fours.

The rainwater soaked into the knees of his pants and he immediately regretted his decision as he scanned the wetness under the vehicle.

The kid was gone.

Resting lengthwise against the inside of the front driver's side wheel was the skateboard.

"Kid?"

Where the fuck?

Michael stood and searched the vicinity of the car, walking a circle around it and stopping at the front bumper once more. A third vehicle turned down the street a block back, beyond the overpass. Its headlights pierced the late evening darkness. Michael moved to the driver's side, crouched and grabbed the skateboard, then stood up and gazed around the vicinity of the car. He called out once more for the boy but received no answer.

The lone car passed.

A moment later, Michael pulled open the door and slipped in. He stared at the skateboard in his hands in the inconsistent light. Scrapes in the wood crisscrossed the underside in all directions and the metal trucks were worn and marred. The wood at the front and rear ends of the board was frayed like crowded chipped teeth. Shadows of rain drops crawled over the crude grip tape and the light from the streetlamp above waned over the entire mechanism through the watery veil of the windshield.

The traffic light ahead turned to green though there weren't any other cars on the road. The eerie glow fell over the interior of the car as Michael set the skateboard into the back seat. For a moment, he imagined if Earth had a green sun and this was its light, pouring over him, and then he put the car into gear. His knees and elbows were soaked through. He waited another twenty seconds before letting his foot off the brake and, even then, only allowed the car to pull itself a few feet before stopping part of the way into the crosswalk. He rolled the window down halfway and dealt with the spatter to see if he could hear anything, God forbid the sound of a kid screaming with his skull popped open.

There was nothing, though.

The boy had fled.

The rest of the evening fell behind the horizon on the way home through the rain. The last flare of the sun in the west fell victim to the night long before Michael had made it into his driveway, performing its death rattle in his rear-view mirror as he cruised over the drenched roads. When he'd arrived and shut the headlights off, there was only the soaking darkness surrounding, barely staved off by the lamps on the front of the neighboring homes.

The garage door opener from the Mercedes thankfully worked as well as it ever had, even attached to the sun visor of this shitty sedan. After pulling the car in, turning the ignition off, then getting out, Michael tried to lock the thing but was reminded of the third issue he'd discovered about this wonderful piece of shit only after having purchased it: the keyring device for the car alarm didn't function. He pushed the Lock button, the Unlock, even the red Alarm button to no avail. *Six grand for this fucking thing and they don't even bother replacing the battery in the lock remote.*

He snatched his briefcase from the passenger seat and left the skateboard in the back. After locking the doors manually, walking to each one and pulling the handle to be sure, he took one last glance in at the kid's ride through the car window. It was one hell of a magic trick, the kid disappearing from sight, then fleeing before he could be noticed. There was something about it, though, something that couldn't quite explain itself in Michael's mind, a nagging of some sort. He could swear something ridiculous like he should've *felt* if the kid had fled somehow, a difference in the dark wet air when he'd stepped out of the car to investigate or... *something*. It sounded crazy, even to himself, but it was a feeling that hadn't left him since those few minutes under that overpass.

He turned from the car, the strange unaccustomed machine lying dark and dormant in its new home within the frigid garage, and moved up the few wooden steps to the door into the kitchen, tapping the garage door button on his way in.

*

There was the sensation of opening his eyes but Michael saw nothing at first, save for darkness. He felt the breaths of air heaving in and out of his slack gaping mouth and how his lips and tongue were parched, dry as sand, even though a puddle of drool had soaked into the pillow beneath his cheek. When he turned over and rubbed his barely cognizant eyes, he felt how they burned and he swapped between blinking and rubbing them until he could scan the black room surrounding. His groggy focus found the glowing green digits of the alarm clock on his nightstand.

2:18AM.

Stale saliva stuck to his chin and he wiped it with the back of his hand. In sleep, his mind had been focused on something, a specific something, and yet, not seconds after waking, all identification and reflection upon whatever that something had been was gone, completely. What it *was* could not be remembered but the very fact of the interaction of his unconscious mind on this unremembered thing remained, like an obscure imprint in the mud of his grey matter or some unidentifiable scent left in the space between dream and reality. Like exhausted musculature, he felt the latent after-effects of prolonged mental focus of a kind, but he remembered none of what had transpired in his sleep. There was a small part of him, though, a tiny beacon inside that shouted of being awoken from that now unknown dream by something else, something that triggered a not so urgent but very extant alert within his biology, like the sudden feeling of being watched, or similar to that strange form of vertigo that occurs when one experiences déjà vu.

Something had brought him out of those nebulous dreams.

The soft rug sprawling out from under the bed tickled the underside of his feet when he stood. He shuffled toward the bedroom door, the first few steps taken shambling like the walking dead. The numb hibernation feeling of REM sleep dragged at his limbs and eyelids as he moved out into the hall, as he descended the stairs to the first floor.

Moonlight cut through the blinds of the kitchen windows, striping darkness and luminescence across the entirety of the sink and dining table. His throat burned dryly when he swallowed. The glass he'd used during dinner sat next to the sink, so he grabbed it and filled it under the faucet. Standing in the shadowed kitchen gulping down tap water, Michael's mind honed through its lagged state to pinpoint what was striking that chord in the back of his thoughts. Sleep had been interrupted for some reason, he wasn't sure for what or why, but the image of that skateboard was in his mind and, whether it had been a facet of those fading dreams now remembered or something new in his waking consciousness, he wasn't certain.

The door to the garage stood silent and bare and he stared at it as he drank. A compulsion of a kind, a drive to see the skateboard, rippled through his stiff limbs. Like having the sudden necessity to listen to a song stuck in his head in order to exorcise it from his psyche, he strangely needed to witness the thing again.

The dim clock on the microwave said 2:32AM. Today was Friday and he still had to get up for work in about four hours. The fixation on the skateboard was starting to wake him properly, however, and overwhelmed his own mental warnings regarding how much Future Michael was going to hate Past Michael for taking away from Future Michael's sleep with this bullshit.

When he'd finished with the water, he moved to the door

leading into the garage, collecting the car keys from the hook sprouting from the plaque on the wall to the right. The door opened and he was blinded and stunned temporarily by the glare that poured through. He'd left the garage light on when he'd come home earlier in the night, forgotten completely in the wake of the evening's events. The silver sedan was perfectly silent under the glare of the garage door mechanism above, and the string with the bead at the end of it attached to the device barely swung back and forth, almost imperceptibly.

Michael descended the three wooden steps to the garage floor, the cold concrete shocking the pads of his feet. Through the back-seat window, the skateboard lay motionless on the pale upholstery exactly where it had been left. He clicked the Unlock button on the keychain by force of habit but, of course, heard no subsequent mechanisms inside the car clicking or turning, nothing to indicate anything had actually happened. *Needs a new battery*. He saw the salesman's face in his mind again, Victor or whatever his name had been—it didn't matter—and mumbled "Fuck you, Victor" under a tired breath as he slid the key into the driver's door handle and turned it.

He reached in behind the driver's seat, unlocked the back door, then opened it and picked the skateboard up from its place of rest. The frayed wood pricked at his palms. He turned the thing once in his hands, then flipped it over. The worn underbelly was marked with gouges in the wood and the faded words SHIT FLIP were barely visible behind the scars. If anyone had asked, he wouldn't have been able to describe why seeing and touching the skateboard wasn't satisfying whatever itch had taken him from sleep and sent him down here in the first place. His fingers glided over the scratches just as his mind moved over the recollections of the evening, trying to parse out what exactly had happened. The kid moving out of sight under the car, seeming to disappear...

He had an idea, then, of what the itch in him craved. It was illogical but, driven solely by some indefinable force, curiosity or otherwise, he needed to *look* again. He needed to see underneath the car once more, just to be sure.

The frigid pavement under his feet had eliminated, by sheer contact alone, whatever remained of the grogginess Michael had dragged from bed. He returned the skateboard to the back seat and crossed the garage to the shelves he'd nailed into the south wall last summer. There hadn't been much use for them as of yet, but he knew at least that he'd placed a flashlight on one of them amidst some other odds and ends. He found it, grabbed it off the shelf and clicked the beam on before moving to kneel down next to the passenger side door. Half of him expected the see the kid huddled up in one of the wheel wells or pinned around the exhaust system leading down the entirety of the underside of the vehicle. *Of course the kid wouldn't be there. What, did he ride the entire way home under the car, soaking in rain water and grinding against the speed bumps leading into the neighborhood? If he had, would I even want to see what he looked like now?*

Michael leaned over with the flashlight.

There was no kid, nor any sign of teenage brain-spatter or guts and gore. Scribblings of something like chalk were written scattered across the undercarriage—perhaps from previous mechanics of the machine who wrote their notes like the characters of alien alphabets, he imagined, and there was a lot of it written—aside from which the space looked unlived in, unmolested, exactly how the underside of a car ought to look.

The space in Michael's mind was warm compared to the cold here in the garage and this space reminded him of the sleep that awaited him upstairs, in the sheets of his bed, if only he'd get up now and go to it. He sat back on his calves, closed his eyes and let go of another sigh, a long and tired one, then stood to brush the bits of dirt off his knees and palms. He placed the flashlight back into its space on the shelf. The door to the back seat made a *whump* when he closed it, leaving the skateboard to its own devices inside. He moved back around the rear of the vehicle and up the wooden steps toward the door into the kitchen, reaching for the doorknob and turning. With his free hand, he flicked the light switch. Darkness enveloped the garage as he pushed the door open. He took a single step into the moonlit kitchen—

And then he stopped.

The moment stretched on quietly into the next. He turned.

Michael's shadow stretched out ahead, perfectly still, backlit by the stripes of moonlight coming through the slatted blinds in the kitchen behind him. In a barely registered detection of stimuli, in that moment immediately after flipping the light switch off, he'd seen something, an unexpected something. His eyes searched the dark: there was nothing but the black outline of the car, the random shapes of the things on the far wall shelves. He remained unsure of what he'd thought he'd seen. His eyes moved to stare off into the back upper corner of the garage, and there was nothing in that darkness, but then...

Then he saw it.

If he kept his eyes still, as if he was staring into an optical illusion planted up in the corner of the garage, he could see it in his lower peripheral but only barely. Somewhere in the center of the garage, on the other side of or underneath the car, was a glow. It was a dim obscure light, the source of which seemed strangely displaced. Michael's immediate logic figured it to be more of the moonlight coming in from the kitchen behind him, but there was another part of his instincts that shouted otherwise, yelling that the angle at which the moon's light was coming from couldn't lay in that manner, that it was wrong somehow.

He brought his foot back in and let the door to the kitchen shut.

With the light from the kitchen eliminated, Michael didn't need to keep his eyes still, as the glow was definitely there, huddled low in the darkness of the garage. A soft current of anxiety made itself known within his veins as he rested his hands on the handrail of the landing, as the sensation of the wood met the flesh of his palms.

The gloom shone faint, hardly visible, and it came from underneath the car.

What the fuck?

The blood pumped loudly in Michael's eardrums. He turned and fumbled his hand against the wall briefly before finding and flipping the light switch back on.

The garage was once again bathed in the bright light of the halogen overhead. He stood at the top of the landing, searching over the profile of the car, stared into the shade underneath it. Unease flared under the flesh of his chest as he moved down the steps and toward the shelves to snatch the flashlight once more. He knelt to the ground, clicked the flashlight on once more and directed it under the car.

It looked no different than it had just a minute ago—no sign of the glow he'd seen on his way inside, no obvious indication of its source. With the glare above from the garage door mechanism combining with the flashlight beam he swooped across the dim space underneath the vehicle, nothing should've been able to escape being seen, and yet that is what he saw: nothing. Though he clicked the flashlight off, he kept his gaze below for a moment longer, waiting to see anything. He stood from the concrete and then moved back to the door into the kitchen, this time setting the flashlight on the far side of one of the wooden steps of the landing rather than replacing it on the shelf. He flipped the light switch and the garage went dark again. His eyes searched the dark.

He thought at first that the glow had dissipated, no longer visible in the black, but as he turned back toward the light switch, the glow caught his peripheral from under the car once more. It was faint, the equivalent of a whisper in the audible spectrum, but it was definitely there. He didn't move for a long moment while he watched the luminescence out of the corner of his eye. When he'd abandoned his focus on the darkness ahead of him for that which lay in his peripheral, it was then that he noticed a subtle but noticeable reverberation in the glow, a pulsing that seemed to grow brighter, then dimmer, then brighter, every few seconds. The garage light was void above.

Michael descended the wooden steps to the concrete floor for the third time, collecting the flashlight as he went. His feet hit the concrete and he turned and moved toward the driver's side of the car. As he approached, he watched the otherworldly gleam iridesce over the skin of his naked feet, then stood still to look upon the light pouring out from underneath. It wasn't a light of any sort of intensity but, instead, appeared as a dim reddish-purple haze, waving like an aurora of some kind. There was only a moment of hesitation before he knelt once more to his knees to look again underneath.

Reality, however slightly, seemed to unhinge in that moment he gazed upon the source of the glow. The thing he stared at could only be described by its movement, as if it was swimming, as if it existed in an invisible ocean, somewhere between the concrete and the underside of the vehicle. It appeared like a tattered cloth, floating in an unseen current, remaining somewhat flat but undulating along its form. Its essence was like that of some deep-water creature, flattened by leagues of pressure and bleached by perpetual darkness. Skeins of kaleidoscopic colors fluttered over the surface of the thing like technicolor worms, crawling this way and that with each wave of its stationary dance. It had traits of a liquid mirror or something similar, illumined as reflective as mercury. It shone almost see-through in an ethereal way, producing its own light.

Michael clicked the flashlight on. The beam sent the darkness under the vehicle back into the corners of the garage. The floating cloth-like thing disappeared entirely. The beam shined beyond the underside of the car to the base of the south wall of the garage, alighting nothing unexpected in between. He covered the flashlight's glare by muffling it with his shirt, then. Once darkness had returned and his eyes had readjusted, the thing materialized back into existence, hovering like a ghost just under the central tubes for the exhaust system. When again he uncovered the beam, and directed it underneath, the anomaly disappeared. Its subtle existence must've easily been drowned by the glare of the flashlight. Michael watched the space where it had been, to see if it was still there yet somehow shrouded in the light, invisible to the eye but existing nonetheless, or if the light made it truly disintegrate from reality.

The flashlight clicked off once more and he set the thing down onto the concrete. The swimming mercury returned, floating noiselessly and beautifully. Something mammalian screamed within him, shouting that this thing wasn't natural, a flare of instinctual heat rising in his chest and neck. His curiosity, though, kept his eyes wide and observing, watching the thing in its seductive stasis. It didn't seem threatening but the non-terrestrial nature of it had Michael's heart pounding in his chest. It frightened him to allow his mind to sense some sort of sentience within its dance, as if the thing were somehow alive. The curiosity grew with the caution and, after a few moments deliberation, he stood from the floor.

The barrel of yard tools was hardly visible in the corner of the garage. After making his way to it, he pulled the lightest of the tools out, a shitty garden hoe he'd never used, gifted to him in an uninspiring White Elephant thing at work a few years back. The wood of the hoe's stock still had the plastic feel of little to no use.

He moved back to the ground in the dark, guided only by the strange luminescence, and positioned himself on his back. Transfixation seemed his body's only response to seeing it again, that and a light but eerie nausea boiling in his stomach from witnessing something of such alien form.

He shifted his body, rotated the hoe in his hands to position its blade upward and began moving it toward the mirrored floating thing. The concrete was cold on his back. The tension in his arms grew the further he extended the hoe, as did his anticipation of some sort of reaction from the thing once the tool had reached it. In his mind, he saw it twitch or recoil once contact had been made, like a creature shrinking away from a predator. Its inevitable reaction to being probed was completely unforeseeable. The object was already appearing to defy the laws of physics by remaining where it was just under the car, swimming in unseen liquid. Michael's throat spasmed and constricted with a brief suffocating feeling while looking at the thing, as if the air he breathed was actually on the verge of *being* water, some illusion created by falling prey to the thing's movement.

As the blade of the hoe reached the point in which it ought to have touched the bizarre wavering mirror, no reaction was had. Rather, the end of the tool seemed to sink through the entity, disappearing entirely into its form.

Michael pulled the instrument back. The blade reappeared, popping back into existence as it emerged from the sheen. In the dim but vivid glow, it appeared unscathed, dry and intact. He moved it again toward the floating cloth and the blade disappeared once more. This time, he kept slowly pushing. A few more inches of the stock made it through, then a few more. From this angle, he figured he ought to have hit some part of the car's undercarriage by now, should've scraped against some part of the axle or frame. Yet, there was no obstruction, and then he had given so much of the garden tool that things didn't make sense and a type of strange feeling came upon him, setting the hairs along his neck and arms on end, setting his sight off-kilter for a brief moment.

The blade of the hoe wasn't being pushed through or beyond the floating cloth but *into* it.

Michael retracted the tool completely out from under the car, clicked the flashlight on to observe the end of the instrument, his sight and hands twitching every half second with the heavy blood pumping through his body. The cheap metal had the same plasticky sheen on it, with no marks or signs of wear or disturbance. With apprehensive fingers he touched along the edge of metal. Its temperature was slightly chilled but otherwise a dry normal.

The result of the interaction between the garden hoe and the thing under the car seemed impossible and, as his mind attempted to wrap around the impossibility of it, Michael's perspective hitched, a slight but significant readjustment, like staring at an illusion for an extended amount of time only to finally see the real true image break through. Perhaps it wasn't a floating tatter of cloth or mercury, an entity separate unto itself, or maybe it still was. Maybe, though, it was a gate of some kind, a rip or tear in the fabric of reality. The thing hadn't reacted to his prodding because perhaps it wasn't a living creature. The hoe had disappeared *into* the mercurial aurora. If it was some kind of entrance or portal, a fissure between the normal world and another, if this really was a gateway of some sort, then there was a space beyond its mesmerizing visage, a space of unknown extent. The mere thought of this nebulous 'other side' left a heavy apprehension in him, left his confused yet awestruck mind with only a single burning question:

What the hell is on the other side?

He needed to see. To see might be to understand and to understand might be to relinquish the mixture of flaring anxiety and the almost electric curiosity at this thing's arrival. To see and to understand would be to take back some sort of hold on the reigns of a reality that had escaped his will for too long, having come to a head at this strange point in his life.

Something like a video camera would do the trick. In his mind, Michael pictured the old VHS camera he had in the closet, a relic from his late mother, duct-taped to the end of the garden hoe. He was pretty sure it had stopped working years ago, though, not much more than a clunky paper weight by now. He seemed to remember Olivia bringing it out of the closet a handful of Christmases ago, back when it was the two of them versus the world. He didn't remember much of that night, save for her look of playful dismay when the thing's POWER button didn't appear to work, that and the Santa-themed lingerie that hugged her curves in the best way possible, an image he was fairly certain he would never forget, a part of her he'd keep forever inside of himself.

The first thought to replace the previous was to head to some overnight store, maybe a Walmart, and buy a camcorder or something. It hadn't taken much convincing to get his faculties on board with the plan but then he remembered that his smart phone had a camera, and it seemed to him that said smart phone camera would do the job without costing him hundreds of dollars and a trip out into the night in his pajamas.

Michael stood from the concrete and moved to the staircase, his fingers growing numb from the chilled air of the garage. He ascended to the wooden landing and opened the door into the kitchen, still holding the garden hoe. The clock on the wall above the key rack read 3:04AM. Clouds must've covered the moon as the blinds were no longer parted by its luminescence and the kitchen was in almost complete darkness. A sinking uneasiness weighed heavily in his stomach, not from the impending day of work only a few dwindling hours of rest ahead of him but from the connotations of that which he'd witnessed so far, and the indescribable discoveries that he thought may await him on the other side of his upcoming efforts.

He continued through the kitchen and headed upstairs, two steps at a time.

*

Though the adrenaline of this new discovery had charged Michael with an unexpected energy, the fatigue of interrupted sleep soon made brief moments here and there feel dreamy, glossed almost. There was even a fleeting thought on his way back down the stairs that he'd imagined it all, everything that had happened since having awoken earlier and, like a dream, it might all go away if he simply returned his head to the pillow waiting for him in bed.

It was 3:18AM when he returned to the kitchen. He held a makeshift contraption like a knight would hold a sword. This weapon, though, consisted of his mobile phone duct-taped to the wooden stock near the hoe's business end, camera out, just under the blade.

Before reaching for the door into the garage, Michael flipped the kitchen lights on. They glared from the ceiling above and would be useful if he needed to leave the garage in any sort of haste, to have the path before him properly lit. However, this sense of security was only momentary as, once he entered the garage and the door closed behind him, he was again enshrouded by the darkness within.

It was only a moment before his eyes adjusted. He descended the few steps to the garage floor, his eyes already locked onto the phantasmal glimmer ebbing out from underneath the vehicle.

Though he'd done it multiple times throughout the night so far, the cold concrete shocked him as he lay down next to the driver's door, his body having acclimated to the warmth in the house during the assembling of his camera-on-a-stick. He shimmied the bound phone up toward his face by readjusting his hold on the hoe. His fingers fidgeted with the touch-screen, unlocking the thing and navigating to the camera app, and then he glanced beyond the device, once again looking upon the undulating shred of alternate reality. Its silvery incandescence glittered in its almost liquid suspension, churning and roiling. It was beautiful and it held Michael's gaze for a long few seconds, caught him in a pseudo-hypnotism like before. He tapped the RECORD button on the screen of the phone and the bulb embedded in its back side flared brightly. In the device's light, the wavering gateway had gone near invisible. He scrolled through the options UI and disabled the flash. The space under the car went dark again but, shortly thereafter, was reignited by the portal's eldritch glow. The red dot on the phone's screen blinked every few seconds, indicating that the recording was live.

The heavy end of the hoe swayed slightly as he drew it out further toward the paranormal thing. The radiance of the anomaly seemed to overtake his vision, turning what little was visible throughout the garage in his peripheral into a deep grey black, for only what lay ahead could he see, and he extended the tool toward it like some sort of proboscis. All that existed in that dark moment was the portal and the phone.

And then, as it made contact, the device disappeared into the mirrored portal, swallowed like sustenance.

There was no way to tell how much room was on the other side but Michael figured he'd get at least a foot of the hoe inside before trying to maneuver the camera around, if the space beyond would allow it. He thought that he'd gotten at least that much in the first time he'd prodded the thing.

When he'd pushed a sufficient length of the tool into the gate, he repositioned himself to better support the stock of the hoe, and then slowly turned it clockwise a few times. Outside the garage door came the sound of a car driving by over wet pavement. Otherwise, silence lay like a thick film over him, save for his own breathing and the subtle sounds of his grip readjusting. Though not seen, the weight of the phone could still be felt as he rotated the handle, trying to obtain a 360-degree capture of whatever place the camera currently resided in. When he'd rotated a few more times, he then held the hoe still.

Michael counted to ten in his mind, then began pulling it back.

The business-end of the makeshift tool popped back into reality. The phone's screen was still aglow. That it appeared to still be functioning was a good sign. Michael slid out from under the car and sat up, his fingers already fighting with the duct-tape to unbind the phone from the stock of the hoe and, when he had successfully done so, he tapped the RECORD button on its screen to stop the recording. The device felt normal in his hands and appeared undamaged. When the phone had finished loading the recording, he positioned himself on his side, to watch the video while being able to look directly beyond to the floating gateway, looking as beautiful as it was foreboding.

The first thirty-five seconds of the video were erratic, taking place after he'd hit the record button and had been scooting himself into position before moving the device further under the car. When the perspective became less turbulent after all his adjusting, and it slowly moved in the direction of the anomaly, Michael's heart began to race in his chest. The anticipation of what lay beyond… The camera grew slowly closer to the source of dim light. A subtle but audible breeze sounded through the phone's little speaker, as if it were closing in on an open window or passageway. The video had captured this sound with clarity though he hadn't been able to hear it on his own before. It grew louder as the camera panned over the concrete floor, the cracks and stains of which grew in detail as the dim gleam became more saturated.

And at the moment in which the phone ought to have penetrated the portal's membrane, the screen went black.

Michael tapped the screen to ensure that it was still playing properly. It was. He sat up, scooting back against the wooden landing and under the rail of the short staircase to the kitchen door. The gentle light still radiated off of the lower half of his sitting body but his attention was on the bright black of the screen he held in front of him.

The breezy sounds had silenced completely. It seemed at first that the phone recording ability had malfunctioned the second it had gone over to the other side but then he heard something, a sound amidst the recorded abyss. His index finger searched for the nub on the side of the phone and tapped it until the volume was maxed. It sounded like a shuffling at first, distorted by the low-quality speaker, and then, with the passing seconds being counted off by the recording's timer in the bottom corner of the screen, the sound morphed into a repetitive, drawn out moaning or mewling. It sounded like...

Someone was crying.

It sounded like someone young, a kid.

Michael's hand fell over his mouth and he mumbled *Holy fuck* under his breath. The events of earlier in the evening, which had been dwarfed by the discovery of this thing underneath the car, came rushing back to him. He remembered the skateboarding kid's face and how he mouthed *Sorry* through the rain-warbled windshield. The sounds of falling water off of the overpass, splashing to the concrete below, now echoed in his thoughts.

The portal...

To Michael, there were only two possibilities, it seemed, and the less plausible one was seeming more plausible by the moment. Either he hadn't noticed when the kid decided to run off from the car earlier that night, or the portal is somehow attached to the car and the kid went under to get the skateboard and never came back out. Occam's Razor said that the former was true, but if the boy really had ended up inside this thing, this gateway, then there existed the possibility that the boy was the one crying on the other side and that he was in danger. The audio seemed to move positions in the speaker and he guessed that this was the point in the recording in which he'd spun the device in an attempt at the panoramic shot. Either the space beyond was pitch black, with no light whatsoever, or the phone's earthly technology was unable to visibly record what was beyond. In both scenarios, he was still hearing the crying and that meant that, if nothing else, the space beyond had breathable air and the kid was still alive.

A fervor overtook Michael then. Something had to be done. He figured calling the police was out of the question. *Hello, 911? My name is Michael Chamberlain and there's a twelve-year-old boy stuck in a portal underneath my car. Can you by chance send someone over to help?* No, the boy's life was in the balance but that story would only leave Michael implicated, leave him judged by the unbelieving eyes of any officer that showed up and then most likely shackled and shoved into the back of a cruiser, whether accused of having something to do with the boy's disappearance or regarded as a psychotic for creating such an elaborate fable. If the boy belonged to any sort of normally functioning family, there was probably already a missing persons filed for him or, if not, at least a worried set of parents at home.

Michael's mind rolled through the possibilities of attempting a rescue on his own. The heaviest of his doubts was that he had no clue of what to expect on the other side. The idea of sticking his arm in blindly to try and find the kid terrified him. He needed to make a window somehow, to see inside without *being* inside, to garner any sort of idea of what to expect if he was going to have to reach inside to get the kid or worse, stick his head through to see. The most unexpected aspect of all of this was that, in that moment, he wondered what Olivia would think of his attempts at a rescue, if she would think him brave, if she would think it enough, *believe* it enough to come back to him.

He shook his head.

Goddamnit.

Another glance at the floating aperture in the dark, to make sure of the reality he'd been experiencing, didn't alleviate the uncertainty that seemed to be mounting inside of him. The feeling of vertigo he'd awoken with crept through the pit of his stomach again in that moment and the totality of all he'd experienced that evening, and in the last few months, washed over him, knotted with the steady tension of ill sleep.

Glass, he thought. *Some form of glass might work to see beyond.*

There was a drawer of Pyrex dishes in the kitchen, one or two of which might be deep enough to fully penetrate the unknown thickness of the portal. He would need to get directly under its threshold, though, which was a thought that creeped him the fuck out. As he gazed at the paranormal tatter, shimmering in its strange undulation, it was apparent that there wouldn't be enough room for him under the car. A smaller person, definitely, but not him with his beer gut and not with the low profile of the sedan. His mind moved from squeezing under the vehicle, to raising the vehicle somehow, to using the stationary car jacks sitting in the far corner of the garage under the bags of stove pellets. They were a gift from his cousin a few years back. He'd never needed to use them, until now.

Michael stood, still holding the smartphone, and moved up the steps, through the door and into the kitchen. In the drawers below the coffee maker were the bowls, plates and Pyrex. He grabbed the largest glass bowl in the stack, about ten inches across, and slid the rest of them back into their spots and closed the cupboard.

Upon his return, he flipped the light switch and the garage lit up. The large Pyrex bowl he'd grabbed from its drawer was heavy in his hand. The concave of the bowl was about four inches and he hoped that it would be enough to get a glimpse of what lay on the other side. He set it on the wooden steps and then moved to the far corner of the garage.

The jacks were rusted things. They screeched against the concrete when he set them down and scooted them into position, as did the wheels of the rolling hand jack that had been dormant in the same corner for about as long as he'd owned the home. He wiped the spider webs from its handle and positioned it underneath the frame of the vehicle, then started pumping. The vehicle was raised a liberal amount before he slid the stationary jacks underneath its frame. He released the pressure from the hand jack and the car sank down into its new angle of stasis. He slid the hand jack out from underneath and set it against the inside of the garage door a few feet away and returned to a crouch to look once again at the writhing cloth-like thing. At this angle, in this light, it wasn't visible but Michael's breath caught in his throat anyway.

There were symbols, everywhere.

Circles of letters and unknown integers spiraled around in bizarre patterns, scattered neurotically amongst the mechanical undercarriage. The grotesque prose formed sentences and phrases Michael could not understand, yet the feeling in his gut told him that they were somehow bound to the creation or maintenance of the portal. Whomever created this tear in reality must've been the author of the jagged carvings, which he'd originally thought to have been the scribblings of the vehicle's previous mechanics. Regardless of the origin of the text, it vexed him with a heaviness he hadn't anticipated and with questions now plaguing his mind regarding the prior owner of the vehicle, the languages used in the scratched calligraphy—obviously not English or even containing anything resembling the Roman alphabet—and the actions he was to take from here forward.

A million paths and all led to him still attempting to get the boy out from inside whatever space lay beyond the portal. He couldn't help but feel that he'd been thrust into something much deeper than was ever meant for someone like him. Strange happenings were at work and he felt small in their wake.

The night had lay robust this evening. Goosebumps prickled Michael's arms from the cold seeping in from outside. Before grabbing the Pyrex bowl from the steps, he moved passed it up to the door and into the kitchen once again. Draped across the couch arm in the living room was an old black hoodie of his, the one he wore while lounging when he'd gotten home and changed out of the suit most days. There existed within him a deep-seated resentment for that fucking suit. It served as reminder that he was working and playing in some other man's game, working on someone else's dreams rather than his own. He slipped the hoodie on, pulled the hood up over his head and zipped it up to his neck before moving back into the kitchen. As he passed the phone, he stopped briefly, staring at it. Instincts told him that this wasn't a one-man job, especially if that man was *him*, and that this required equipment and testing far beyond his own capabilities. He thought again of calling 911. The phrase *There's something wrong with my car* kept repeating in his mind, a way to get the authorities out here without using words that might paint him as some sort of pedophile or kidnapper of the boy lost beyond the veil. He shook his head and entered the door into the garage, flicking the light off, grabbing the Pyrex. He moved down to the concrete floor and decided he would call the police if absolutely necessary but, for now, this was his bag.

Swirling patterns of phosphorescence waned along the concrete under the angled vehicle and, by simply crouching rather than getting on his hands and knees, Michael was able to garner a decent look at the thing shining so otherworldly in the dark under the car. The cloth-like phenomenon billowed in the air silently and, to his surprise, the thing was angled now, too, as if bound in parallel to the tilt of the car by the text splayed out above it via which he figured it was summoned. No longer facing the concrete floor, the surface of the swimming thing was more visible, now. It moved in a way that made it almost seem alive.

Michael laid himself to the ground, holding the Pyrex bowl. Feelings of awe, apprehension and confusion were all competing in his mind, but something about the light, the strangeness of it, kept drawing him to look at it, to lean toward it, to be *near* it. The attraction was magnetic. He also knew that the kid in the portal was depending on him, though, and that he had no way of knowing how long the boy could survive in the space beyond, or even what the space beyond *was*. The possibility of the kid being hurt was very real and Michael thought then of the potential of having to go in and retrieve the kid, shuffling his growing-into-middle-age body through the small gateway to do so. Harrowing thoughts fluttered in his imagination of being suffocated in a strange inhuman space beyond, a place void of any oxygen or water or other sustainability needed for human life. If there were something so drastically wrong with that other side, though, the boy shouldn't be able to breathe, let alone whimper and cry. This understanding did nothing to alleviate Michael's fear, however, of experiencing the sensations of anoxia.

There was a good amount of room to slide under now with the jacks in place, though the underside of the car was still going to be less than a foot from his face, and the portal, once he'd gotten underneath it, a few inches closer still.

Michael repositioned his body and started shimmying closer to the enigma in the dark. And when he was fully positioned underneath it, he found that his hands were shaking, his limbs trembling. The edges of his vision wavered with each heavy heartbeat. For a long moment he watched the pulsing thing, listening to the gentle breeze like the sound he'd heard in the phone recording. It was a faint but sharp whirring noise, like a constant inhale. In the background of that, the crying was still there, still audible, a whimpering from just within.

Michael Chamberlain took a deep breath, a breath worthy of the slight lightheadedness he received for it, then grasped both sides of the Pyrex bowl. Even with the room provided by the jacks, his proximity to this gateway, so foreign in nature, was alarming and part of him wanted to stop all of this, run into the house and lock the door to the garage. His body did not respond to these thoughts of flight, however. His hands, instead, started moving the bowl toward the anomaly. The portal writhed and squirmed and its colors glinted off of the smooth contours of the glass, colors that, even when studied from this close, Michael could not fully decipher. The thing was grey and blue and technicolor and yet, when he tried to focus on a single ripple in its form, a single wave or a crest of color, his eyes seemed unable to focus. The patterns were evasive, warbling furtively into each other.

The bowl reached the surface of the portal and the underside of the glass was kissed by the multicolor light, as if being slowly submerged in liquid. Around the sides, the weird light touched Michael's fingertips and it was cool against the skin of his knuckles. And, like an eye opening in the color beyond the Pyrex shield, a spot of darkness appeared then in the center of the bowl and grew to encompass the entire bottom side of it.

The glass had made it through. The window was created.

The light around the circumference of the glass rippled over the tops of his hands. All he could focus on, though, was the darkness beyond the bridge he'd now forded between his world and this other. There definitely appeared to be a space beyond but it was aphotic and indecipherable, void of all light in great contrast to the multicolor gate, itself. In the background of the din made by the gentle breeze and his pounding heart, the boy's crying drifted out of the obscurity like the whispers of a ghost.

"Kid?" Michael said. "Hey, kid!"

A few moments passed.

"Kid, I'm here to help. My name's Michael. Are you okay?"

No response. There was an interval in the crying, though, and almost seemed a little louder when it picked back up, a little closer to the other side of the portal.

Michael cursed under his breath. Nothing was visible in the murk beyond the glass. Even if there were a source of light somewhere in the dark, he wasn't sure how distorted the view would be due to the contours of the bowl. He thought again of just reaching his hand inside and trying to grab the kid's pant leg or something, seeing as his fingers had already been submerged into the other side and seemed to be without molestation, but the thought of gripping onto unimaginable stuff that *wasn't* the kid, like ectoplasm or the dregs of otherworldly gutters, scared the shit out of him. *Fuck that.*

He pulled the bowl back to his chest. The portal was whole once again, returning to its previous glowing form, dancing above him. He scooted out from under the car and snatched the flashlight off the concrete. When he returned to his position under the portal, he clicked the flashlight switch to ON and once again held the Pyrex bowl up but this time with the flashlight held against the right side of it, combining both items into a window plus a source of light that would hopefully show him the location of the kid in the dark beyond.

The technicolor mirror furrowed over the glass again. The chilled liquid light rolled against the backs of his hands. The darkness opened up once more on the other side of the glass, as if the abyss were opening a single eye to stare directly at him...

And when the flashlight broke the veil, shining its light into the amorphous space ahead, it's beam illuminated a mound of some material, smeared and slick in the spotlight, sitting only feet from the glass and the open portal. And then it came to Michael that it looked like skin, see-through skin, stretching like a membrane. A long slender snout, deranged and misshapen, formed the centerpiece of its shape. Boils appeared clustered all over the thing, seeming to push at the flesh. Below, at the bottom of the thing, was a quivering hole lined with dirty brown protrusions, shredded lips and drooling some kind of effluence.

The crying was coming from the twitching fleshy opening.

It mimicked the sound of a boy's crying.

And then, in the moment that terror exploded within

Michael's lungs, but before he could retract the glass, the boils, set asymmetrically in the thing's bulk, seemed to rip open. Black bulbous orbs stared out of those newly torn lids, fogged pupils dancing in their centers, spasming.

Michael screamed.

The bowl fell from his hands, bouncing off of his chest to shatter against the concrete. The flashlight fell, too, whipping its beam in all directions in the dark as it tumbled. In a flurry, he scrambled out from under the tilted car. Shards of glass embedded themselves into his knees and palms. He tripped over himself rushing toward the wooden steps that led up to the door to the kitchen, barely catching his balance on the handrail before bounding up the four steps to the landing. As he grabbed the doorknob, he stole a frightened glance over his shoulder to the car and the light underneath it.

Something was coming through the portal:

Akin to the shape of a horse's head, covered in bare glistening flesh, it gibbered its rotten needle teeth, exposed from chewed lips and a shredded snout, as it birthed from the light. Its jaw moved and ground spindly incisors against themselves. Beyond the crying mimicry, still hiccupping out of the thing's throat, a growling came from the gutters of its being, sounding like gravel dragged by skidding tires. Crooked claws emerged from the portal to clack against the concrete, attached to twitching limbs lined with skin that sagged horribly.

And in the blink of an eye, it emerged and was skittering over the garage floor, rushing toward Michael and the open door.

Michael fell into the kitchen. Instinct closed the door immediately. Fear locked the deadbolt right afterward. Massive thumps erupted against the other side of the door, the sounds of a paroxysm that sent Michael's mind further into the gloss of horror. His breaths came viciously in that ringing state of nightmare, the image of what was seen under the car and that which clawed at him from just beyond the door repeating erratically in his thoughts, over and over. He held the doorknob tight. "What the fuck! What the fuck!" he screamed through clenched teeth. The door shook on its frame, rattling with each beating.

And then, as quickly and violently as it had come, the slamming stopped.

The moments of silence seemed to stretch forever. With each passing second, Michael's breaths became shallower but no less difficult for the oxygen didn't seem to be doing anything to abate the tremors shaking his bones.

Then, the gentle whimpering came again, creeping into his ears from the other side of the door. The boy's crying voice...

The breath constricted in Michael's chest, wrapping around his throat and lungs like a python crushing him of life. He let go of the doorknob, stepping as quietly as he could backward toward the hall, his body still shaking with adrenaline. The cell phone caught his peripheral and he snagged it before he'd backed into the entrance hall.

On the other side of the door leading into the garage, the crying went quiet.

Michael stopped.

The silence waited beyond the threshold of the hallway into the kitchen like some beast holding its breath, like the moment just before exacting the killing stroke. Michael stood for a moment longer, then stepped further back into the hall, angling toward the front entrance.

His heart nearly stopped at what awaited him.

Radiating like a beacon in the dark of the entry way, waving and contorting in the air just inside of the front door, was another portal. It glimmered and moved menacingly in the space between Michael and his salvation, shimmering and sparkling with fathomless cosmic coloration.

The slamming came violently once again from the other side of the door leading into the garage. The distinct sound of splintered wooden door frame crackled out of the kitchen. Michael's mind went into overdrive:

Escape—
Upstairs—
Window—
Shotgun—

The shotgun, the one Michael's brother had given him a few years back to 'protect the household', he'd said, was upstairs in the office closet. He could use the window in that same room to get outside.

Michael took his first step toward the staircase.

The glowing veil just inside the entryway parted as something birthed from it, slithering into reality: the beginning of another mangled gibbering snout came through, followed by a skinless head and body. This one had massive cloven hooves, multiple sets on the same limbs, wretchedly visceral as it crept out from the mercurial light.

It was an abomination.

Michael bounded the first set of stairs to the middle landing before the turn up the latter half of the steps to the upstairs hallway, leaping two and three at a time. He envisioned the shotgun sitting in its box up on its shelf in the closet, envisioned loading the shells one at a time into the thing, and pumping a round into the chamber. It was survival. It would be his defense. He could load it, then open the window and move out onto the awning above the front doorway. The drop to the lawn below would be rough but doable, so long as he didn't land wrong on his ankles. That was the plan and, in the state of hyper-terror in which he moved, breathed and existed, *a* plan was better than no plan.

He turned right at the top of the stairs and rushed into the office, slamming the door shut behind him and locking the knob before flipping the light on. In the years he'd lived here, all those fights with Olivia and those countless other times he'd slammed this same door, the wood never felt so noticeably flimsy as it did now compared to the door into the garage from the kitchen. This one was a cheap thing, purchased when they'd first moved into the place from the discount aisle at Home Depot.

After securing the door as well as he was going to, Michael's hands fumbled with the closet door and finally slid it open on its tracks. The long slender case on the top shelf was heavier than he remembered, though his adrenaline made it easy enough to handle. The box of shells tumbled off the shelf to the carpet below and burst into a cluster of never-been-used buckshot.

Anomalous thudding came from the staircase out in the hall, a rapid rumbling ascending to the office. Hooves smashed against the outside of the door. It shook on its hinges as if made of cardboard.

Michael kneeled to the ground, unlatched the case and pulled the shotgun out of its cloth imprint, then slid to the floor after one of the shells.

Shards of the door spattered into the room against the far side of the computer desk. A slick mutated hoof penetrated through a hole in the door. Growling and gurgling and child-like crying goaded from the other side.

Only two of the shells were loaded when the door burst fully inward. The force of it slammed the door knob against the wall, producing a concussive sound so loud that Michael jumped, thinking he'd misfired the shotgun with his uncertain hands. It was the sounds afterward, though, that drew his attention away from his weapon and toward the entrance of the room, instead.

The thing that moved slowly through the aperture and into Michael's sight petrified him into a state of pure disbelief. He'd purchased an extra bright bulb for the office light for him to work under and this light was now clinically illuminating every contour of the thing that unfurled before him. The way it ambulated, the glistening coagulate that seemed to grease every surface of the twitching thing, amnion from its bizarre birth into this world...

It was all accented beyond comprehension, driving the whole situation into some space of true madness in which there was no coming back from, by the childish human-sounding lamentations coming from deep within the teeth of its bestial orifice.

Michael couldn't breathe, and so he pumped the fore-end of the shotgun, aimed and then fired. What happened next did not go the way his mind had, in that micro-moment of absolute instinctual survival, imagined it would: in his mind, he saw the flesh of the thing shredded from the buckshot, forcing it back and leaving a hole the size of a grapefruit, except that his first shot didn't seem to do anything, as sure as his aim had been. The projectile only sunk impossibly into the wall behind the adversary. The second shot didn't follow the plan, either. It, too, splintered the drywall beyond the creature.

The shots had passed through cleanly as if he'd been shooting at something imaginary, as if the projectiles had intentionally ignored that which Michael most wanted to be affected by them.

The creature, if one could say it was ever whole, was no worse for the wear after the two shots, though it did display a reaction to Michael's attempts at wounding it. The hooves that crowned the ends of its crooked limbs dug into the carpet and its head shook and rattled side-to-side, then came to stare directly at the human in front of it. It gazed with its clusters of misshapen eyes, scattered like a galaxy across the bone plate protruding from its skinned horse head. The largest of the creature's eyes, embedded in the crest of its grotesque display, bulged then and slid out of its socket, trailing with it a pudgy grub body. And then the rest of the bulbous black eyes, one at a time, popped out of their homes and fell to the floor, all varied sizes writhing in the carpet like freshly beached worms. The congregation of nightmarish grubs inched their way forward underneath the beast's swollen bulbous belly. Poised low and predatory, all the while babbling and biting and salivating, the creature crawled slow over the now fetid soaked carpet. It's gibbering began to form words and, in these words, he heard things he'd never dreamed of.

As the head of the second beast moved into sight from the doorway behind the first, Michael's hand grabbed listlessly for the other buckshot shells but found none. Though his fingers still searched the soft carpet almost autonomously, his gaze remained otherwise hexed by the serpentine back-and-forth gaits belonging to those unbelievably wretched things that now closed in on him.

*

In the still air of the studio apartment, a sharp annoying sound obliterated the comatose silence.

As he sat up in the darkness, Jim Trent, having just been ripped out of his death-like sleep by his shrill and repetitive alarm clock, half-consciously growled at the thing. He rubbed his eyes with the palms of his hands and then hacked up some shit from the back of his throat, likely deposited there as a bit of after-love from the six-pack he'd killed on an empty stomach before going to sleep last night. His sleep-addled mind toyed with the idea of laying back down and seeing how long he could zonk out with the shrieking alarm still calling out and, when he decided that he couldn't actually take it any longer, he leaned forward to the small desk under the window, pushed the alarm to OFF, then sat back on the bed.

4:30AM.

It was a cold and early one, as usual. This place never retained heat during the autumn or winter months, and the night chill had crept through the thin single-pane glass of the old window while he slept. Underneath it, the antiquated heater sat long dead like the discarded rib cage of some animal's skeleton. He'd wondered to himself countless times as to why he was paying almost two grand a month for this shit heap in the middle of the city, with its outdated structural integrity, its limited space and lifeless heating implementations, and in that moment Jim wondered it again. In his slowly waking haze, he could swear he caught glimpses of fog when he exhaled. His blankets lay strewn over the far corner of the bed, kicked away at some point during the night. Goosebumps prickled his arms even though a latent cold sweat clung to his brow. The skin of his arms and shoulders was chilled. The morning gloom glowed dimly through the blinds.

Jim stood from the bed and moved to the kitchenette in the corner of the small studio. He realized then, as he had realized yesterday morning after using the rest of it, but doing nothing about it at the time, that he was out of coffee grounds. He flipped the lid of the coffee maker open and the still damp grounds and stained filter from the morning prior lay dormant inside.

Yesterday's grounds it is.

The shower was uneventful. It didn't wake him the way he'd hoped. Jim's hangover had been stumbling around inside his temples like a drunkard in a coat closet throughout the entire twenty minutes he'd spent under the steaming water, which he'd maxed to its hottest temperature even though it still felt depressingly lukewarm. He'd decided nonchalantly that he'd commit suicide by shower this morning rather than going into work today, but when he tilted his head back and opened his mouth for the water, Death did not come. Instead, he coughed at the jets of water hitting the back of his throat and noticed the return of his seemingly perpetual headache. Even the second coffee he'd downed after drying off had only traces of caffeine left to fuel any sort of energy in his system, though it had curbed the throbbing behind his eyes a bit and, for that, he supposed he was grateful.

When he walked outside of the apartment building at 5:22AM, after locking the deadbolt from the outside and taking the stairs slowly as not to irritate his bad knee, Jim was met by the sounds of the city's early traffic, muffled by the fog that blanketed everything, and by Detective Kyle Stedner leaning up against an unmarked police car parked at the curb. The young detective held his own cup of coffee and the shit-eating grin he always had equipped on the mornings in which he came to pick Jim up for work, which was almost every morning nowadays. The kid was only twenty-nine years old, twenty-one years Jim's junior, but Jim knew him to be good nonetheless. Stedner was a bit of a goof, sure, but he'd also been at the forefront of an internal corruption case two years prior, had sat boldly in front of a supreme court judge and aided in the convictions of the two dirty investigators staring murderously at him from across the bench as he testified. Presenting the evidence he'd gathered and the methods of his investigation, he won the title of Detective with that case. Jim had been wary of his inexperience when they'd been assigned with one another but had grown to trust him over the three years they'd worked together, had seen the kid able to handle himself with a deep-seated resolve that seemed rare, as ridiculous as he could be at times.

"Morning," Jim said.

"Morning, crypt-keeper. How'd you sleep? You look like shit." The young detective made slurps at his coffee, which steamed open-lidded in the chilly morning air.

Jim chuckled as he moved to the passenger door. "Same to you, princess."

The grey morning was choked with fog and Jim watched it pass outside the passenger window, rubbing his right temple to ease what was left of the ache. All the world seemed obscured by the dreariness outside, aspects of which didn't seem to take taking form until the car was within a certain proximity of them, at which time buildings and telephone poles and parked cars seemed to manifest into existence like ghosts made flesh from some spell of inspection. Stoplights looked like phantom glowing orbs in the haze, reminding him of how clouded his own thoughts were in the mornings, increasingly foggy the older he got, it seemed.

The sun began to rise from somewhere in the east as they rounded the last corner to the station. The sunlight was indistinct among the fog but set fire to the color of that early gloom. Jim's phone vibrated while he stared out his window and, when he glanced down to it, saw a text from his sister. The preview on the screen said *Can you take Timothy to his therapy session tonight? I need to work the late shift for…* He clicked the phone back to sleep and returned it to his jacket pocket. His nephew had been one of a myriad of aches and pains he'd had to deal with these last few months, albeit Timmy's circumstances were different than the old joints and shitty back the seasoned detective had to put up with. Some time ago, Timmy had gone almost mute, left with but a few things to say by some experience he'd had in the woods with his friends. The details of what had actually happened were obscure at best, considering none of the kids he'd talked to were willing to tell Jim anything other than describing some segment of time the neighborhood boys had spent messing with an old tree trunk that had scared them half to death. Though Jim's first thought had been that they'd simply frightened Timmy the way that young boys usually did with each other, the very real silence Timmy exhibited spoke of a trauma that couldn't be brushed off as standard childhood tribulations. Prying into that was another problem for another day, though. With a stack of case work on his desk for weeks now, and three of his colleagues retiring in the last month, Jim had his work cut out for him without being swallowed by his sister's domestic issues, no matter how much he cared for her and, by proximity, the boy.

*

The familiar door to the briefing room, tacked all on its front with printed announcements and policy changes, was shut when they arrived to it. Stedner moved in a wide arc to get a better look through the slim window of the door without making it obvious that he was inspecting the inside.

"She's in there with one of the new guys," he said.

Jim nodded in response, then gulped the last bit of his third coffee down. It had lost all taste to him, save for the bitterness it left in the back of his throat with each swig. Thank God he'd given up cream and sugar. He could only imagine how that phlegmy lactose residue would feel in the back of his throat right now, so on the verge as he was to throwing up anyway. He'd forgotten to eat dinner last night, something that seemed to be occurring more and more as of late, and the alcohol was still taking its toll on him.

The corkboard they stood next to, on the hallway wall

opposite the door, was also covered in notices—position openings, business cards, mug shots with stats and pictures with descriptions, even a *Free car wash at Dale's!* coupon. Twenty-two years on the force, twelve years as a detective, and Jim still remembered exactly what the position opening notice looked like all those years ago, when he'd seen 'Detective' in bold print and decided to take a chance and apply for it. To get off the standard beat, to get back into normal clothes and step away from traffic citations and domestic disputes, that's what had driven him then. The stress was high, sure, but going back to patrolling neighborhoods and ticketing bad parking jobs was not something he wanted in his future, if he had any say in it.

The door to the briefing room opened. Chief Samantha McClary held it open for the new patrolman, Gregger or Greguar or something, Jim couldn't remember, as he left the room and went down the hall toward the main hub of the station.

She turned to the detectives. "Come on in, boys."

The lights on the ceiling in the briefing room were especially bright in the mornings, though Jim couldn't ever really tell if it was the bulbs or just him, especially when they seemed to be even brighter if his hangovers were particularly bad. Chief McClary had left the middle row off, though, so the light wasn't too terrible on his aching eyes.

"Got a weird one for you two," she said, sliding a manila folder to each of them. "I know you've got your other cases but hopefully this will be an in-and-out for you. Maybe no more than a day. Jefferson is out with the flu and I don't want to make Cordeaux do it on his own, seeing as he's retiring next week and senioritis is all over his expressions like face paint, though I might send him out later to give you two a hand if needed.

"Neighbors of a guy down in Stone Hills said they heard clattering and pounding noises from a house in the early AM, around three-thirty or four. Then there were shots fired. Only two reports heard. That's when someone called 911."

Jim opened the file, thumbing through the first couple pages of the brief, still warm from the printer.

"When our units arrived, no one was home. The door was locked but, after our guys broke it open, they found a shotgun upstairs and slugs from two buckshot in the wall of the bedroom.

No inhabitants, though. No blood, no signs of mortal wounding. Just the shotgun and the expended shells but the carpet in that room was soaked in something foul. We got samples of it but toxicology is so backed up right now that it won't be able to take a look at it for a week, if not two.

"I'd like you boys on it. Take a break from that Dynam corruption case. Go see what you can find. Get it wrapped up ASAP, if you please."

Jim nodded and then glanced to Stedner, who was smiling his shitty smile at him and slurping at his coffee again. Stedner clapped him on the shoulder and said, "Ah, don't worry, old-timer. This'll be cake and then we'll get back to the Jamison case tomorrow. You'll be retiring soon enough."

*

The morning fog had begun to clear by the time they'd reached the freeway though the overcast sky beyond seemed like a further extension of the stuff. Thick globules of grey cloud cover hung overhead but, in the distant east, patches of blue sky were making way for the sun as it rose.

It hadn't been until about that point, as Jim started to read over the report in earnest, that he'd begun to fully wake up. He mulled over the report aloud, his breath still reeking of coffee. "Officers responded to the call, found no one home. Buckshot in the wall and two dispensed shell cartridges in the upstairs office. Shotgun was nearby. Car was on jacks in the garage and there was broken glass underneath it. Blah blah blah. The missing man is a Michael James Chamberlain. Forty-two years old, Lead Data Analyst for a telecommunications company, recently divorced..."

"Anything on the ex-wife?"

Jim scanned. "Nope, save for her name being Olivia."

A long moment passed as the car drove smoothly down the freeway.

Stedner smiled. "She sounds hot."

Jim snorted and shook his head.

*

The clock on the car radio ticked over to 6:31AM as they arrived at the house. Two patrol cars were parked outside the place, one in the driveway and the other in the gravel along the outskirts of the front yard. The lights on the latter were swirling silently and there was an elderly woman speaking to an officer standing near the rear of the cruiser. Stedner drove past them a short distance, then put the car in reverse and angled to parallel park in front of the patrol vehicle. He pulled the parking brake, grabbed his pack of smokes from the center console, gave Jim a smirk, then got out.

The air hit Jim's nose like a wet towel when he stepped out, muggy and still tainted by the rain that had passed during the night and that morning. He took a deep breath, smelling a tinge of cigarette in the air. When he glanced back, Stedner was stepping away from the scene toward a ditch on the other side of the road, already puffing away. Jim had smoked on and off for ten years when he was younger, and had luckily quit when he'd entered into his thirties. He'd given Stedner shit here and there for not quitting but didn't give it to him too much—to each their own and all that. He'd told Stedner on a few occasions how much better food had tasted when he quit, how improved his outlook on life and the future had started to get because of that improvement, alone. *Did I ever listen to anyone telling me the same type of thing back then, though?* No, he hadn't. Ten years, smoking like a chimney, and it took Jim finding a stranded driver during a snowstorm years ago, half-buried in the white embankment on the side of the road, and then helping said stranger push the car out to the road again, to realize just how bad his lungs hurt and how far he'd let his body go, just how close to an inevitably painful death those years of smoking had brought him. After that, he'd decided he'd had enough. *Cold fuckin' turkey.* Nothing like the fear of God to put a stop to a terrible habit, Jim knew, yet that fear of God must've diminished drastically this past decade, slowly decaying when he'd had his attention elsewhere, for now the drink had its greasy claws in him. It was a means of relaxation, of destressing. Those were his excuses and he hid from the truth of it all, that he was sliding further and further away from any sort of graceful movement into retirement age, like a child hiding from his parents for staining the walls with magic marker.

If there were any silver lining to Stedner's smoking, he was at least quick about it. He'd finished up and was back at Jim's side, carrying with him a miasma of cigarette reek, in the time that Jim had only had the chance to scan the front of the house and overhear a bit of the conversation off to his right.

The two detectives walked onto the driveway and towards the thin concrete path leading from the driveway up to the front door. The young patrolwoman talking to the older gal had glanced up and nodded when she recognized Stedner, who gave the officer a nod in return. The other officer standing at the front door, one of the newer recruits, appeared not to recognize either of them as they approached.

Jim raised his badge. "Detective Trent. This is Detective Stedner."

Stedner pulled his badge from his jacket and displayed it for a moment, then clipped it onto his belt.

The officer nodded and stepped aside. "Yep."

Jim ducked under the crime scene tape strewn across the doorway. The lights above in the entryway were lifeless, as were those in the kitchen as the detectives passed. The eastern sun was showing its pale beams through the blinds of the window above the sink, over the dark countertops and dining room table. Vertical curtains stood tall and still over the sliding glass door leading to the backyard. The door to the garage stood propped open. Light from somewhere inside and above poured through. From this angle, Jim couldn't see but the very top of a tilted car inside.

A bright yellow evidence card with the number **2** printed on it sat next to a bowl on the dresser in the walkway. Forensics had been here already, it seemed. Detective Stedner had put on his bright blue latex gloves and was rummaging through the keys and change in it, but he seemed to bore of it quickly. Jim moved to the base of the staircase, snapping his own latex gloves on. The stairs were broad and carpeted. He stared up to the midway landing and the window above it for a moment before beginning his ascension. Stedner followed behind.

The bulbs in the ceiling of the second-floor hallway were off but the colorless morning glow through the landing window was enough to light their way. The panel into the attic was closed, though the short string hanging from its handle gently swayed in some subtle moving air Jim could not feel. At the far end of the hall, the door to a room on the left was open wide.

When they reached the room, Jim saw the truth of it, that the door was no longer whole. Only about a quarter of the thing still existed, hanging crookedly on a bent hinge attached to the bottom of the doorframe. Shards and strips of flimsy wood were spread over the carpet toward the wall opposite the entrance to the room, riddled about as if destroyed in some fury. Speckled throughout in seemingly random spots, evidence cards with their own individual numbers on them stood facing every which direction. A specific card, marked **11**, was sitting on the carpet up against the wall to left as they entered, guarding a pair of buckshot holes that were embedded amongst the drywall, with chalk-like innards exposed inside of each one.

Stedner stepped in. "Ugh, that smell. Is that vomit? *Yikes.*" He took two long lunges, avoiding the wooden splinters, other evidence cards and the visibly soaked portions of the carpet, and moved around to the back end of the shotgun lying on the floor near the window. He crouched, staring at it for a moment, then looked up and aligned himself with the gun and the holes in the wall where Jim was standing. His hands came up as if aiming a shotgun with the invisible butt against his shoulder. "So, guy grabs his shotgun, loads two shells into it, fires both at the wall ahead of him..." He made two pumping motions and *kshh-kshh* with his mouth as he fired the imaginary weapon toward Jim, who stood directly in front of the holes. "At some point pukes... Then leaves?"

Jim's eyes searched over the computer desk against the far wall, scanned over the bits of wood on the floor and within the rank dampness, then looked to the window behind Stedner. "There wasn't any evidence of a break in, correct?"

"No signs of forced entry, save for the *obvious* forced entry into this room. Nothing in the report to indicate otherwise, at least. All the windows and doors were locked, according to the first responders. The second story bathroom window was cracked, though that one is the size of a doggy door."

Jim chewed at his thumbnail. "Hm."

At his feet, evidence card number **8** sat next to a large chunk of door that contained the doorknob. Jim's knees popped as he crouched. He fiddled with the knob attached to its own island of wood among the sea of soft carpet. "The doorknob's locked."

Stedner simply nodded with a determined look but, in his eyes, Jim saw the uncertainty he was trying to hide.

Jim stood, moved back to the doorway and turned toward his partner. "The way I see it, there's only really two possibilities, considering the knob is locked. Either the door was locked before our guy could get to the shotgun, and he destroyed the door in order to get to it, or he locked the door *after* entering the room, and someone else busted the door down after he'd reached the shotgun. Either way, the shots are aimed low and the buck unobstructed. If there really was someone breaking into the room, seems strange he'd completely miss them." He motioned toward the stinking effluence in the carpet. "And, of course, at some point did this. It doesn't smell like vomit, though. Smells more like rot, or some sort of infection."

Stedner was now standing and flipping through the report. "Maybe he went crazy. I've heard divorce can do that to a man."

Jim didn't say anything. He'd been married once when he was younger but the divorce wasn't anything to cry about. They'd fallen into it hot and heavy and both realized they'd made a mistake. It'd been a mutual parting, and he'd dated a few women since though nothing had ever come close to the passion he'd felt then, if there was anything he still regretted or missed about it.

Stedner coughed and grimaced at the smell again. "They found shattered glass in the garage, underneath the car held up on jacks. Wanna go take a look?"

Jim waited a moment longer, searching once more over the room. The computer monitor was black as night. Squat stacks of paper and books sat on the filing cabinet in between the computer desk and the wall. Dust motes floated in the morning sunlight beaming through the window behind Stedner, sodden bits of carpet here and there glinting in the light.

"Yeah, let's head down."

In the kitchen, on the counter separating the cooking area from the dining table, there was another evidence card, this one marked with a **13**. A smart phone with a dead screen lay next to it. Jim approached and clicked the power button on the side of the thing. The screen lit with a request for PIN entry. He tapped 1-2-3-

4, and the screen didn't seem to like responding to his latex fingertips. He tapped the numbers once more, this time doing it slowly and methodically, and got an INCORRECT PIN error. A sticky residue of some kind speckled the sides of the phone, and a roll of duct tape sat beside it.

Stedner was already standing in the garage when Jim entered.

The car was small, looking cramped inside from where Jim stood. The license plates were simply advertisements for *Dela Luna Used Cars*, a midnight color gradient in the lettering and a phone number, backdropped on a night vista of a Maui beach or something.

"What do you make of it?" Stedner was crouched looking at the shards of glass spread out under the car.

Jim's phone had just vibrated again and, when he pulled it from his pocket, he saw that it was another text from his sister. "It's glass," he said, distracted. "Looks like Pyrex or something from here."

"No, not the glass. The markings."

Jim's attention returned ahead to see Stedner pointing with a bright blue latex finger to the underside of the car. He slid the phone back into his pocket and descended the steps of the wooden landing to the garage floor. A quick glance into the rear showed him a skateboard on the backseat cushions and a brief thought came to him, that maybe Timmy would be interested in a skateboard, something to take his mind off of whatever had scared him so badly in those woods.

Jim crouched in front of the car, and then he saw what Stedner had been pointing at: symbols marked with chalk, and some scratched into the very metal, crawled out all along the different pipes and panels and tubes of the undercarriage. Some of them were letters he recognized, most of them were shapes of a language he'd never seen before.

And there was something else, too.

At first, Jim thought he had something in his eye, very subtly obscuring his vision, maybe an eyelash or a bit of dirt. He blinked repeatedly and then rubbed the eye socket with the palm of his hand but, when he looked back, he could still see it, like a fog or haze barely visible in the space underneath the car. It was like a faint light emanating from the space, some odd mist or—

A *thud* erupted from upstairs.

Jim looked to his partner. Stedner's eyes were already wide and looking at his.

"Is that one of our guys?" Stedner asked.

"I don't know. I didn't hear anyone else arrive yet."

The detectives stood in unison and moved wordlessly back up the steps of the landing, into the kitchen and toward the staircase leading up to the second floor of the house. When Jim could see the patrolman still standing at the entryway, facing out to the yard beyond the police tape, he drew his pistol from its holster, Stedner following suit immediately afterward. Switching the safety off felt strange with latex gloves on, Jim noted, but his thoughts were stolen by the muffled sounds of movement now coming from the floor above them.

Once he'd reached the midway landing of the stairs, Jim could see the office light flaring and dimming and flaring again. Accompanying the strobing, there was a sound, a sort of moaning or crying. Stedner was his shadow, moving slowly with him as they ascended the latter part of the staircase to come upon the second-floor hallway.

The fetor was the first thing Jim noticed, rank and miasmic, and he hadn't even gotten a full look into the room at that point. Nausea overwhelmed his senses and he stopped for a brief moment and leaned his nose into his shoulder for respite. It was the smell from earlier, from the stuff in the carpet, but enhanced into intense putridity, with a sourness concomitant of sewage or rotting garbage.

"Ugh! What the *fuck*?" Stedner, with one blue hand covering his nose and the other holding his pistol out in front of him, slowly moved around Jim and into the room. "Woah! Hands where I can see 'em, *now*!"

Jim snapped from his temporary daze, shaking his senses back and stepped into the room in which his partner stood.

Stedner had both hands on his gun, pointing it at a shape crumpled underneath the singular window at the far wall. With a backdrop of blood splatter and dripping coagulate over the wall behind him, the shape looked less like a man and more like a soaked animal of some kind. His hair and the hoodie and briefs he wore were drenched through with an unrecognizable excrement, a mixture of bodily fluids like blood and placenta, and there was too much of it to accompany any sort of vitality if they were fluids belonging to the man lathered in it. Writhing around in the puddle he sat in, the man cried and groaned loudly. His eyes were closed and his face was grimacing in some unknown torture. There were no apparent wounds Jim could identify, even though he kept looking for some. The man's face and clothes dripped of the syrupy stuff and the smell that billowed toward the detectives was sour and pungent and burned Jim's nostrils like fire.

And then the man stopped crying, instantaneously even, and lifted his head. His eyes slowly opened to stare up at the light in the ceiling of the room, white spots amongst red and brown and the off-yellow of pus that was slathered over his skin, the coagulate in his beard. These eyes then lowered and came to glare directly at Stedner. An almost visible viciousness crept from the gaze toward the young detective, a searing focus.

Jim tightened his grip on the pistol held out in front of him, waiting for any hint of movement.

"Identify yourself," Stedner said. "Now."

Only silence answered. And then a breath escaped the bloody man's mouth, followed by a single sob.

"Are you Chamberlain? Michael Chamberlain?" Jim's own voice sounded strained, hoarse.

A few more sobs came from the man's throat, deep sobs, his shoulders racking with each one. Snot dripped from his greased nose. He sniffed and began to speak:

"The... the things... showed me."

Stedner looked to Jim, then looked back and said, "What?"

The man's dripping hands rose to grip at his own face. He cried into the shelter of his palms. His voice was raspy, morose. "It said I was... It said I was the vessel and I was supposed to be it, all this time, somehow. It... Fuck... They won't let me go. I'm just as much a part of them as they are parts of me. I... hear her voice, telling me it's time. I don't want..."

"What do you mean," Stedner asked. "What happened to you?" His pistol had lowered to point towards the floor between he and the suspect. Jim left his pistol where it was, aiming directly at the man's heaving chest. The years of service had wrung the old detective's instincts taught with a tension Stedner had yet to develop, a tension that didn't allow Jim to drop his guard as easily as his young partner.

The man cried again and inhaled through a visible exhaustion. Deep tremors ran through him with each breath. The fluids slathered over his arms and in his clothes glistened with a lurid sheen. He leaned forward over his own lap and vomited into the already sodden crotch of his briefs. Stedner's pistol came back up. Both detectives took a step back before the man let out another belch of the stuff, grotesque chunky gore that looked to consist of blood more than anything else, trailing threads of something black in it as well.

Spittle hung from the man's curled bleating lips. "I don't want to be a part of this. I just want to be okay. I just— *Aaaagh!*" The man leaned over once more, his arms wrapped around his stomach. And then Jim saw that those arms weren't cradling his stomach but pushing against it, as if holding something in. "It's time. Oh, God. Oh, fuck, it's time. It's when it was meant to be ohmygod *uuugggghh*—" A guttural sound burst forth from his mouth, unreal and bizarrely animalistic. A squeezed croaking noise followed.

He was choking.

"Oh fuck," Jim said. He took a step toward the man but stopped when something grey and slick slipped downward from the man's hanging mouth, sliding out of his throat onto the wretched carpet below. A fat pale grub, the size of a bratwurst, lay in the puddle of refuse. A new stench, even more fetid than before, reached Jim's nose and he turned and vomited against the wall to his right, unsuccessfully fighting back as much of it as he could.

The bloody Michael Chamberlain leaned back on his calves, trying to recover his breath. "H-help me! Help me— *uuggghh*." And then another bulbous grub sloughed out of his mouth to the floor. This one immediately began to writhe and twist and curl. Upon seeing it, the bloody man's eyes went wide and his breaths shallowed, and he began leaning back against the wall and moving to stand up.

Stedner's pistol was shaking. "Stay where you are! Sir, stay the fuck where you are!"

Adrenaline was rushing through Jim's hands as he turned back to see. His gun, now raised again, was shaking, too.

"I *will* open fire!" Tension raised the octave of Stedner's voice. "I said stay where the fuck you are!"

Jim held back the bile in his throat, looked to his partner and tried to speak. "Kyle!" He spat to get the grease out of his mouth "Wait!"

"*Nuuuuhhhh--*" the bloody man mumbled as he stood. And then he lunged for Jim's partner.

Pop!

One single shot erupted from Stedner's pistol, sinking through the man's skull and sending him back to the wall, adding more dripping gore to the macabre painting of blood and fluid already there. The latent brightness of muzzle fire burned in Jim's vision. The body slumped into the puddles of stuff below and spouts of blood pumped out of the new hole in the bridge of the man's nose with the erratic beats of his fading heartbeat.

Stedner retched onto the floor.

There were shouts from downstairs. The other officers had entered the house and their footfalls were moving up the stairs. Jim didn't take his eyes off the body lying in front of them. Curds of bloody matter dripped from the glass of the window.

"You saw him take steps toward me, right? I wasn't—" Stedner spit the rest of the puke from his mouth, his hands shaking. "I wasn't seeing things, right? He stepped toward me, goddamnit!"

Jim nodded, though he wasn't sure if his partner saw it through the shock that had obviously overtaken him.

Stedner took an unsure step toward the body, then another. Jim stood still in the doorway, his pistol aimed at the corpse. There was a brief moment, as Stedner stood over it, in which the silence seemed to be almost overwhelming. Jim found himself staring directly at the white-eyed face of the man that had been horribly alive only moments before, at the hole that trickled blood down the nose and lips and chin and down the neck.

Stedner pointed toward the floor. "And what the fuck are *those* things?"

The two officers from outside came into the room, weapons drawn.

"We heard a shot," the patrolwoman said. "You two alright?"

Jim answered. "Yeah, I think we're alright. The guy lunged at Detective Stedner so he put him down. I can attest to it." When he glanced to his partner, the young detective was nudging the grub closest to him while wiping his mouth with the back of his sleeve. Even though the worms on the floor were motionless, they still looked bulbous and wretched. A look of unease lay heavy in his eyes. Jim knew the kid had never shot a man before.

"Where'd he come from?" the patrolman said. "I cleared this floor myself before you guys arrived." The two moved around Jim and came to stand beside the corpse with Stedner, just outside the puddles of gore and the two apparently dead maggot things.

"Ugh, what the hell is *that*?" The patrolwoman motioned toward one of the two grubs.

Stedner raised a boot and nudged the foot of the corpse leaned against the wall, his pistol at the ready. At first, as the four stood in silent observation, no one moved—not the detectives, the officers or the body below. But then there was a twitch, a slight wiggle from the dead man's torso, and the officers drew in sharp breaths and raised their weapons. The stomach of the man moved in and out, an unnatural type of shifting, separate and willful from the rest of the limp lifeless body. The head lolled to one side with the movement, leaking more dark blood from the hole in the head to the carpet. The stomach under the hoodie bulged and wriggled, and the bottom of the man's shirt slid up as the mass swelled, as if some feral fetus was trying to claw its way out of the man. A slow rolling motion ascended the corpse's throat and Jim watched the cheeks swell and the mouth part for an emergence.

It was another grub. It slithered out of the bloody gullet and down the man's soaked chest to the floor.

"Oh—" one of the officers started. "Oh my god..."

Jim took a single step back toward the hall, and then another, his pistol still held firm and aimed true. "Guys, I think we sh—"

And then there was a terrible sound, a ripping or rending and, even with the officers partially obscuring his view of the dead man, Jim saw everything: like the tight skin of an overcooked sausage, the bloody man's swollen stomach stretched out, as if a basketball was hidden under his shirt, and then burst through the hoodie he wore with a deep *bloop* sound, almost comical in its horrible audibility, leaving his flesh gaped open. A mound of milky worms fell forth from the vacuous hole and spread out at the feet of the officers like some grotesque ritual offering.

Stedner leapt from his position back toward the door, as well as the patrolwoman, but the other officer started yelling and lifted a foot where he stood. "What the fuck!" the patrolman yelled. "It's biting me, get this fucking— *Aaaghhh*!" And then he dropped to the floor. Like a small army with one mind, one consciousness, a cluster of worms crawled up from his shoes, into his pant legs as he tried to scramble backward. Within moments, half a dozen of them crawling on the outside of his clothes seemed to disappear and Jim then realized they were burrowing, digging themselves into the officer's thighs and hips and buttocks.

Pop-pop! Pop!

The patrolwoman backed toward the computer desk, firing at the grubs that crawled hungrily after her through the carpet. The gunshots shook Jim from his horrified gaze. A look of wild fear had the woman's eyes wide in their sockets.

Pop!

Stedner took a shot at one of the worms heading toward the doorway, stepping back and yelling, "Oh fuck, oh fuck!" while swinging at something low. Jim backed into the hallway, felt his back press against the banister that overlooked the staircase to the first floor. Writhing up his partner's pant leg was one of the pale things, unreal in its speed and intent. Stedner batted at it with his pistol but the thing clung to him, hooked into the denim of his jeans. When he'd breached the doorway into the hall, Stedner fell to the carpet and tried scooting toward the staircase. The bulbous thing appeared to be chewing into his knee.

"Kyle!" Jim screamed. He sidestepped, then swiped at the thing sticking out of his partner's leg but, by the time he'd attempted it, the creature was already half-buried into the kneecap. He grabbed at the thing's slimy little bulk and was immediately hit with a searing pain that leapt across his palm. A slit was open, shallow but wide, across his hand. Out of the ass-end of the worm, glinting in the office light, was a slender almost invisible hook-shaped stinger. Another attempt at bashing the worm with the butt of his pistol left Jim's pinky finger sliced open like a fillet. The pain was something indescribable, and the ache quickly spread to his entire hand, stared moving up his forearm.

A curdled scream erupted from inside the office. When Jim glanced toward the sound, instead of seeing the remaining patrolwoman rushing out, there were only the endless worms moving as a tide out of the room. There were multitudes more than could've logistically fit inside the dead man's stomach, fat and glistening and in a wave that undulated like a blanket of molting snakes. The screams of the patrolwoman were cut off, choked into a gurgling silence somewhere back in the office, beyond where Jim could see.

The detectives had scooted back all the way to the staircase but another of the worms had reached Stedner's bloody dragging leg. It seemed to sniff around the heel of his shoe and then it began to chew into the rubber of it. Jim stood and punted the thing with a forceful kick. There was a heavy *smack* when he did, the thing weighing much more than he'd anticipated. It splattered against the door of the linen closet at the end of the hall, exploding like a water balloon filled with pus. By the time Jim glanced back down to his partner, two more worms were chewing into the same foot and Stedner was screaming, his hands tight around the thigh above where the first grub had entered his knee, squeezing it hard like some last resort tourniquet.

Jim pointed his pistol at the mound of worms coming out of the room and fired four shots into the heap, though it seemed to do absolutely nothing to stop the oncoming things, moving in a roiling singular clump. He holstered his pistol and grabbed his screaming companion under the arms, dragging him down the first two steps of the staircase. Before he could get to the landing, though, he felt Stedner's body go slack.

"Kyle? Kyle!"

And when Stedner's head rolled back to rest against Jim's chest, Jim saw something squirming out of his partner's eye socket, a set of rapidly moving mandibles. He leapt back with a shout, stumbling down the last few steps to the landing and almost falling over the small end table underneath the window, knocking its lamp to the floor with a clatter. He struggled to find his balance, grasping at the curtains of the window and blinding himself with the morning sun that lay beyond.

Stedner lay limp halfway down the steps from the second floor. It seemed only a moment of Death's peace was allowed before Stedner's body was swallowed by the swarming scourge, a single-minded mass of biting and gnawing, wringing gouts of blood from the body. Straggling grubs fell through the staircase balusters, smacking to the hardwood of the first floor below. They squirmed, fat and bloated, and crawled to block the path of escape.

Jim sprung toward the latter section of stairs. He made the first step, then the second, then bounded over the things inching toward him and slid into the foyer. He pulled the walkie from his belt, tried to press the push-to-talk button but his thumb slid off the thing at first, his injured hand having made the device slick with his own blood. When he'd gotten the button pressed down, just before he'd met the police tape across the entrance, he yelled into it.

"Dispatch, this is seven-Adam-six, Detective Trent! I need backup now! Multiple officers down! There's some kind of... Some kind of fucking infestation here and something—"

He burst through the police tape, screaming his location into the radio. He stopped and turned to pull the front door shut behind him, and then ran out into the morning light. When he'd reached the yard beyond the small line of planted shrubs, the morning dew from the grass having already begun to seep into his shoes, he turned to look at the house and the entrance, stumbling backward toward the patrol cars. The dark windows stared down at him like unblinking eyes. In one hand, he held the raised pistol, in the bleeding other, the radio.

"Dispatch, something is happening. Jesus Christ..."

He didn't know what that something was, though. The moments of silence before the response over the radio seemed to stretch on longer than his mind could justify, and then just as he was about to shout into the thing for an answer, the dispatcher's voice came through sharply, crackling from the speaker into the still dawn air.

"*Detective, two units on the way. ETA three minutes. What's happening? Two units were on scene before you arrived. Where are they?*"

"Something is happening," Jim said again. "There's... worms and..." His mind had lost the words to describe what he'd seen, the horrific bloody mess that had unfolded in front of him. Kyle Stedner, his partner for the last three years, just a damn *kid*, was gone, horribly exsanguinated, along with the other two officers and the man who lived in the home, yet his words were weighted on his tongue, unable to formulate these things, incapable of leaving his terror-locked jaw.

The growing sun shined through the fog onto the white frames around the windows of the house, onto the awnings and the gutters, and brought life to the baby-blue paint elsewhere. To simply look upon the place, one would never know the horrors that awaited just inside, creeping worming horrors.

"*Detective Trent*," the voice came again. "*Who is down?*"

The breath swelled in Jim's lungs with each inhale, burning with fright and hyperventilation. Adrenaline clouded the edges of his vision. When he stepped back against the rear bumper of one of the patrol cars, he yelped like beaten dog, and then side-stepped around the vehicle, all the while keeping his eyes on the front door of the house. In the distance, sirens rang out. In his hysteria, he'd forgotten the sound's purpose, what it meant and why it was incoming. The reeling whine only seemed to combine with the ringing in his ears, sending him further into his horror.

Kyle...

"Stedner," Jim said into the radio. "My partner, Detective Kyle Stedner. And... and the two units that were here before. I don't know where these things came from but they're worms and one of them got into his knee, one tried to get into his shoe but—"

And then the sound of the house's front door latch stopped Jim in his words and in his movement. Like some yawning beast, the door groaned slowly open. Though the sun was brightening and the sky was clearing, the interior of the entrance hall appeared as dark as the void, a portal to nothingness. There were no shapes nor movement, no crawling things or anything else.

There was only darkness.

Sweat mixed with the condensation of the morning and dripped down the detective's neck into his collar. The pistol was shaking in his hand.

"*Detective, you're cutting out,*" the dispatcher cut through again. "*I can't hear you anymore.*"

Jim didn't hear her voice, though.

He heard nothing. He *saw* nothing, except...

Out of the darkness and into the light of the morning walked the young Detective Kyle Stedner.

Jim was overtaken by a unique emotion, then, the feeling of reality no longer making sense at the sight of the man he'd thought dead only moments ago. Stedner ambled slowly out into the grass in Jim's direction but his eyes did not look ahead. Instead, they were focused at the pale sun beyond the diminishing fog, staring off as if to a distant place. Clustered sores and gaping holes were scattered over his body, and little things peeked in and out of those holes as he walked. Slick strings of coagulate marked each slow step of his right foot in the grass below, left by the holes in his leg. His clothes were soaked in blood, his skin a purpling shade of lividity.

"Jim..." the thing said. It was Stedner's voice, Jim could hear, but it was off somehow, too croaky, not full enough, as if this thing pretending to be his partner was speaking with little to no air in his lungs. But it spoke, nonetheless. "Jim, Jim, Jim-Jim," it rambled. "It's beautiful, Jim-Jim. It's beautiful and it, it, it—" A grub slid from a hole in the imposter's neck, cutting off the words and then dripping itself to the ground below, leaving a slick trail on this thing wearing Stedner's body. "It begins with us, Jim-Jim. It begins with us, with us, with ussssss..."

It wasn't the bizarre undertones of the voice, or the even the worms sliding in and out of the wounds on his body, that petrified Jim. Rather, it was the rachitic inhuman gait his young partner moved with. The limbs and tendons of his body seemed to extend and retract on their own, though somehow still maintaining a walk, still coming closer and closer in an alarmingly unnatural way.

The dispatcher was calling out over the radio but Jim still couldn't hear her words, which were reduced to an indiscriminate background noise as he was too focused on what approached from ahead.

"Kyle! Stay back!" Jim yelled. "Please, just stop until... until I can..."

He'd never seen a human move in this way and the observance of such a thing paralyzed him with disbelief throughout his body, filled him with the electricity of impending madness. Adrenaline shook his hands. Images flooded his mind of his pistol's muzzle fire exploding outward and a bullet zipping through the air into his partner skull, ending the life so prematurely.

Jim's voice cracked when he shouted again. "Please, Kyle! Stay there. Please don't make me!"

"Jim-Jim. Jim, can't you see? Life and Death, there is no

difffffffff-diff-diff. Jim, Jim, jimjimjimjimjim—" Stedner turned his head to face the old detective and his eyes were all the way rolled back and solid white in his head. A few steps closer and Jim was able to see:

Fat worms rolled around in his partner's sockets instead of eyes.

It was at this moment that the thing playing as Stedner, the creatures animating his body, shrieked some unholy sounds from deep in the throat and Detective Jim Trent fired three rounds towards the chest. Two landed in the upper rib cage and the third sunk through the neck. When the gored and bloodied body fell back, it was as if it'd been held together by mere stitches or tape for, when it slammed against the grass, the stomach flesh of the thing that once was Stedner burst open, as did the swollen legs and the neck. Grotesque balls of worms and snake-like things slid from the newly gaped cavities, with streams of the things pouring out of the excavated heels of his feet.

The smell hit Jim like a sucker punch and he couldn't hold back. Vomit erupted from his throat once again, splashing into the gravel on which the patrol car and his own were parked. He coughed out the rest of it and spat, a stinging sourness clinging to the insides of his nasal cavity. He gasped and, as he took his recovering breaths, something twitched in the grass of the yard, only five or six feet from where he stood.

The distant sirens took a sharper tone as two interceptors sped around the corner of the block, just down the street a few houses.

There was a hiss in the grass and then long bloody snakes, headless save for circular mouths, slithered toward the car.

Jim leapt to the driver's side of the car he and his partner had shown up in, opened the door and slammed it shut. His eyes searched frantically over the interior of the vehicle, checked all around the pedals, over his legs and by his feet, down the cracks between the seat and the parking brake. Quick flashes of movement seemed to haunt the outskirts of his vision though nothing appeared to have slipped inside the vehicle. A thud against the driver's side window made him blanch, sent him reeling halfway over the parking brake and into the passenger seat.

Sucking against the outside of the glass at eye level, looking more like a lamprey than a worm, a circular mouth full of strangely human-like teeth ground and bit together and, impossibly, sent cracks like forked lightning through the glass with the force of its gnashing.

Even in the daylight, the blue and red lights of the approaching cruisers rolled over the interior of the car as the backup promised by the dispatcher closed in from the street behind. The first interceptor came to a skidded halt next to the cruiser left abandoned by the now dead patrolwoman. The newly arrived officer stepped out of the driver door and drew his weapon, leaning and saying something into his shoulder mic.

"Get back in your car!" Jim shouted from inside his own vehicle. "Don't let 'em touch you!" He waved, trying to get the attention of the officer, to motion him back into his own car, though there was a certainty that he couldn't hear what was being yelled. Jim's hand instinctively reached for the window switch but then he heard another crack in the window and the snake thing sucking on the glass brought him back to the sick reality of his situation. Another shape crawled serpentine up the windshield, another of the fat grubs. This one reached halfway up the glass, then suddenly burst, covering the windshield in bile and necrotic gorged blood.

In his hysteria, Jim popped the windshield wipers on and then placed the end of the pistol against the inside of the glass of the driver's side window, lined up with the snake thing sucking at it from just outside. Before his mind could tell his hand otherwise, he pulled the trigger. The report from the shot exploded in a deafening sound. The glass shattered into countless twinkling pieces flying all over the interior of the car. Shrieking tinnitus sang in Jim's ears.

The snake was nowhere to be seen but now the interior was exposed to the outside and anything else that could be crawling toward the opening.

Jim slid the keys in and turned the ignition over. The engine started immediately but he could hardly hear it. As he put the car into reverse, he shouted at the other officer, "Don't let them on you!", but his voice sounded far away, as if it were someone else's voice instead, shouting to him from some great distance. The windshield wipers smeared the fetor, back and forth.

From the entrance to the house, out of the passenger side window, something caught Jim's attention.

A silvery glinting shone only briefly from the dark entryway of the house, something slick catching the light. And then a horrid thing moved out of the shadows into the light of the day. It was like a dog, on four legs, but was much bigger, its head elongated, shaped like some malformed horse's. Its back and spine were twisted yet sinister and predatory, its claws were misshapen but massive, deadly. A steady stream of fluid dripped from its mouth of strange teeth onto the concrete of the porch.

The officer outside screamed. "Oh my God!"

The creature's lidless cluster of eyes rolled in its skull and turned toward the officer. It stopped its slow walk for only a moment. The sinews of its hind legs rippled as it coiled back and, just as Jim was raising his pistol to fire at the abomination from inside the car, it sprung like a bullet at the officer, over the grass of the entire lawn in a mere moment. The officer screamed horribly when it slipped around the front end of the car and managed to follow him back into the cruiser before he could close the door. The interior of the windshield went black with blood as the large shape moved ravenously inside.

And then, from the doorway of the house, two more shapes emerged.

The two officers from before...

They moved out onto the grass the same way Stedner had before Jim put him down, before the worms came flooding out of the burst flesh. Both were pockmarked with the same worm-sized holes amidst their bodies, holes that things peeked out of and slithered back into, animating the shambling bodies like marionette puppets.

Jim threw the pistol into the passenger seat and slammed the acceleration down. The car jumped into reverse, crunching into and skidding off of the freshly parked third interceptor behind him. He stuck the gear into Drive once he'd cleared the car and driveway, then pushed the pedal to the floor. The windshield was still smeared with the rotten stuff from the grub that had exploded on it. He clicked the button for the spray of washer fluid. The juices dripped and poured in through the broken driver's window as he began to gain speed.

Caught under the tires of the car, meaty little shapes burst beneath the weight, accompanied by *popping* sounds as if Jim was driving over some kind of bubble-wrap. Worms and fleshy snakes flooding the road...

As he sped away, his terror convinced him to check the interior of the car once again. In his rearview mirror, growing smaller by the second, an officer from yet another patrol car stepped out and approached, gun out in front of him, to the bloody mess of the other interceptor. The large creature bounded out of the vehicle onto the officer, looking like some type of rabid dog in the distance. Jim could see the muzzle flare of two shots fired before the shape overtook the man. Far beyond, even more lights were coming into view.

Jim cried with each exhale. "Jesus fucking Christ. Jesus fucking Christ..."

As the scene faded into the early day behind him, Jim's limbs shook with furious horror. His eyes darted around the floor of the car and the seats behind and next to him. Madness was setting in. His knuckles were white with the tension of his grip around the steering wheel and his lungs were tight with crippling constriction. He could hardly catch a full breath.

The sun was high in the east beyond the fog and it shined off of the remnants of slime smeared over the windshield of the car. The daylight lit a world that passed by in a glaze for Jim, a glaze of shock. Even when another interceptor flew passed him going toward the very place he was escaping, it hardly registered.

Nothing else registered for him.

Justifications for the things he'd seen and smelled and heard seemed to manifest within the attempts at rationality his mind employed, then dissipated in the face of the reflection of such otherworldly events, unexplainable memories now burned into his psych. There was no way that Detective James "Jim" Trent could've known, when he'd woken up that morning, drinking the fruits of day-old coffee grounds, thinking of his sister and plight of his nephew, that he would bear witness to the beginning of the end of all things that he knew. There was no way he could've known that the infection wouldn't be confined to this one house, this one town block, but would spread like a ravenous horde of locusts and never slow, extending from land into ocean and to other lands, plaguing and overpowering. There was no way he could've known that all continents would fall to the dominion of the hungry dark things that had come, that the existence of man would face its cessation with the cries of suffering, to be met only by the indifference of the deep spaces hidden within the endless void of death.

The Gate and the Star

The night seethed and almost boiled in its darkness. Great fires burned in all distant directions, backlighting the broken silhouettes of the gnarled and blasted desertscape with a dim perpetual orange. The smoldering color shone up into the skies, which were low with a black overcast, separating the horizon with a thin line of glowing flames. The terrain's gloom was the color of the void, out of the cracks and holes of which rose grey-black smoke in plumes, thin and silent like charmed serpents, as though the whole plane was burning just underneath its surface.

The muscles in Esha's legs were as if bathed in those distant flames. The final bit of adrenaline was turning into exhaustion, though she still moved as quick as the wind, striding deftly over the burn encrusted dirt. A quiver on her back held the last two of her serrated arrows and they rattled against each other with each swift step she stole.

Don't look back. Don't look back—

The mantra repeated over and over in her mind, emboldening her pace and, even though her lungs felt scorched by the ash in the air, she held onto the image of what lay ahead:

The gate.

Fathomlessly tall, it appeared as an immense monolith against the backdrop of the inflamed horizon, standing higher than any structure she'd ever seen. It ascended at least half a league into the air. In this perpetual night's murk, the profiles of the ominous titans could barely be made out, humongous guardians etched out of the stone on either side of the great doorway. Attached to no wall or other building, the gate stood on its own like a lone god against the blackness of this twisted world. Radiance from between its great bronze doors shone as a sliver of illuminating gold among the shadows of the realm surrounding. The darkness left thwarted by its brilliance undulated like a throat, coughing and choking, as if trying to swallow the light whole.

To traverse it was to reach an alternate reality altogether.

To traverse it was Esha's mission.

A savage mass, gross and curdling, nipped only yards behind her heels. Ferocious barking accentuated the rest of the bizarre calls of the legions that pursued, footfalls of which were growing louder in her ears. Joints cracked and jaws clapped, snapping open and shut at her scent. Wretched cries of a single unified hunger, belonging to some kind of kinship between living beast and the dead, sounded off to war horns from the demented unseen at her back, riding on the snarls of a swelling devilry.

Don't look back. Don't look back—

An individual point of this many-mouthed intent, a singular piece of the pursuing horde, had gained ground on the right flank. The feathers of those last two arrows grazed Esha's fingertips when she reached back. She unsheathed one from the quiver, drawing and nocking it and turning to aim at the bold thing closing in. That micro-moment stretched and, within that dilation, the tingle of learned pyromancy coiled in her knuckles and under the flesh and nerves of her fingers. The arrowhead burned orange with heat and then she let it fly. As it sang through the air, the projectile caught fire mid-flight and sunk into the abominable shape, erupting into a small explosion. The heat blasted against Esha's face. Her skin, left cold by the frigid setting in which she was fleeing, drank it like sustenance.

When she turned back toward the gate, the internal mantra no longer repeated through her, silenced by the glimpse she'd caught of the horde that ravenously carved its way through her wake. The hellish shapes had moved like maggots over the terrain, digging and burrowing and tumbling over each other, eating the rotten landscape beneath them. This necrotized scourge rolled as a flood of doom, a persistent wave of the dead converted into thralls, slaves of bewitched animation. They meant to consume the one that ran from them, to absorb her into their ranks…

Esha's hand moved to her swollen belly and she gave her thoughts and soul to her womb. *We will not be like them. This place will not be where it ends for us, my little sun, my star.*

A monumental sound came then, almost deafening and loud enough to unleash avalanches. The golden light from the gate ahead began a dwindling as, on their ancient hinges, the doors slowly moved to close.

Slick tongues lapped violently behind, licking and speaking languages of a realm beyond the living, getting closer and doing it quickly. The blood raced through Esha's veins. The final arrow was nocked and drawn, an action done more out of instinct than anything, occurring almost before the two humanoid things galloping like beasts came into sight on her left. A strange lifeless intent was visible in their shadowed sockets, one of an endless wanting, a jealousy. She released the arrow, decapitating one of them where its head met its bulk, then slid the dagger from the sheath at her hip and threw it at the second abomination's front limbs. Both tumbled into the sand and were overtaken by the following multitudes a half moment later.

And then the abyss above, the one that barely lit her path as she fled, changed. There was no moon, no nocturnal sun, but the hue of whatever sour lambency existed beyond the overcast altered, morphed into a deep crimson illumination and glowed through the black clouds with the color of blood. Everything became saturated in the newly produced light and, within the bizarre heavens, great masses floated overhead. Though she couldn't see them, she could feel their weight in her ear drums, pressing down from above the clouds. Underlying the distant firmament, the color of the fires changed to that of a boiling redness.

The mountains in the far horizon began to shift, moving impossibly like titanic entities awakening from eons of slumber. They trumpeted their grand calls over the leagues of land that lay between them and her. Esha felt the horrible bellowing in her bones. She threw the bow from her hands to the passing ground. Her eyes returned to the gate that stood ahead. Her hands moved again to the round of her belly and cradled the bastion of hope from which she drew her tired breath, the small life that grew inside of her. With every hard step, she said *I'm sorry, sweetie, I'm sorry, my star, I'm sorry*, but the gate's loud closure rumbled the ground. There wasn't time to slow and, truthfully, she reveled in the pain, the pain of maternal responsibility, of existential purpose.

Two hundred paces...

Esha hurdled over a crumpled mass in the sand, then another. Gleaming in the dim bloody radiance from above, bent and broken limbs and bones lay scattered in the dirt, bodies of humanoids and beasts alike, the remnants of a bloody battle fought recently. All she had left was being spent on her swift movement while the sounds of clawing and gnashing intensified behind her.

A hundred paces...

At the base of the towering doors, a crescent of monstrous corpses curled around the opening. Beyond the skeins of crippled figures, unreal in their alien forms, Esha could see the sheen of armor and the slashing of steel. A heavy shield moved back and forth, the counter-weight in perfectly executed strikes of a glinting silver sword. Opposite the one in armor, something scuttled and snapped like a deranged animal. The knight twirled in a dance and, as a slash from the creature glanced off the shield, the long blade swept in a whistling arc, cutting cleanly through the thing's neck and sending its snouted head tumbling to the ground. The knight turned. Black blood soaked his hair and face, dripping in threads from his armor.

"Strad!" Esha yelled.

A second wind came for her in that moment she saw her brother. And then she spoke again to her child. *We have to give it one last go, star of my life. One last push and then we'll be alright.* She sent as much of herself as she could into the love she poured over the thing inside of her, to muffle and dampen the trauma of her ambulance.

A subtle, almost imperceptible, little movement bumped from under the skin of her belly in response.

I love you so much, she pleaded to it. *I love you. I love you. I love you.*

"Sis!" Over the mound of bodies, Strad vaulted, sprinting toward her. "Duck!" he yelled, and so she did, sliding amongst the dust toward the doors. The thick shield spun like a disc overhead.

There was a heavy crunch that followed, a shriek from behind. When she looked up to him, her brother stood with a weighted front stance, staring beyond her position to what chased her. The sword he held in both hands now glowed with crystalline light. The moment she passed him, she heard the blade slice through the air, followed by a thundering sound, shaking the ground beneath them. A flash of emerald light erupted behind her. Whines of searing flesh and abominable throats soon followed. She leapt over the half-ring of corpses and landed against the closing doors.

Behind, Strad slashed and moved like a warrior from children's tales. Covered in the blood of his foes, he parried here and countered with a riposte there, his form perfect, mesmerizing even. Impaled and decapitated things writhed in heaps around him. He slammed the sword to the ground again and emerald light erupted once more from its blade. The dark acres ahead roared with its green flames. More of the things came flowing over the distant swollen hills, though, replacing those lost in the conflagration with their endless numbers.

The doors were still closing.

"Strad, you have to hurry!" Esha put herself between them, mere feet left of their opening, and pushed as hard as she could against the immense bronze things. "*Strad*!"

The knight turned toward her. His eyes widened. In the flash of a moment, he was rushing. His plate armor clanked as he bounded off of the skulls and ribcages of felled foes, toward the gate.

He was too far away.

Just before the great doors shut, Esha saw it in Strad's eyes, the realization that he wasn't going to make it. She saw him slow his pace, saw him turn back toward the oncoming horde, wretched things bursting forth from crevices in the ground like ooze rupturing from cavernous infections. He descended the mound of gore and raised his sword, backdropped by a horizon of green fire and a rushing scourge.

She watched them overtake the lone knight, and then the massive doors closed with the sound of thunder, obstructing her view.

*

Reality crept back in.

Esha breathed deeply.

Black panels gridded her surroundings, separated by thin lambent blue lines. It appeared like the inside of a construct of some kind, overlooking a starless universe, like an underwater photographer looking out into an ocean, guarded from the unknown by the cage she floated in. The Virtua-Deck gave the illusion of a dark infinity waiting beyond the grid in the walls and played with the perceived geometry. In function, they enhanced graphical output of most simulations, but this ancillary sensation left her strangely calm.

Esha removed the peripherals from her hands and then her face and then lay there staring into the darkness between the glowing lines. "There goes eight hours of progress," she said.

Her brother sat up from his own table a few feet to her right. "Relax," he groaned. "It's not like we won't try again in a few hours."

It was noticeable how thin he'd gotten when he slid off the table and walked to the door leading out into the hall. The cyber-jack implants in his temples and arms looked like tumors under the malnourished skin. She hadn't seen him eat a thing in days. They'd already had that discussion many times, though. Instead, she said, "I can tell you've been practicing. Your moves with the sword are getting better."

He stopped near the exit but didn't turn around. In the dim blue glow of the room, with his knobby shoulder blades visible through the thin cloth of his shirt, he looked like a standing corpse. A moment passed, then he said over his shoulder, "Thanks, sis." He tapped the button on the wall panel. The door slid open with a hiss and, after he left the room, it closed on its own with the same sound.

Esha laid back and rested a hand on her belly, or lack thereof. She closed her eyes. Her fingers moved along the contours of the sunken flesh around her hip bones and pelvis, over the boney ribs through her ragged shirt. Her judgment of Strad for not eating seemed hypocritical when, now that she was willing to admit it to herself, she hadn't eaten in a while either. The acidic pangs of hunger, and the roiling stomach bile that sometimes erupted into the back of her throat from lack of substance to digest, was something she'd grown used to. She could hardly feel it anymore, that drive to remain whole in the physical world. It came with being a big sister, though, to worry about the wellbeing of her little brother even if her own body meant next to nothing to her. Apathy had a way of dulling alarm, that was for sure, and the latest update of the game had changed everything. Three weeks ago, when the massive download had completed, she'd found a renewed purpose in that virtual world that left her wanting to leave the physical realm completely behind.

The reviews raved about it, and Strad couldn't stop talking about the new realms to explore. Esha had her own reasons for a new obsession within the virtual experience. Both she and Strad had broken plans elsewhere and called out sick from work numerous times in the past in order to login for hours on end, but it was never like it was now. Before, she'd actually been cutting back, checking out other mindwares and games. Now, she'd returned, been pulled back in full swing like an addict returning to smoke sticks. Now, the other world gave her something unique, miraculous even. It gave her the feeling of a hole inside of her, an emptiness, being filled. It didn't matter if it was fake or real. It *felt* as real as she ever thought pregnancy would. More than anything, it satiated the need to feel the weight of creating life. It was a weight of hope and of possibility. It was a weight of a future, much more fulfilling than the sagging emptiness of the true reality she'd been living in.

The words the robotic nurse had printed across its faceplate years ago during one of her physicals, *PREGNANCY INCAPABLE*, were the only images sitting in her mind at this moment, glowing bright yellow in the darkness behind her eyes like they had back then. The words came with the memory of the faint antiseptic smell of the hospital and she could swear the scent was in the air around her now. She'd tried to brush it off after she'd understood the diagnosis, pretended she didn't want children anyway... The years crept by, though, and the desire to hold a new life, to watch it grow and to keep it safe, had all but consumed her in times since.

Her stomach let out a long groan, for sustenance or something else, she couldn't tell. The noise seemed far away. When she sat up, it wasn't hunger she felt but the child that had been inside, some residual sensation of its simulated existence. Her mind hung half focused on the quiet scene around and half lost in the world she'd just left. She envisioned herself standing and moving to the door into the hall, finding food in a reality that had grown so vacant of meaning and of satisfaction...

Her faculties followed a different plan, though.

Boney hands attached to thin arms she hardly recognized anymore moved almost autonomously to reattach the sensor gloves and slip the headset back over her greasy hair. She leaned to her left and suckled on the water straw sticking out of the table before tightening the facemask over her mouth and nose, then punched in a code on the panel to relaunch the software. The still-warm cerebral prods slipped back into her skull, and the shock of neural synchronization flooded her senses once again. The screens of the headset came to life and, beyond their transparent lenses, the black panels of the Virtua-Deck morphed with animated shapes and bright colors and fell away into an almost Mandelbrot complexity.

*

The maelstrom of light swirled around her as she fell through dense black clouds, roiling with a tempestuous force. Lightning cracked all around while thunder shook her eardrums. Icy rain stung her skin as she sunk through, its frigid temperature soaking into her hair and clothes. She tried looking down to see the clouds breaking open and to see the dark desert coming up to greet her but the wind was too much and the atmosphere whipped at her face. It was only after she'd fallen through the dark overcast, right before slamming into the desert crust, that she had been able to see the tenebrous lands that extended in all directions.

The impact was hardly felt but it was loud, undoubtedly alerting the hordes to her presence. Rocks and pebbles pattered to the broken ground all around, cracks wormed out from the spot of her landing like a spider web. The dirty puddles nearby rippled like bizarre liquid mirrors, lit by the crazed flashes from the sky.

Esha stood and sniffed with renewed breath. The scent of the dirty rain seemed to baptize her. Under that, the air smelled of smoke and charred corpses with the iron tinge of some kind of corrupted blood behind it all. Her hands moved to her belly. When they beheld the mound once more, she half-laughed half-cried with something like gratefulness mixed with a helping of sorrow. In this world, her flesh was full of life and her soul was full of something maternal, glowing inside of her like nothing she'd felt in her corporeal reality.

Shining constructs manifested themselves in the high pit of clouds above. They were bright letters spelling out a message:

WELCOME BACK, ESHA.
TIME OF LAST LOGIN: 03:23AM AST 2 JUN 2074.

Then the text evaporated, eaten by the viscous overcast blocking whatever unnatural stars existed above this place. The rain fell in sheets that sounded like white noise from every direction. Beyond the music of the storm, the calls of the horrible legions were already manifesting. A crescendo of roaring and lashing grew with the incoming force. They'd heard her arrival, she was certain of it, and knew they could smell her humanity. Like static electricity running through the air, she could feel them, those thousands of biting mouths and wretched bodies crashing through the dark lands, honing in on her position.

The hue of the skies went like blood once again and the mountains in the distance woke from their rest with horns that shook the shadowed world. Gargantuan beasts broke through the clouds, oozing out of electrified portals and turning their assemblage of compassionless eyes toward Esha's direction.

And yet, she couldn't help but smile and send all the love she had, all the love she could ever generate in a million lifetimes, into the life that grew inside of her. *You ready?* she asked it almost whimsically and, a brief moment later, there was another gentle bump underneath her hands. Her eyes, blurry with a mix of rain and grateful tears, lifted to the dark heavens. She breathed in the smells of a permeating odor, the soaked aroma of blood and dirt and bodies rotting in the winds, bizarrely warm like dragon's breath. She breathed to feel the fullness of the star that burned brightly in her womb...

And then she ran.

Master

A long concrete hallway ran like an artery just beyond the back perimeter of the shoe department, pumping nothing but cold air produced by the vents that ran throughout the mall complex. In this hallway were employee entrances to the adjacent sections of the store, as well as a handful of storage rooms and janitor's closets, the doors of which stood lonesome like stalwart guards under the ceiling lamps that ran the length of it. It was during his first trip back there, returning a wad of dirty rags, some cleaner fluid and a used bucket of brown water to one of said closets, that Connor noticed the cooing sound coming from the far end of the hall. There was a door there, and it appeared ajar but only barely. That far down the hallway, it was impossible to tell who was in there and what they were doing, but the light inside was on. It shone as a sliver of yellow through the cracked door, intermittently blocked out and shifting its shades of color with the movement of whomever was inside. The sounds were soft, drifting out like the whispers one might produce when soothing a child to sleep, gentle tones meant to comfort and sedate.

Connor had started work at King's Department Store the day before yesterday, for $8.21 an hour, on a Monday that'd greeted him with pouring down rain and an ache in his groin that seemed to show up as soon as he'd first stepped foot into the building, which he'd chalked up to sleeping on his balls the wrong way the previous night. For two and a half days now, while he'd been trying to memorize intercom codes, check-out procedures and which go-backs went to each department, the soreness had ebbed and receded somewhere deep inside his groin or colon, but never seemed to fully go away. Bowel movements provided no relief, neither did stretching, deep breathing or even masturbation, the latter attempted on both of his fifteen-minute breaks those first couple days. The strangeness of it was that it didn't seem as pronounced, or he at least didn't notice it much at all, when he'd leave in the evenings to go home, and there were no other symptoms that accompanied the sensation—only that low ache.

Now, in this employee hallway, as Connor stood one-foot in the closet directly across from the north entrance of the shoe department, he began to feel a new surge in that dim ache.

His attention had shifted from his task of replacing the cleaning materials from where he'd gotten them, to the door at the far end of the hall, kitty-corner to the electronic department entrance. He stared into that distance and, as he stared, the pangs in his bowels evolved into something else, something less painful and, instead, more of an urge, a tingling biological response to a stimulus he'd never experienced before. It was a feeling of being coaxed by something gentle, initiated by an invisible thing he could not discern. The lights in the bland concrete hall seemed to dim, the lumens of which shorted out and flickered with the pull in his intestines and groin. The more he tried to focus on that door at the end of the hall, the more his sight lost itself in his attempts.

The edges of everything were blurring.

He hadn't noticed that he'd left the rags and bucket on the floor of the janitor's closet, that he'd turned and walked away without shutting the door, and that he'd made it the entire way to the end of the hall, until he was standing right outside that far door. The sounds coming from inside were easier to make out, easier to understand now that he was within such close proximity. Indeed, there was a nurturing happening within, one accompanied by lubricious sounds of a repeated motion. He hadn't even seen inside the doorway yet but he felt something, that thing that changed the ache in his groin into a strange driving pleasure. He knew *it*, whatever *it* was, was inside of there but he also knew that there was someone else in there with it. A sense of possession, one rimmed with the fire of jealousy and a bloating anger, crept into him like a million bugs crawling from in the flesh of his limbs, through his musculature and into his grey matter, building slowly at first and then ramping into a crescendo. He wanted the thing beyond the door, or maybe that wasn't the truth. He couldn't tell at first. Some new part of him wanted it, a part that had just reared itself into being, a part that wasn't there before but manifested as a product of the sensations that were overtaking him. It was a primal lust to which he now found himself losing control.

He wanted what waited beyond.

He *needed* it for himself.

Connor's hand neared the doorknob. The whispers and slick sounds from inside grew more pronounced, joined by a drawn-out moaning. An overwhelming numbness ran through his limbs. This numbness transformed into a range of vibrations, emanating from his crotch, seeming to caress and call to him, promising pleasure just beyond the threshold. Deep beneath the want, the now relentless desire, was a mounting terror at the loss of his own will, but that emotion, too, was squelched by the indescribable need for possession.

When his fingers grasped the cold metal of the knob and then pulled the door the rest of the way open, he could see that this closet was only about half the size of the one he'd come from. There was a single muted bulb above. Shelves along the three inner walls were cluttered with boxes of detergent, plumbing equipment, paper towel rolls, buckets, and packages of latex gloves amongst other things. Down below, kneeled and leaning back on his haunches, was a middle-aged man, naked from the waist down, reaching out and feeling into the darkness under the bottom shelf. And there really was a darkness there, one so viscous and thick that its unnaturality was undeniable. Even in his bewitched state, Connor shuddered at the sight of the absurd blackness.

The man on the floor groaned and these groans sounded of the razor-thin space between ecstasy and suffering, sounded of a letting-go of something Connor knew in that moment that he had and that he wanted to let go of, too: the last ounces of control. And he noticed, through the alien veil of custody over his senses, the noodle-like appendages that had extended from the black below the shelf, thin and burgundy like wires of blood. They were coiled around the man's erect penis, with a portion fanning out beyond that to stretch around the man's torso, gripping over the shirt like a passionate lover with a hundred squeezing fingers.

Connor's eyes adjusted to the gloom in that low bit of wall and, in the ambiguous light, he could see what was in the darkness, that which the creeping probosci belonged to.

A fracture in time ripped him from the moment of seeing the creature's beautifully hellish form to a moment only seconds later in which his hands were around the throat of the man in worship upon the floor. There was no time in that interim, for the actions were taken by the desire, not by his waking mind.

The blood pooled in the arteries Connor now struggled to close shut. He could feel them bulge under his fingers. The man didn't attempt to fight back, only gave a distant look of pleasure as the blood bloomed under his features, a look of almost acceptance. Connor felt the tendons in the man's neck grow taut like guitar strings under the skin and, after readjusting his grip, heard a knuckled sound when he collapsed the man's windpipe with his thumbs. A sucking wheeze had barely escaped the throat before the man crumpled into a heap against the linoleum.

The tendrils unclenched and slid seductively away from the body of the freshly dead. Tears of confusion and disbelief fell from Connor's eyes as he watched those things snake into the darkness below the bottom shelf. There, in his confoundedness, he gazed upon the shape that undulated and quivered its demented orifices, and the curves of its horrid black flesh.

*

Over the course of the next few hours, Connor ambled in a fog of disorientation from one end of the shoe department to the other, picking up and immediately putting down shoes, prodding sale displays, appearing busy, all the while his mind seeking any excuse to return to the employee hallway. He hardly spoke to any of the customers that came in, even blew one off when she approached him about a price-check on a pair of heels. Every twenty minutes or so, which felt an eternity when experienced from within the state of agonizing desire in which he'd found himself, he'd retreat from the world of commerce to the back hallway and, each time, *it* would whisper into his ears and into his mind to leave the door ajar just a bit, because it had spent so much time shut off from the rest of existence. It would not allow itself to be confined in totality any longer. In exchange, it let him look upon its unearthly sex and its countless nipples and holes, let its thin appendages snake over his flesh, to stroke and enter him and drain him of the vacillating misery in his loins. He'd never felt so debased, so out of his own hands and given over completely to the whims of primality and sexual release. The thing, this *master*, was of some other realm entirely and exacted a cost each time it seemed to feed from him, breaking off a piece of his soul whenever it coaxed the ejaculate from his strained and powerless body.

Toward the end of the afternoon, when the sun had turned a blood red in the western horizon and shone through the front glass doors of the store, there was a shift change. Connor's immediate manager Mark was to be replaced, as he was every evening, with the swing-shift assistant manager whose name was Angela. Connor was tidying up the children's shoe section, unmade by a tornado of little snot-nosed banshees not ten minutes prior, when Mark approached with the woman at his side.

"Connor, you remember Angela." He said it more as a statement than a question. "My shift is about done so she'll be the manager on duty after I leave you for your last couple hours."

Connor reached his hand out and she took it, shaking only for the briefest of moments before letting it go. They'd met in passing the first day on the job but he hadn't spoken to her since. He didn't care about meeting this woman again, nor about any sort of title or responsibility she held.

There was only one priority, one reason to breathe.

When he'd parted company from the manager, Connor slinked back around the men's clothing section and through the door near the dressing rooms leading into the back hallway. It had been about forty minutes since he'd been back here, a torturous forty minutes of desire and of a burning need to return. And so, he returned to that closet. With his pants and underwear around his ankles, and the wriggling tentacles protruding from that dark under-corner like sentient roots to squirm over and in him, the ejaculate pumped from within once more, placating the ache like an addiction being fed. He looked to the bulb at the zenith of the closet ceiling and tears fell from the corners of his eyes. He sobbed at the release of that resonating pain in his balls that enslaved him, at that small part of himself totally lost in this communion, screaming to understand what was happening to his mind and his will, to understand why his body was no longer his own and why he couldn't stop the drive to submit to the beast in the closet.

*

Thirty-five minutes later, after having made a half-assed attempt through the go-backs cart, Connor once more began his way toward the exit into the back hall. His movement felt driven by something outside of him, as if he was a passenger on the ride called Connor's Body and had no say in where it went, what it did, adrift in the back seat.

As he slipped between two registers and down one of the aisles of hiking boots, he spotted something out of the corner of his eye. Angela, the assistant manager, was peering at him from over one of the shirt racks in the children's apparel department. Connor slowed his gait, pretended to check something on a shelf behind him for a long moment. When he looked back, the assistant manager was no longer where he'd last seen her but was instead moving toward the far door leading into the employee hallway. A sudden thought came to him, one that stung like a splinter being driven into his mind:

She *knew* what was back there, and she was going to take it away from him.

A flush of panic flooded his veins. Without waiting for his mind's consent, his body quickly scrambled toward the entrance to the back hall closest to him. His entrance to the hall was farther from the closet than hers. He knew he could make it in before she could, but only if he hurried.

A man approached from the main entrance of the department.

"Hey there. I'm looking for some size twelve—"

Connor bullied past, sending the customer into a rack of jackets, and b-lined it straight for the hall door. He barely heard the man behind him yelling something about talking to his manager before slamming the door open and exploding into the hall.

Angela was nowhere to be seen.

Connor could only thwart his movement for a few seconds before he started to jog, then sprint, toward the door at the end of the hall. The pain swelled within him as he closed in on the closet, the used soreness of his cock following suit. Already his body greedily sought the touch of that thing in the grotesque darkness beyond.

When Connor opened the door, the aroma of deep animal cunt gripped him by the nostrils, pulled him down onto his knees. His hands moved on their own to shuffle his pants down, his escaped erection standing like granite. He stared into the beast's beautiful panel of eyes, deep pools of red and black flecked with the gold of some sort of divinity. The strange pupils seemed to glow, searing their images into Connor's thoughts. The appendages from its numerous holes unfurled and coiled toward him over the dirty linoleum and he gave himself to those creeping things once more. They circumscribed his testicles, embracing them, and slid down into his urethra to drink the seed directly from the source.

Buried underneath the weight of this horrible ecstasy, Connor barely heard a shuffling noise behind him, the subtle sounds of a presence standing over him. When he turned, he could hardly see the assistant manager standing there for, in his vision, the world was breaking up with the tingle of psychedelic orgasm staticking through his groin. Slats of everything he saw were being pulled apart like panes of glass and, in between these shards of reality, he saw the bloody chasm of anguish into which his master was pulling his soul. Even as Angela's face looked down upon him with its savage expression, the lines and spaces that made up the world shattered and amplified that dreadful background which awaited to swallow him whole.

While her hands reached for his neck and pushed at his throat with her thumbs, Connor felt the final chords of his orgasm, diminished now into complete painful suffering. As his throat collapsed, he felt the *taking* of himself by his interdimensional master, the one who moaned from the darkness under the bottom shelf, from whence cool rotten breath flowed to rub his skin into goosebumps, giggling coyly into his mind at the impending personal calamity. It sucked the very essence out of his body along with his cum, drained him of his heart, and began the slow eternal process of digesting his hopes, fears and memories.

In the last bits of sight he could glean from his earthly life, after he'd been dropped to the floor and as his body was pulled like a puppet on strings into the space under the shelf, Connor saw the assistant manager, pants and underwear down around her ankles, fall to her knees and, there, she stared with reverie, awaiting the sensations of the master's touch.

The Midnight Baby

It was a strange sort of experience, after three days of breathing that sterile hospital air, to notice the way the weather had turned out, considering what Jen had expected it to be. One might've figured that times of despair ought to have been crowned by overcast skies or strangled by dark clouds, bloated sentinels pouring torrents of autumn rain into the gutters, flowing coldly into the sewer drains along the city's streets. She expected something perhaps a bit more *apt* to accompany the span of days in which a person heard words they wished they could unhear, words that changed everything. The days in which one saw things that never left one's mind, those were the days that ought to be choked by the electric humidity of an oncoming storm, or permeated by the musty dirty smell of a smog-ridden fog under darkening skylines.

And yet, instead, on this day that she finally left that artificially bright environment of the maternity ward, almost feeling as if it still had its IVs and wires jammed into her veins, on this day the sun was at a perfect height so as not to blind her on her drive home. Not but a few wisps of cloud hung in the vast blue above. The rest was an endless sea. To Jen, in her haze of shock and confused reflection, it was interesting that the sequence of events that had led to this very moment, of driving in her car and leaving that godforsaken hospital, had dragged her through misery on what might otherwise be considered a rather beautiful day.

She hardly perceived the road beyond the windshield and the

steering wheel gripped by her white-knuckled hands. There was a reel, something like a movie clip, that played through her thoughts, repeating and reiterating itself again and again: she was back in the hospital waiting room, desperately holding onto that moment in which she'd first confirmed that she was pregnant a little over eight months ago, trying to stay in that space of happiness. *Jennifer Lansky*, the nurse's voice had said, coming from the bright hallway leading further into the heart of the medical center. In this memory, Jen didn't transition from sitting to standing but, instead, was simply sitting one moment then moving toward the voice in the next, as if floating or skipping through segments of time. Then she was in a patient's room, sitting on the papery sheet that covered the examination bed. Her mind perfectly reenacted the knock on the door and, after the doctor stepped into the room and closed the door behind him, he said *You are definitely pregnant, Jennifer*, with a smile that, at the time, seemed genuine and made the weight of all that stood before her a little more bearable. The memory of this distant moment of relief and of happiness had lost its flavor, however. It was bland on her tongue and in her heart compared to the pain, that nauseating anguish, that her soul now held in the present.

The next clip that followed in the theatre of her mind had her lying on a different hospital bed, her body full to the brim and her bones feelings as if every one of them were being stretched. The contractions had been powerful and there was a dread that had come with each one of them, something outside of the pain or fear of her own mortal death. She had known that something was wrong, that it wasn't just a premature birth, that something else was wrong with her son. This feeling had lived under her skin for days, coiled in her stomach and neck, a feeling of sourness, of some corruption that she couldn't pinpoint creeping through her tissue. This sensation seemed to have fermented during the eighteen hours she'd spent in the hospital bed before *it*, the event, finally happened. When she brought her concerns to the nurses beforehand, they dismissed them as unfounded worries, the same paranoia all mothers go through before they get to see their beautiful healthy child.

The sunlight beyond the dirty windshield of her pickup truck seemed to grow brighter with each moment spent in the slow traffic on its way out of downtown. All that Jen saw appeared bleached by the bright glare.

Roan was his name, like *rowin' on a boat*, she remembered saying to the nurse. She had chosen it because it was the most beautiful name she'd ever heard. Even now, she wasn't certain where she'd first heard it spoken. Her vague memories played some unremarkable voice calling the name over a playground at a daycare in her childhood, or some other time and place just as ambiguous. Either way, and ever since, the name had been something special to her and always sounded just as enchanting when she said it aloud.

"Roan."

The word was by itself, alone with no substance to attach to within the muffled silence of the interior of her truck.

There'd been panic amongst the maternity ward staff. For a few seconds, when they'd first pulled him from her, Roan's little body white and blue, motionless, Jen still trusted the nurse, still waited for that moment in which the 'beautiful healthy' side of this natural event, of these supposed present truths, was to be shown to her. When it was done and she'd heard the words *I'm so sorry, Jennifer* spoken, but hadn't quite grasped why they were telling her that, she begged them to let her hold him. They told her of the stillbirth, a word which, at the time, she couldn't properly cognate. They said how they could not resuscitate her son and how sorry they all were for all that had happened. Hysteria, anger or something else had driven Jen to an edge she could no longer prevent herself from falling over and, for some reason, in that moment, she believed that within the contact between her skin and her son's body, there was an answer, the secret to the location of the ledge where she could catch her grip. In that embrace of his little self, she could manifest a suicide net to prevent her total collapse from the fall of whatever all of this was rapidly turning into. She just needed to hold him and then maybe she could understand and, with understanding, there could be relief.

And yet, when they handed him to her, with sympathetic eyes staring from just above their safety masks, it was the lightness of his dead weight against her chest that broke her completely. So then she fell through that instant in time into the dreadful abyss from which she begged both doctors and God to help her escape from, but out of which she could not climb. The fingers of her soul and sanity slipped on the greasy embankments of disbelief and slid, instead, further back down into the obscure grey of shock. That was some days ago, and yet she still felt the vertigo of freefall as if she'd never stopped dwelling in that gown and bed and tangle of indiscriminate wires, never stopped staring at the bright TV without seeing, watching those voiceless heads of daytime television and listening to the heart monitor without truly hearing its *beep*.

She didn't know exactly how many days they'd kept her. *Do you have anyone that could come pick you up*, the nurse had asked before she was discharged, to which Jen had simply shaken her head. *What about the father?* To that, Jen had shaken her head once more.

The rest of the drive home from the hospital was a stream of colorless stimuli, oozing past her peripheral while the tunnel vision her gaze dwelt within started to lose its focus. Street signs glinted in the refracting sunlight, pedestrians strode the sidewalks, dogs barked playfully from beyond low yard fences and cars drove by with their sunroofs open and music blaring. She felt none of it, heard none of it, *saw* none of it. These things were meaningless, or it was impossible for her to give them meaning when the numbness of apathy had already settled so heavily into her perspective. She even cracked her window at one point but everything she saw, and the air she tasted, were warped by the droning indifference of her trauma. There had been a type of death that had grown inside her, for how long throughout those last two months of her pregnancy she knew not, and its form took the shape of her dead child. Her body had gone from slowly swelling with a maternal fullness to now being deflated, used up without completing its true purpose, in what felt like a blink of an eye in retrospect. She was supposed to have given proper birth to a living breathing child. Ambulating this husk of a body, laying in it, *being* it in those achingly long moments of stark reflection was a torture that could never be described. Some part deep inside of her craved to escape the flesh she now dwelt within, this heavy feeling that encased her struggling soul.

Snug in the driver's seat of her truck, how vacant she felt, both physically and emotionally, now that she'd been emptied of her Roan. And this vacancy must've clouded her recollection of the drive home because she couldn't remember parking her car, nor could she remember how it had already reached the late evening. The hospital had only been a thirty-minute drive from her apartment every other time she'd driven to or from it, and four hours had passed since she'd left, according to the glowing clock in the dash.

The light in the entryway of the apartment complex flickered overhead, doing something odd to her vision as she entered. Her mailbox was set in the same spot it always was, an arm's reach from her path to the staircase, but she left it untouched. The second-floor hallway surrounding the door to her apartment was quiet when she arrived. The stock framed pictures and two potted plants along the walls, between her door and the adjacent apartments on either side, appeared to be waiting silently for her to do what was expected, which was to open her door and disappear from their inanimate sight.

Her keys jingled in some distant part of the world, impossible to pinpoint due to the tinny quality of the sounds that fell upon her ears. As she slid the key into the deadbolt lock, her weary eyes happened upon an envelope half buried in the thin space between the door and a lower section of the door frame. She slipped it from its spot and beheld it under the hallway light above her.

The paper of the envelope was crisp, slightly misshapen due to exposure to light moisture of some kind, perhaps atmospheric. The misshapenness felt unexpectedly coarse, almost violently visceral against the sensory of her fingertips. She stared at her own name printed in cursive on the front of the thing but, like the television in her room at the hospital, she could barely see it, no matter how long her eyes stayed on the writing. Instead, her site blurred and her thoughts drifted, though toward what concepts she also couldn't hardly grasp. Waking life felt almost dreamlike, simultaneously weightless yet undeniably cumbersome.

Down the hallway, as if in answer to her quiet stasis and rumination, a subtle crack occurred in the floor near the stairwell, pulling her attention out of the numbness of malaise that had started to creep over her again. She saw nothing save for an empty apartment complex hallway with terrible carpeting and blandly painted walls but, then again…

There *was* something.

Between the waves of unfulfilling sleep, delirium and just plain exhaustion, the time spent in that hospital bed had been something like a play, acted across multiple stages, each stage being either reality or the dream world, and she was forced to witness the dance these perspectives cycled between with each other, shifting in and out, while she hung onto dwindling consciousness. There'd been a gamut of different dream scenarios, ranging from horrible to falsely hopeful, dreams in which Roan was still alive or she was still healthily pregnant with him, to dreams in which she'd watched him pulled from her by some dark beast that consumed his little body as soon as the air had kissed his skin.

During one particular morning, in which she'd arisen and fallen back to sleep multiple times, with a throbbing pain in her gut accompanying each of these resurfacings, she'd dreamt of a great expanse of cars. They were all parked bumper-to-bumper throughout both lanes and shoulders of a highway, an eerie quiet highway, one that, from where she stood on it, stretched off into the horizon for miles, no turns or curves, straight into a distant firmament that lay orange and full of fire. Great plains of cracked dust and black weeds lay ancient and reaching for the distant mountains beyond the guardrails on either side of her. There were no drivers behind the steering wheels of the cars, nor passengers navigating from their seats. All was desolate, abandoned. And then moving and scurrying between the cars, opening doors and entering and exiting them, opening trunks then closing them, were nurses in pastel colored scrubs. They shuffled along through the quiet traffic like aimless bees in a hive. Their actions were erratic, their purpose unclear. At some point during her observation of them, a second sight in Jen's mind picked up a signal within the dream-world, a shock of intent or willful observance directed toward her, staring *at* her, stinging like licking a battery would and alerting her of an unintended presence within this dream place. Twenty feet ahead of where she stood amidst the petrified traffic, and partially obscured by the tail end of a nameless delivery truck, a dark shape lingered. This shadow did not move nor shift, only stood alone against the cloudless sky without any actual form to cast it. It was not a malevolent intent she felt from the presence. It was still unknown, though, menacing in its obscurity. It watched her. She watched it. It seemed an observer from somewhere else, a wanderer from a different world, perhaps a different dream.

In that moment of partial speculation, the sounds of scurrying went quiet. The nurses were no longer there. That wandering shadow, however, stayed.

In the dream, the skies above had grown dark, then. The glaring sun was obstructed by sudden and horrible clouds of black dust. Strangely, the wanderer remained full and present as the world darkened. Beyond the shadowed entity, far off to where the perfectly straight highway met the flat line of the horizon, a bright light burst into sight. It mushroomed up over the mountains in the distance, blackening the skies around it even further. A shockwave moved out from the explosion, advancing quickly and building in height and, just before it consumed the very spot Jen stood upon, she saw a smear of mirrored glass shimmer out from the center of her vision, to bleed over all her sight, her corneas burned by the instinct to glance at the light in the distance—

And then she'd awoken.

Throughout those remaining few days at the hospital, she had slipped in and out of the weak grasp on her own imagination, found herself witnessing other places and worlds from her bed though none of these memories could she recall as clearly as the one in which she'd seen the wanderer and that great cataclysm beyond it. When she'd been awake, or thought she was awake, she'd begun to see shadows where they ought not be in her room, an occasional warbling of the lines in her peripheral or the flicker of the light in the small attached bathroom closet in the corner. At one point, in between nurses entering and exiting her room throughout the haze of feeble sleep, she'd seen a tall shade standing near the doorway. It had looked in at her. She'd felt it regard her. She'd sensed the way it observed her but she couldn't remember if it had been a human or a shadow, as confused as she was from the overlay of dreams.

In this moment, as the anxiety strung out the last bit of her adrenaline, as she stood perfectly still in the apartment hallway, staring through wired eyes, she found herself confronted with the truth she'd been either avoiding or too blind to see: when she lost Roan, she'd been thrown into recurring nightmares that, after she'd finally come out of them, left something attached to her like a parasite, something that didn't want to stay where it was. Though she could not see that same shadowed thing at the staircase leading down to the first floor of the complex, she could feel it there. She sensed the presence of it, its weight, its staring invisibly through the aether into her.

When she entered the apartment, the sourness of old fruit hit her nostrils. Through what energy remained in her logical thought processes, she locked the deadbolt, making sure to double-check the knob lock, but then questioned her efforts, imagining that this would most likely not keep an entity made of shadow out of her home, should said entity decide to come in. Her emotional undermind screamed otherwise, though, and followed through with the motions of securing the door like a protective ritual. For a few long minutes, she stood there leaning against the door with her hand over her mouth, unsure as to what she was waiting for but knowing that she was listening for something. She couldn't help the expectation of, at any moment, a hand smacking against the other side of the door, or to hear a series of whispers licking out in the hall. The silence stretched and then it stretched more. Finally, her hand slid from her mouth and she stepped back.

It wasn't until she'd set her bags onto the couch, moved to the dining room table and held the envelope under the light, not actually seeing it for how many minutes she knew not, that she'd finally noticed the return address. *Thor Lansky*, her uncle's name, was marked in old slanted penmanship. The address was a P. O. Box in the Caribbean. It'd been a trend that small families sprouted from her lineage and, when her mother passed almost a decade ago, it left her uncle as the only blood relative Jen had left. She hadn't heard a word from him in years, since the funeral. He'd mentioned during the service, a mutter under his breath, how this could've been prevented, how his sister, Jen's mother, could've been alive if it wasn't for what he called her *ignorance*. Jennifer hadn't understood what he was ranting on about at the time and, instead, had lashed out at him for his insensitivity.

That was the last she'd heard from him, until now.

Inside the envelope was a hand-written letter. As she beheld it, she looked over the scribbled writing, taking in its contours against the page, before reading even a single word. Somehow, within the examination of those miniscule troughs of ink existed what it took to pull her focus out of her thoughts of Roan, of Trevor, of the hospital and the nurses and that wandering nebulous shadow, even if only momentarily. With emails and text messages and social media, communication like this seemed a rarity. She couldn't remember the last time she'd received a written letter.

Hypersensitivity burned in her eyes. She rubbed them with the palms of her hands before beginning to read.

Jenny-Bear,

I'm almost certain that today marks seven years since your mother was laid to rest. I won't bore you with pages of uninteresting updates about my own life. I will, however, say that I had a feeling that it might be a good idea to reach out to you—something in the wind, perhaps. Though we aren't nearly as close as we were when you were a girl, we're still of the same blood and perhaps there's more to that than we are aware of.

I'm a sentimental old coot. I believe your mother's passing was the last time I got to see you, my wonderful niece, and I should like to amend that soon. I may have said some things back then that weren't exactly prudent, but I have it in mind that us meeting once again could make both our lives a little bit easier. I have acres of land and plenty of empty rooms on my property. Inside the envelope with this letter is a one-way ticket. Should you choose to come, you can stay as long as you like and we'll get you a return ticket when you've had your fill of this place. It's quite alright if you're not interested. The cost of the ticket was nothing to me and I wouldn't care for you any less if you chose to decline the invitation.

No matter how you decide, as long as I still breathe, you'll always have a place here with me if things get too heavy.

I look forward to hearing from you.

Your Uncle Thor.

It was her uncle's words that reminded her that last week marked the seventh anniversary of her mother's passing. It wasn't an insignificant thing. Every year, she'd remembered to visit the grave on that particular day or a day surrounding it. Yet, with all that life had thrown at her, with Roan and Trevor and the pregnancy, it simply hadn't registered this year. And then her mind was on Roan again. Horrible thoughts built in her along with a terrifying warmth, an anticipation that there would come a time in which life would pull her one way or the other, so far in some direction that she would forget her son, too, that the anniversary of his birth wouldn't register some year like the anniversary of her mother's death hadn't this time around. She wondered if Trevor had already forgotten about her. She hadn't seen him since that night they'd spent together, the night that sent her life down a completely different path than that which she'd known prior, and he never knew Roan, at least not the way that she had. No one could've known her son the way that she had after she'd felt the weight of him inside of her, held him with every ounce of her body and flesh.

The temperature in the apartment was freezing when she'd entered yet there was, in the air, a burning kind of field, like static, toying with her sense of smell and the hairs on her arms. From where she sat at the table, where she'd read the letter, she had an unobscured view of the door to the room in which she'd planned for Roan to sleep, where she'd daydreamed of hearing his cries and laughter and sleeping coos coming from. It was slightly ajar. Darkness waited beyond. In the black, Jen could not see but knew there was a crib that she had decorated with a mobile that spun little airplanes and birds around. Somewhere in the black depths of that room, there was a dresser stacked with fresh towels, baby diapers and a container of wipes waiting to be used for their intended purposes. She also knew that framed pictures of her mother watched from positions scattered about, sitting silently in the dark, as well as pictures of her father whom she'd hardly known except through the grateful loving words her mother described him with. He'd died shortly after Jennifer was born, an accident involving a negligent semi-truck on the freeway, an accident her mother never liked to talk about.

All of it—the pictures, the supplies, the mobile, the memories—was useless now.

It seemed almost out of her own control that her hands simply set her uncle's note back onto the table, that she got up and moved toward her bedroom, pulled the empty suitcase out from under the bed and started packing. She hadn't noticed at first the slight moan that eased out of her mouth as she breathed and wept. Tears drowned her vision, dripped from her nose and fell onto her hands while she folded clothes. She felt the open black of Roan's room out in the hall behind her like an open wound, a vacant space to remind her of what possibilities were no longer possible.

...you've always got a place here with me if things get too heavy.

Things *had* gotten too heavy. Reality was up for grabs now that Plan A had been thrown to the wolves in the worst way imaginable, the life she'd thought she'd had being seemingly eaten right in front of her, devoured by a gullet of groping latex gloves and incessant apologies. That invasive heat of knowing nothing would be the same dug its talons into her spine the moment she saw Roan's body pulled from her, feeling the ability to predict or hope slip away, and it was still there now, burning. It was a feeling she knew she was running from, a weight, invisible to the eye, perched on her shoulders no matter where she was. This weight was birthed from her dreaming reality, of trying to accept certain truths and a knowledge of irrevocable change, but being unable to let go of that *something*, that corner of life that held her baby.

Things had definitely gotten too heavy.

In the back of her mind, somewhere in the subconscious part of her senses, Jen thought she heard something in the hallway outside the apartment, something that sounded like the faint footfalls of nurse's sneakers drifting down a hospital corridor. She glanced over her shoulder, through the bedroom doorway into the living room.

The front door was still closed.

The place was empty and the walls looked as if they were breathing beyond her tears.

*

The next morning, navigating the trip from home to the store for a few toiletries, then to the airport and onto the plane, went by in a blur of autonomous movement, of the body ambulating but the mind being stuck in some silver muck of fleeting memories back at the apartment, or back in that hospital bed, or in some space and time in between. It wasn't until she'd already been buckled into her window seat on the plane, staring out at the sun barely beginning its dawn over the black tarmac, that Jen's thoughts awoke from the void she'd seemingly spent the last twelve hours in.

She'd tried to stay up before the flight. Back at the apartment last night, when she'd called, the airport customer support line informed her that their earliest flight to Orlando, from which she would get the transfer to the islands of the Caribbean, wasn't until 7AM. She'd made coffee to try and stay awake. The thought of sleep, and the nightmares it might bring, sent a sick feeling into her stomach. The black burning drink had seared her throat with the anxious way she'd sipped at it, unable to pull her eyes from the front door of the apartment. She'd even tried turning the television on but it only reminded her of the hospital room, so she turned it off immediately. It wasn't so much fear that had held her stare to the front door as it was... anticipation, of something she couldn't quite identify but felt wholly. She could sense that presence, the wanderer, as if, through the front wall of the unit, it stared at her, as if she sat in a cage of glass and it watched like an observing doctor of a kind, as if no matter where she went, it would follow her. Upon rereading the letter from her uncle again, she couldn't help but feel that small possibility that escape from the presence and from the horrible reality she'd fallen into lay only a plane ticket away. The night stretched along like taffy and these were the thoughts that repeated themselves over and over, riding along the tattered borders of her neurosis, thoughts of an escape she felt she could hardly believe in.

At some point, she'd set her coffee down and grabbed the alarm clock from the nightstand in her room, finally succumbing to the pull of sleep. She'd plugged it into the wall next to the couch under the waning glare of the standing lamp in the corner, and restored the blue glowing numbers to their proper time. The alarm was set for 4AM. The single suitcase and bag she'd packed were leaning against the wall near the closet. By that time, there was nothing left to do but crumple onto the couch in that sorrowful exhaustion and ride the tenor caffeine into unconsciousness, so she did exactly that.

And now, in this cramped seat on the plane, she was awake.

The lights sprouting from the underside of the baggage compartment above looked like burning eyes staring down on her.

Their gaze revealed a seatbelt pulled tight over her stomach and the clothes she'd worn the evening prior, unclean and sleep-stretched. In fact, they were the same clothes she'd worn home from the hospital yesterday. She could smell her own souring body odor, could feel the ripe dampness in her groin, mutilated from the birthing process, the refuse of which was absorbed only by the diaper-like wrap she'd been dressed in before they let her leave the hospital not twenty-four hours prior.

To her immediate left, sitting in the aisle seat, was a tall thin man with headphones over his ears and his eyes closed peacefully. His knees were together and his palms were face down on his thighs, as if he was doing everything he could to remain as out of the way as possible while he rested. She hoped to God he couldn't smell her, though, due to proximity, she assumed he probably could.

The window nuzzled against her right shoulder. She looked to the great expanse of landscape that yawned beyond the tarmac, running off into the flat horizon. Snowcapped mountains clustered in one part of the distance under the deep black-blue of the retreating night.

The fact that she hadn't been conscious of her drive to the airport, nor boarding the plane, or that she'd at least forgotten the experience already, was worrisome. However, what plagued her more, strangely, was why she'd even come to at this point in the process. Something had broken her from the spell. She couldn't explain why, in this moment, *that* was what was most important, how she knew that it wasn't just her consciousness coming back to itself after an unsatisfying few hours of sleep and a strange few more of somnambulating. Being awake now was a good thing, a necessary thing, but the thought would not let her alone: *something* had awoken her. Staring out the window at the pinkening sky, using as much intent as her recovering focus would allow, didn't seem to work to distract her of these thoughts. She closed her eyes and leaned her head back against the headrest in an attempt to ignore the feeling.

Only seconds passed before she sat up once more.

She glanced to the thin man, then looked over the other passengers in the seats in the other aisles, hoping that something would reveal itself if she got her focus on whoever or whatever her instincts were driving her to seek. A food cart rolled noisily down the aisle with a flight attendant attached to its back. An infant stood in his mother's lap while she cooed at him a few rows back toward the rear of the plane. Near the front, two teenage boys sat next to each other, both with earbuds in, directing their unblinking stares down toward the smartphones they each held in their hands. An old man with terribly wrinkled hands looked longingly out of his small window portal a few feet from the emergency door. Jen wondered if he'd ever had children. His hands reminded her of the inevitability of Death and so she turned back toward the seat ahead of her, tried to occupy her thoughts on something else, setting her head back once more.

In the moment that her eyes closed, as the very cusp of her lids fell into each other, a chill climbed from the base of her spine up to her neck. It made the hair on her arms stand. Her eyes flicked open and she again surveyed the other passengers: the attendant, the infant, the boys, the old man. Goosebumps prickled at her arms and neck. She wasn't seeing it, but she could sense it, a *something*. She scanned, looking for that which she knew was staring directly at her but that she could not find.

The man next to her briefly opened his eyes to glance at her and then returned to his nap.

There was a rock of turbulence, resulting in Jen's hands clamping like vice grips onto the armrests. Then she caught it in her sight, that *something*, off near the bathrooms toward the back of the plane: extended a little too far along the inner wall of the fuselage was a darkness, a shadow, weird and almost watery. A smiling attendant retrieved a towel and walked right through the patch of darkness on her way to an outstretched hand in the third row of seats. The shade did not move. It only stayed there, seemed to grow in opacity, then fade into a barely noticeable mist, then back into a thickened state. It pulsed as if to the rhythm of some heartbeat of the plane or an oscillating process Jen had no knowledge of. If anyone else saw it, they weren't making it apparent.

The rising tension in her stomach gurgled and spoke secrets in a language she couldn't understand. The agitation stretching the tendons of her hands played long violent notes containing answers she couldn't hear. She turned back to sit straight in her seat and murmured *Oh God* under her breath. She closed her eyes and moved the fingertips of her shaking hands to her temples, swirling them in slow methodic circles. She knew that no one else could see the shadow. Somehow, she just knew. It was the wanderer, the follower from her dreams, from the highway of dead vehicles with all the nurses. The purpose of the entity was unclear and yet Jen's fright told her a great deal about the situation, and she'd learned in her life to trust that little voice, that pull in her chest, when things got strange or terrifying. It was instinct, a deep nature within. The recent past, however, had thrown her internal compass to the gales of a storm she'd never anticipated, one she couldn't seem to intuit her way out of.

An urge came over her then. Why, in that moment, she reminded herself that *Trevor doesn't know about Roan*, she didn't understand. It was like a jolt of electricity sent through her, charging her body with a thought process she had not agreed to have nor to set into any sort of determined action. It was outside of her will, a disruptive interruption of this experience of uncertainty and creeping fear, a distraction. *He doesn't know about Roan, and he doesn't know that Roan is gone.* Jen reached to the phone on the back of the seat in front of her. It clipped out of its cubby like the flimsy hunk of plastic it was and she turned it over. The cheap thing shook in her anxious hands. She thought about pulling her cellphone out to check the number again but the truth was that she had memorized those ten digits of Trevor's number the better part of a year ago. She'd stared into the lit screen of the phone, at the string of numbers she'd dialed so many times trying to get a hold of him, to tell him about her pregnancy, about Roan, about their child together.

He wasn't going to answer. He never did in the past. Only the one time after that single night they'd spent together did he answer. She'd called the very next morning. She couldn't remember what she had said or how she'd greeted him but she remembered each and every one of his words: *Hello... Oh, Jen, how you doin' beautiful?... Not bad, not bad. Hey, I'm right in the middle of a thing here. Let me call you later this evening... Alright, talk to you soon.* She had said *Okay, bye* at the end, she remembered that, but he'd only responded by ending the call. She never heard his voice again. The words, themselves, the ones he spoke, were etched into her memories like initials carved into tree bark, *J + T*, but she could no longer remember the intricacies of his voice. It made her lungs fill with sorrow when she thought on it, that there could be so much disconnection after a night of what she remembered as being such a breathtaking experience. Nobody had ever made love to her the way he had. No one she'd been with before had smelled like him, that same cigarette, cologne and gasoline smell that drove her tingling into primality. No one had ever kissed her with those same soft lips...

And no one else had ever given her Roan like he had.

After her thumb pressed the keys in the proper order, it hovered over the call button. A few months had passed since she'd last tried to reach out to him. She'd resolved a while back that there was no reason to continue trying, that she could handle whatever came on her own. Her job at the insurance company was giving her two months of maternity leave and she had some vacation hours saved up to use afterward. Even without Trevor's support, as aching as that realization was, a plan had seemingly come together: she would raise Roan on her own. This plan had held her up, kept her chin from dropping for at least a little while. That was until she had produced death from her womb, until she'd brought into this world a child made completely of decay and wasted potential. Then the plan no longer held. The road down which she'd pictured her fate transpiring had hit a roadblock, more like a brick wall, and she was sitting upside-down in the overturned vehicle of her life, watching the gas drip and waiting for the inevitable conflagration that would consume her totally.

Her thumb dropped to tap the button with the green icon. She lifted the phone to her ear and stared out of the window to the ozone that was set out in front of her. *We're sorry. The number you have dialed is no longer in service. Please check the number and try again.* A sob came out in a rushed breath. She felt fresh dampness surge inside the diaper thing they'd put on her. That was something they never mentioned before she was pregnant, that, afterward, she'd bleed more than any menstrual cycle could've prepared her for. There was a chance that she'd dialed the incorrect number, though, so she tried again, this time comparing with the number on her cell phone. Her thumb dialed carefully, then she returned the phone to her ear.

We're sorry.
The number you have dialed is no longer in service.
Please check the number and try again.

*

She hardly realized she'd arrived in Orlando, then boarded the transfer to the Caribbean, before the second flight landed.

The passengers all stood at their own speeds and unloaded the overhead compartments, and with that came wafts of stale body air moving around the cabin. Jennifer's olfactory sensitivity compounded these smells with the heightened stress from the long ride through the clouds and the despair that had grown stale in her heart, intensifying her desire to simply get off this fucking plane, especially because she was certain that her own odors were making their generous contributions to the rank recycled air. Her body groaned with pain the moment she moved to stand. She felt more dampness in her groin and the loose feeling of her belly. On her way to the exit, she chanced a look toward the bathrooms, the area in which the shadow had sat for most of the flight.

It was gone, and then she remembered she was on a different plane than the first, and then wondered if, in her delirium, she'd seen the wanderer on this plane, too.

The lever was pulled and the plane's main entrance door opened. Jen watched through a window as the mobile staircase pulled up the tarmac to come snug against the aircraft. Tourists and travelers walked down its throat, single file, slowly descending to the concrete below. When Jennifer breached the exit of the plane and moved out into the tropical air, the heat of the day lingered, even though it was late evening. A salty warmth rode the sea breeze and waves made their calming sounds in some not-so-distant surf. The sun shone red and orange in the far evening sky, setting the horizon aflame, its vibrant rays seeming to blanket her body. Above, a few stars had already birthed in the darkening eastern atmosphere. She thought of how much Trevor would like it, then chastised herself for giving in to such idiotic sentiments and, instead, thought of how much Roan might've enjoyed the view.

Coming with the feeling of touching her feet down onto the

black concrete so close to sea level, instead of being strapped into that hunk of metal barreling through the empty skies, was a very palpable feeling of relief. Yet, even at this tropical island thousands of miles away from everything Jen knew, the anguish still flexed and moved its bulk in the dark within herself. The hospital that Roan never left was back in Portland, but the loss she'd experienced had congealed somewhere in the space between realities, where time and distance held no authority and the desires for her individual soul to escape this torment were met with a deep cosmic silence that followed her everywhere. So many things had come with her, so many parts of her life desired to be discarded. Though splayed out in front of her was a vista not unlike that of some kind of tropical dream, the reliefs felt were noticeably fragile, skittish and ready to fall away at any moment.

The trail of passengers, shuffling like visibly sore and jet-lagged zombies, led off toward a squat building in front of a parking lot about a football field's length toward the dying sun. A hundred feet or so along this path was a black vehicle parked on the tarmac. It was an old car with an even older man standing next to it, holding a sign that read *Ms. Jennifer Lansky*. This was not Thor Lansky that she looked upon, as this man was about a foot and a half shorter than she'd remembered her uncle being. Plus, this man still had some red hair whereas, even in her childhood memories, Uncle Thor's hair was completely white by the time he'd entered his forties. Strangely, though, she felt she recognized this man somehow.

The soreness in her muscles and hips sang a constant tone, disharmonizing with each step she took toward the vehicle.

"Hello," the man said, smiling as he greeted her.

"Hi..."

"Jennifer?"

She nodded.

"Name's Gary Taylors." He stuck his hand out. "I help your uncle when he needs errands run now that he's getting on in age, even though I am, too." He chuckled and smiled. "He's been a great friend to me over the years."

Jen shook his hand.

"Please, this way."

The man opened the back door to the car, motioned her into it.

Instinct once again kicked in, directing Jen's eyes back toward the plane, scanning the tarmac around it, glancing under the mobile staircase and into the aircraft's black doorway, for any sign of the shade that had followed her from her dreams. When she saw no sign of it, she slipped into the leather seats and darkness of the backseat of the old car. The closed the door behind her.

They departed the airport, taking a smooth looping track around the parking lot and out onto the main road as Jen watched the sunset, muted by the tinted window.

*

At some point, though she couldn't remember when, they'd left the main road for a dirt and gravel path leading off into a forest. The gravel moved loosely under the aged automobile's tires. Though it had looked presentable from the outside, the car bounced on old shocks and screeched like a rusty hinge when it hit some of the larger pot holes. The remains of the sun peeked through the palm trees leaning from either side of the path leading up the mountain. Eventually, the rest of the evening light dissipated beyond the encroaching forest.

There was a sharp right turn in the path and, after the car bounced slowly beyond an outcrop from the cliffs leading further up the mountain, faint lights could be seen in the woods ahead. A black iron gate met them a few moments later, in front of which the car slowed to a still. The old man in the front seat rolled down his window. There was a single black pole sticking out of the ground, crowned by a chrome keypad. The old man punched a code Jen didn't catch and the gates slid back to either side of the road, allowing them access to what lay ahead.

A few bumpy minutes later, the car came to its final stop.

The complex was built into a steady slope moving up the jungled mountain, which summited far above and beyond like the stump of some giant ancient tree, perhaps felled in some biblical storm. Jen imagined the paintings she'd seen of the fabled massive world tree, Yggdrasil, and thought that this wouldn't have been a bad place for it to have been, thought of what it would've been like to stand at its base, to pray to it. She wondered if it would've had the power to give her Roan back to her.

A great gabled roof peaked above the main entrance to the place like the top of some wooden obelisk. Ornate carvings of dragons, chimaeras and other mystical creatures snaked up extravagant totem poles that guarded either side of the huge oak doors. The totems seemed almost out of place and strange in this tropical biome. Standing a few stone steps down from the entrance was another old man, one that, even after seven years, she recognized immediately. Her uncle Thor had always been a tall man, but lanky and pretty thin. Though the darkness of the night and the flickering light of torches along the staircase moved shadows over him, she could see the warmth in his eyes. She saw her uncle, the only blood relative she had left, and the memories of her childhood came back to her. And she felt it then, an undeniable tugging inside. She unbuckled the seatbelt, pushed the door open and rushed out of the vehicle.

Before she could even reach him, she was sobbing. When she fell into his old arms, smelled the same scent he'd worn for decades, the world seemed to let go, then, as did her weak knees. It all let go of her and sent her soaring through the infinite sea of her own emotions, as if she'd been holding her breath for days, months even, and now, finally, it was pouring out of her so that she could seek a cleansing breath of renewal. This breath tasted of sea salt and vintage cologne.

"Oh, Jenny-Bear." The sound of his voice made her cry all the harder. "I've got you. I've got you."

In this momentary lapse of tension, as it filled a small portion of her vacuous sorrow with warmth, she felt the presence of the wanderer, that thing from the hospital, detach then, removing itself from her, at least that was how her mind perceived this sensation. She slid as much of herself as she could into that small blessing, regardless of how afraid she was of its inevitably temporary nature. When all the world remained for a few long minutes in that seemingly motionless state, with her uncle Thor's arms around her and the stellar abyss looking down upon them, she finally closed her eyes. The sobbing was heavy, produced by the totality of her soul, and seemed a necessary exorcism of the madness and weight that had built up in the dilation of these last few days.

After a while, her uncle said, "It's alright, Gary. I'll take her from here." Her eyes were still closed, sealed air tight by the tears that soaked them, when she felt her uncle move to direct their standing embrace through the entrance to the complex. When the *whump* of the great doors came from behind them, the echoes of the night ocean and nocturnal animals went quiet. The heat from a hearth in the wall of the dark entryway settled over her. The homely atmosphere caressed her skin as she let her uncle take her further into the building. In the muted world left beyond the walls of the place, the vehicle that had driven her here came back to life and rumbled away down the gravel drive.

*

Window panels ran floor-to-ceiling along the east side of the cozy dining room, looking out over a wall of jungle that pushed right up to the balcony underneath. Dim lights lit the corners and dark shadows trailed the ritual masks, crude tribal weapons and sculptures hanging throughout. More examples of the totem poles, inlaid with fantastic beings, stood along each wall of the room.

Glazed onions and greasy pork glistened from Jen's plate in the candlelight. Steamed vegetables sat off to the right. She'd told her uncle about the pregnancy, about everything, while he cooked, but had hardly said a word since he'd finished preparations. It wasn't until they'd sat down in front of their plates that she'd realized how hungry she'd been. Being able to eat a good meal, especially in the company of her uncle, seemed to lessen the pressure of the recent past. Prior to dinner, he'd led her to one of the richly ornamented bathrooms, in which she showered and, under the hot streams of water, tried to scrub the grime from her physical body as well as her mind. With each bit of hot food she now swallowed, she felt herself uncoiling in the same way.

While chewing on a particularly large bite, her eyes wandered to the light and shadows around her. Pictures hung scattered throughout the artifacts on the walls. Behind her, there were two separate paintings of a phoenix, great birds of fire done in vivid paints and oils that seemed alive in the gloom. Her earliest memories reaffirmed that her uncle had always been interested in exotic things, artifacts of lost cultures, societies and religions. She hadn't appreciated the charm of the ancient craftsmanship when she was a child, though.

"This place is beautiful, Uncle. I never... I never expected I would get to be somewhere like this in my life." Amidst the heartache of the last few nights, there really was a part of her that felt a type of relief here, being so far away from the home she'd known, the people she knew. She'd lost her child but she couldn't help feeling a separation from all of it, now that she was here on the island, with her uncle Thor, so many miles removed. It was a lightening that she felt, an easing of the burden. She didn't have the imperative to explain anything to those who'd seen her pregnant, because they weren't here with her. That anxiety could be left until later. Here, in her uncle's company, there was sanctuary.

Her uncle had finished eating more than a quarter hour ago and had simply sat with her while she ate. His bushy white brows animated above his glinting eyes and the slightly crooked smile he'd always had, a genuinely unique face for a genuinely unique man. "Well, I'm glad you're intrigued by it," he said. "I admit, a part of me wishes I'd have moved out here when I was a lot younger, when I had more strength to explore and climb trees and the like." He chuckled. "Still, this place has given me something I couldn't get anywhere else. Even for an old-timer like me, a place like this has secrets still to be discovered, to be nurtured and brought out into the—"

He coughed, hacking heavily into a red handkerchief he swiftly pulled from his pocket. It was a terrible grinding sound. When he'd stopped after a few seconds, his eyes were watering. He looked back up to her. "Brought out into the light," he finished. "Excuse me."

"Everything alright?" she asked, nodding toward the handkerchief he'd folded and was stuffing back into his pocket.

"Oh yes. Don't worry about me," he dismissed with a wave of his hand. "I'll be fine. Everything's good."

Her uncle smiled and Jen responded with a weak smile of her own. A sense that he was hiding something nagged at her a bit. Her hands slowly moved to her stomach, the deflated round of her belly, and she was hit with a tinge of that reality, the one that waited for her back home: an apartment that had been prepared for a baby, yet there would be no baby, a few friends that had spoken of all the potentials and unknowable traits of the little soul, and yet there was no soul to be had... It all still burned in her. The ripening of that ache seemed not yet at its fullest power, but this place was dampening it somehow and for that at least she was grateful.

When Jen had finished her second plate of food, the old man stood from his seat.

"Come," he said. "I'd like to walk for a bit. Think you're up for it?"

Her uncle's eyebrows were bunched together like two caterpillars and his hand was outstretched toward her, accompanied by another of his smiles.

"Sure, Uncle."

She took his hand.

They moved through the many hallways and rooms of the main building. To call it a *house* would be an understatement to the highest degree as, on the first floor, second floor and in the basement, there were offices and bedrooms and exhibition rooms lit by dim candles and wall lamps, one more room seemingly beyond every turn or corner in the dusky hallways.

Outside, they moved along perimeter balconies that overlooked a dense jungle shrouded in the dark of night. Clustered palm trees and overgrown ferns waved in the gentle ocean breeze and, out over the endless dark horizon of waves, the Milky Way was sprawled like an arched spine, holding up the lurid black of the void.

As they rounded a specific turn in the balcony, her uncle stopped to lean on one of the railings, coughing heavily, and hurriedly pulled the handkerchief from his pocket once again. It was only one or two hacks but they were coarse, ruthless, and Jen could swear she felt it in her own lungs and throat as she watched, compelled to look away from the very real and very apparent vulnerability of her last living relative. In the moving light of a wall torch, she saw that the piece of fabric he'd been coughing into wasn't in fact dyed red.

It was splotched heavily with blood.

"Uncle, what's wrong?" She wrapped an arm over his hunched boney shoulders in comfort but her hands were shaking, tears welling up in her eyes. "Please… don't lie to me."

After a long moment of labored breathing, her uncle straightened his back and cleared his throat after wiping his mouth. "Ah, well," he smiled. "I'm seventy years old, Jenny-Bear. A body can't last forever..."

She was unsure of what to say. She could smell inevitability on him in a way she hadn't noticed until right this moment. It'd been covered up by his cologne, the sea air, by nostalgia. The odor was there now, though. "What is it?" she asked.

Another few moments passed in which the old man looked out to the dense trees and the starlit ocean beyond. The torchlight wavered over their backs and, together, their faces were drenched in darkness but she could still see his eyes, reflecting the stars and the sea upon which he gazed.

He cleared his throat once more. "It's lung cancer."

A feeling punched her in the stomach then, spreading over her, a feeling of being alone on the bow of some unnamed ship she did not recognize, watching as her life stood on land and she drifted backward away from it, taken by the greedy tide of entropy and of the annihilating reality of all things. Visions of a slow but steady untethering... These last gentle roots of her life, which seemed to miraculously hold her stable in the face of all else, had already begun to rot and, with the ineluctable passing of her uncle, Jen felt the oncoming loneliness like a black wave, coming to capsize her vessel and drown her in the oppressive deep.

She would be alone, truly and utterly alone.

"But, you... You've never smoked, have you? I don't remember you ever smelling like cigarettes or..."

Her uncle Thor shook his head slowly. "No, no. Never touched the stuff. Save for smoking a few joints back in college, never smoked anything." The old smile crept over his face but it was one that, even in the shadows, Jen could see was being forced against a small twinge of something that ran along the contours of his eyes—maybe anxiety, maybe pain, doubt, fear. He'd always been a man of confidence and entelechy in his kindness, yet just under the surface, there was now a subtle but very noticeable kind of strain. He'd never looked so old. Everything was changing, or maybe it had always been changing. Perhaps, Jen thought, she'd never really had any sort of stable footing. Perhaps each day, each second, had been a continuation of a heartless process of sorts started a long time ago without regard for her, her being the one through which this process and its indifference would be experienced.

At her uncle's insistence, they walked further around the perimeter, moving slowly along the balconies that lined the southern westerly sides of the complex. The night air was light and smelled of the ocean water, a rich salty smell that mixed with the fragrances of the surrounding flora and rode the breeze in from the beach. Her uncle coughed frequently as they continued their walk, excusing it by saying that it happened more frequently right after eating, and, with each cough and hack, Jen felt herself wince, felt herself swallow, as if she needed to clear the blood and phlegm from her own throat every time he did.

When they'd turned down the north side of the property, Jen noticed, separate from the rest of the home and down a small stone path, a strange structure squatting in the dark. It looked like a single room house made of glass, segmented geometrically by dark wooden beams. She thought it to be some sort of greenhouse at first but she couldn't see through the glass, as if it was coated from the inside with paint or curtains. Even under the light of the glowing moon and stars, no forms within were visible. Perhaps they were only tinted, the dimness of which was potentially accentuated by the dark.

Her uncle nodded toward the structure. "Want to check it out?"

"What is it?"

The old man looked down over the balcony toward it and coughed once more. When he'd recovered, he smiled and said, "That's the greenhouse."

"That's what I was first thinking," she said. "Why does it look painted? Is light not able to get into it?"

Her uncle smiled that same smile, reminding Jen of his weakness, driving the facts of the newly understood reality further into her heart, that he was going to die soon and that she would be left alone until the day she killed herself, or until the day the world did the job for her. She felt heat burning in her tear ducts when she smiled meekly back at him.

"No light," he said. "The plants that grow inside *there* do not require sunlight."

Jennifer wiped a rogue tear from her cheek. "You mean they use artificial lights?"

"No, I mean they do not require *any* light."

She scanned the contours of the small building, searching for anything to give away what it was that was contained within, what it was she was feeling at the sight of it. Curiosity, yes, but the way the black glass looked in the night... "Weird," was all she could manage in response. Something else was a part of this scene that she couldn't quite place, a separate invisible part of what she was witnessing. Something awaited inside the dark walls of glass, and she knew this not just through her uncle's proclamations of such. It was more than just nocturnal plants. She could feel it from here on the balcony, thirty yards away.

Her ruminations were broken by a wrinkled hand on her shoulder.

"Come with me," her uncle said. "We have much to discuss."

*

The study looked more like a library than anything. Probably a thousand square feet just by itself, an exhibit of book cases lined the walls on all sides and every shelf was filled to capacity. Jen walked slowly along them, regarding the ornately bound texts: tomes of horticultural studies, collections of mythological stories and origins, homeopathy, occult astrology, and aged books on the topics of ritual divination and prehistoric structures all stood shoulder to shoulder with one another. Multiple books on the origins of the phoenix in myths and ancient cultures were scattered throughout.

"This collection is amazing, Uncle." She'd always felt a strange connection to the very tactile sensory input of an old book, its smell and feel. Her fingertips traced the embedded relief of the firebird on the spine of a book titled *The Rise of the Phoenix: On the Myth of the Fallen, On Death and On the Rebirth Thereafter*. It had always seemed that, regardless of the topic, aged texts were like elders that she could sit down with and listen to stories from without requiring anything from her but time and a little bit of attention. She was reminded in her brief whimsy of a quote she'd heard once, something about books being the *quietest and most constant of friends*.

The clink of glass and subtle sounds of chugging liquid preluded her uncle's approach to where she stood. His hands contained a glass tumbler in each, both a quarter full of a brown syrupy liquid, one held out toward her. He smiled. "The phoenix, the bird of rebirth, the creature that awakens from the ashes of its own perceived mortality. Paradoxically, its immortality is defined by its constant reoccurring mortality."

Jen took the glass from her uncle's outstretched hand and swirled the liquid, smelling the aroma of the alcohol. It had been the better part of a year since she'd touched anything alcoholic and, even with everything that had happened, her no longer carrying the responsibility that she had been, no longer carrying her Roan within her, she still felt odd considering the drink. She felt the emptiness inside of her, refocused her attention on it only briefly and, when her heart felt that ache that she'd managed to somewhat stifle while listening to her uncle talk, she put the tumbler to her lips and drank it all back in one swig. Her mouth and face burned immediately. The warmth spread through her chest and in her lungs and stomach, and then she held the glass out for another.

Her uncle watched her, then put his hand out to take the empty tumbler from her before taking the first sip of his own.

At some point, her uncle had begun to speak again of the flowers and the phoenix, of knowledge kept hidden from someone or in some place, but it wasn't until she could no longer hear him that she realized she hadn't been able to hear him for minutes now or, if she had been able to, her attention was too unfocused and directed elsewhere other than her uncle's words. Her perspective dragged along the carved mouth of one of the totem dragons near the room's entrance. And then she was sitting in one of the chairs closest to the roaring fireplace. The heat of the flames licked the skin of her chest and arms and face. Her uncle's voice was a low intermittent hum in the background, words she still couldn't make sense of. The aperture of the fireplace began to warble and shift in its dimensions. At first, Jen thought that she was imagining some similar room to the one she was in but, when she blinked rapidly and rubbed her eyes, trying to focus on something, *anything*, but being unsuccessful, she understood that it was her reality, *the* reality that was transforming and making the fireplace appear like a maw of some kind, opening and closing. Her eyes felt heavy, as did her head and arms. "Unc..." was all she could manage to say before realizing her lips were completely numb, her tongue feeling like a foreign worm wriggling in her mouth.

The world dissipated in a mist of smoke or fog. Everything faded. Strangely, she could then hear her uncle's far away voice saying *It's alright, Jenny-Bear. I'm sorry but this is the only way to... cooperation in this process... been searching for an answer to... I need you. It's...*

And then there was only the abyss.

*

A harsh pungent smell ripped her from the darkness, shooting fire through her senses. Jen's eyes tore open. Adrenaline pushed through her system, jumpstarted like a car battery by a bolt of lightning. Her instincts tried to send her hands to rub her burning eyes but they were bound. Restraints were snug over her wrists and, when she blinked the daze of a short sleep out of her eyes, she saw the straps that held her in position. She was no longer in the chair by the fireplace but was held in an antiquated wheelchair, further back in the study toward one of the corners. Over her shoulder was one of the totems, staring down at her with its exaggerated features, still slightly warbling from the effects of whatever had sent her into the black of sleep to begin with.

Standing near the fire, which had died down a bit from its earlier vivid blaze, was her uncle. He was all shoulders and bones underneath his papery-looking clothes. The light poured around his thin profile, a cryptic silhouette lined in a fiery aura. He pushed the small pouch of whatever it was he'd held under her nose into his blood-stained handkerchief, then tossed the combination into the glowing embers.

"What is—" Uncertainty mixed with growing panic into a potent cocktail, surging under her skin and in her blood. "Why am I tied up? What, what're you doing, Uncle?"

He turned and, though she half-expected to see some sinister look on his face, his eyes met hers with only sympathy, with shamefulness. "You see, Jenny-Bear, I've brought you here because I need you. I didn't initially want to force you into any—" He coughed into the crook of his elbow. When he pulled away, there was red spatter on the sleeve of his shirt. "Into anything, but I don't have much time, as is apparent."

"What are you talking about? What does tying me up have to do with your cancer?" She pulled at the restraints to no avail.

"Rebirth. That's what I'm talking about. And a second chance for you to raise a son, *your* son, Roan, the way he ought to have been—alive and healthy and grateful for his loving mother."

Jen's head still throbbed with confusion, with a rising anger and frustration, but upon the mention of her dead son's name, the son that never bore witness to the world she'd so lovingly prepared for him, she stopped her straining. Tears streamed from her eyes. "I don't believe... What could you possibly do to change that he's gone? He was born *dead*, Uncle! Let me go, goddamnit!" The fury in her own voice surprised her but the anguish she now fell into somehow made it easy to yell, to scream.

"Well," her uncle started.

He moved slowly around behind her. Jen heard his hands grip the handles on the back of the wheelchair. There was a clacking, an unlocking of something, followed by a small push and then the chair was moving toward the doorway out into the hall. She pulled at the restraints again. The masks on the walls stared down at her with hollow black eyes and the firelight messed with their shapes as they passed into her peripheral.

"I won't let you go until you've seen what I need you to see. I've waited too long for this moment, so much has been sacrificed, so much time spent in anticipation, contemplation... Regarding your son, I'm not sure where to start but I'll do my best to explain this all. And I can promise you this, my dear Jenny-Bear: I will not hurt you. I promise with all my heart you will not be harmed. I just... You are my last hope and I need to be able to *show* you, even if you refuse me in the end. You have to witness it... You have to behold it. And then I'll remove the restraints."

They breached into the hallway and the old man coughed again, roughly, a sound like rocks caught in a garbage disposal. The wheelchair made a steady rolling noise on the hardwood planks—*thud-thud thud-thud*. When they reached the front of the house, her uncle pushed the great double doors open, exposing them to the tropical night. The outside air hit her sweating skin and cooled the flesh of her neck and arms. The moon was high in the starry dark sky now, staring down on her fright like a single gaping eyeball.

"Where are you taking me? Just tell me where you're taking me!" Jen's blood ran hot and anxiety squeezed at her throat. She rocked in the chair back and forth, at one point lifting the right wheel off the ground for a moment before slamming back down.

"Calm down, Jenny-Bear." Her uncle's tone was consoling. "You wouldn't come with me if I untied you... I admit, this isn't a very delicate way to handle this but—"

"Where?" she screamed. "I'm asking *where*! Just tell me, please."

Her uncle Thor cleared his throat and then said, "I'm taking you to the greenhouse."

*

At the staircase leading down to the walkway, which forked to either side of the complex, her uncle turned a hard right with the chair and directed it down a ramp she'd not seen before. The totems standing guard on either side of the front doors played in the torchlight when she looked back to them, the phoenix on each seeming more alive than ever. Though she was being rolled out into a luminous night, in her mind, Jen saw only the black glass of the structure that awaited, the coarse paint chipped away in some of the panels, and that obscure essence of its inner darkness.

"In the year fifteen-twelve," her uncle began speaking, "a Spanish man by the name of Rodrigo de Clemencia claimed to have found evidence of the lost city of *Atlantia*, or Atlantis, during his exploration of what is known in modernity as the eastern coast of Chile." When the wheelchair reached the bottom of the ramp, her uncle coughed again, then cleared his throat. He continued in a croaky voice. "This evidence he described was a lost catacomb from thousands of years ago, buried deep into the heart of a mountain. The walls had been painted in gold and inlaid with ivory, so totally that light reflected off of the surfaces in ways that he described as unearthly, heaven-like even. He said that a single torch held in his hand lit the entire thing for his exploration, rows upon rows of cloisters, a shimmering labyrinth. He found chests of jewels and beads, rare stones and minerals he'd never seen before. There were ornate weapons, gold tempered into shapes he'd never beheld...

"In his writings, he describes happening upon a chest with bizarre imagery carved into it, the likes of which no other object he'd found in the labyrinth resembled. The messages depicted in the reliefs told a story of the creation of Earth, the breaking open of the heavens and the waters pouring over the *faciem terrae*, of the cycles of catastrophe in human existence, and of the gift held within that very chest."

The wheelchair stopped. Her uncle entered a coughing fit Jen almost thought he wasn't going to get out of. Fluids and phlegm audibly curdled in the old man's wheezing gasps with each bone-rattling hack. Meanwhile, Jen pulled at her restraints with what strength she had regained, almost tipping the chair again. The old man was using one of the handles to keep himself standing, though, and it was apparent after her attempt that she was going nowhere. When her uncle managed to compose himself after a good thirty seconds, she glanced up to his face, fixating her angered eyes upon him. Fire flickered in his pupils from the torches that lined the path and reflected off of the tears that streaked his old cheeks.

"Excuse me," he said, smiling weakly. He gave a half-hearted *whew*. "Jenny-Bear, please believe me. I'm not going to hurt you, and I mean that. I won't let any harm come to you and I will let you go shortly, but not until I've shown you what needs to be seen. Please, just… just trust me."

When he continued pushing the chair, she could feel the difference in the pressure, a weakness that had seemed to enter the old man's boney limbs in just the last few moments. She let out a whimper then, one that was a culmination of the situations that had led her to this moment. The darkness from beyond the torches, within the jungles that surrounded, seemed to sap her of her will to fight. Her uncle had repeated that he wasn't going to hurt her but the restraint, being held down, and the murky world that continued to smother her with an inability to focus, was sending shocks of anxiety under her skin and throughout her senses. Her heartrate attested to it.

Please, just… just trust me is what he'd said.

There was nothing for her in this to trust. It was as if her Uncle Thor had died already, given the sudden loneliness and further vacuity she now felt. He may not have meant her harm but this was a major breach of trust, one that would change the relationship she had with him forever.

Uncle Thor cleared his throat once again, then continued the story as he pushed. "In the chest, when Sir Rodrigo opened it, was a great seed. As he described, it was the size of a melon, nestled in a bed of cloth, a bulb of a sort, and he translated the markings on its arch to mean that it was a Flower of Life, though the Latin name Rodrigo had given it was a bit different— *Infantulus mediae noctae*, or the Midnight Baby. This was because the carvings also described the flower's blooming habits, that it would only show its full bloom in the heart of darkness, and that, when it did this, miraculous things could occur."

The path snaked around a stand of trees, then rounded the northeast corner of the main building in the complex. And when the flora pushing up on either side of them opened up, Jen looked out at the clearing and, within its center, saw the greenhouse once again. Its structure appeared demented. Whether it was from the haziness of the drugs still wearing off or the latent effects of the alcohol in which the drugs had entered her, the framework seemed to shiver slightly and transform in the night, exaggerating its geometry in the corners and edges of its architecture. She could sense something beyond its dark panels, breathing maybe, or shapeshifting. Then, as if an understanding was forcibly injected into her thoughts, she recognized the feeling, what she sensed: it was the darkness she'd been trying to avoid for entire days now, the thing that followed her from home, from the hospital, the shadow from her dreams. It was here. It hadn't left. It had only waited. There was intent, and she felt it with every fiber of her being as she stared at the tenebrous structure. She could feel that entity, how it waited for her inside, waited to swallow her or undo her at the seams, *something*. The threat loomed heavily as the wheelchair crept closer and closer.

"So why, why am I here?" she managed to say.

Small torch flames reflected off the grimy glass panels of the greenhouse's double doors. The creeping dark seemed to move up Jen's spine, then, the dark that waited inside, or maybe the dark that surrounded them, abated only in illusion by the torches. It was as if *it*, the wanderer, knew she was approaching and she could *feel* it, that dark thing, and its anticipation emanating from within. The salt breeze no longer whispered through the trees surrounding, nor could she hear the language of the ocean. She wanted to look around, to verify with her own two eyes that the world still existed around her, but her eyes were inexorably fixated on the doors that led into that unknown beyond.

Her uncle moved to stand in front of the doors, then turned to her. "Through some connections, and a hefty amount of money, I was able to obtain the journals and scribblings of others who tried to figure out the secrets of the flower. When I finally got a bulb of my own, I planted it and I took care of it, devoting much of my time to the protection of this beautiful thing. My work took a backseat, as did what was left of the family, hobbies... *It* became my hobbies, *it* was my work. The Midnight Baby. It really is beautiful. I can't wait for you to see it. And you are here because you've lost your child. You've suffered more than many could understand. Through this sorrow, I believe you are the key to my own rebirth."

At that, he turned around and moved his aged hands to the door handles.

Jennifer blurted, "Wait!"

Her uncle stopped and turned once again.

"How did you know that I'd lost Roan? Did you know before you sent the letter?" Endless possibilities ran through her mind, of him somehow spying on her, of having contacts within the hospital or something.

He paused. And then he said, "I did."

How could he know, but then, as she thought this, she remembered a face amidst the delirium, a face she recognized at some point on the trip here. The man waiting for her at the airport, the one who drove her here…

"That guy who gave me the ride, your assistant or whatever. Was he there, at the hospital?"

Her uncle nodded. "Yes, I had Gary look in on you."

She didn't understand. And before she could ask another question, to find out why, he'd turned back around and reached once more for the doors. When they swung open, the entrance gaped and tears poured down Jen's cheeks. The confusion and horror rose within her, bubbling like foam. Her eyes showed her things within the dark aperture, things she wasn't sure existed but electrified her, nonetheless. She pulled at the restraints but still they did not break.

"Uncle! No! Please, no!"

The fear was crippling, the breath shallow in her lungs. She couldn't discern its shape but the *thing* was in that oily blackness, she knew. She felt its stare upon her, though she couldn't find its eyes to meet with her own. She didn't want to find it but her wide eyes searched anyway and, in their fruitless endeavor, the terror grew. Within the bedlam of panic and paranoia, she heard those screeching shoes of the nurses on the dream-bridge, echoing out at her from the black ahead, warped in octave and reverberating endlessly it seemed in some great cave hidden within the impossible confines of the greenhouse. Her uncle did not respond to her pleading but simply returned to his position behind the wheelchair and began to push once more. Jen's resistance ceased when she stared back into the darkness, growing larger as it enclosed. As the doors were shut behind, that darkness seemed to swallow her whole.

The black was total. Nothing could be seen. Jennifer couldn't tell if her eyes were open or not. Rainbow streaks pulsed in the darkness with her quickened heartbeat, a neural reaction to the blood that rushed through her retina.

Uncle Thor spoke softly from the black behind her. "It's okay, Jenny-Bear. Just breathe. I promise I wasn't lying when I said that you won't be hurt. Though things seem the contrary, you are not the one vulnerable in this, which is why you are here. I'm going to need you when the time comes."

Jen hardly heard this. Her breathing was fast and getting faster. The entity was here, it was no longer a single shadow on a wall somewhere. Rather, it was all around her, in each lungful of darkness she breathed. It flowed into her, its presence, and the unknown of it made her want to scream. And just as she was about to unleash one, her uncle spoke again:

"There's nothing be afraid of, my dear niece. Allow your eyes to adjust and you'll see..."

Something between anger and horror surged within her. Yet, eventually, after a few full deep breaths, one after another, she managed to slow her heartrate, to quiet her thoughts. The calmness allowed her to regard the space they were in, a damp and muggy space. The black air smelled of dirt and mulch and a tinge of something iron like blood.

Her uncle's voice came from the darkness again.

"Do you see it?"

Within the moments that passed, her eyes finally adjusted to the black, and then she began to see.

The paint that coated the inner walls of the greenhouse had chipped in a few different spots, allowing small pin-pricks of moonlight to come through. There was one coming through the ceiling that was larger, the width of a flashlight beam. It shone down into the center of the space and, in its cold luminescence, something was visible.

It was a monstrous thing, not in color or texture but in size. It was a flower bud larger than any she'd ever seen. Its colors appeared black in the sliver of moonlight, its shape bulbous, as if its inert pedals were wrapped around a fully inflated basketball. And there was a light, one she had not seen before but now leeched full notice from her. This light came from within the unbloomed flower, a faint purple glow. At first, she blinked, uncertain whether her eyes were playing tricks on her or not. And then, just as her eyes were beginning to grasp what small light it produced, the glow grew substantially, brightening the space within the confines of the black glass walls. The bulb was bizarre, pulsing with light like some dormant beast's heart. Strange sensations squirmed under the skin of her nape as she looked upon the thing.

"It begins," her uncle said. His voice quavered. "Oh, Lord. It begins."

The vibrant light soon drowned out the weak moon beams that her eyes had sought before. Now, the flower was the only source of light in the space. Its glow sent shadows of other smaller plants onto the black painted walls surrounding, their shapes taking the forms of strange things.

"I've waited so long and it's—," her uncle mumbled. "This moment... I have dreamt of this moment for the better part of forty years. The better part of forty... Jenny-Bear, I'm going to undo your straps now. You can get up and you can run out that door if you'd like. You're right, that this is a place filled with darkness. I was a fool to restrain you, to drug you. I *am* a desperate old fool. But I only wanted to show you. In here, if you were to stay just a bit longer, I believe I can make the worst of your woes go away while simultaneously allowing an answer to my own problem, this annihilation that is coming for me. I think the darkness will bear light if we hold out for it, together, but, beyond this point, I will not force it from you. If you do not stay, though, I cannot, alone, be the solution to my predicament. I *need* you, Jennifer."

Her uncle placed a hand on her shoulder and squeezed gently, then began unstrapping her ankles. As soon as her wrists were free as well, what was left of her adrenaline screamed in her blood. She stood and ran for the door, could swear she was already running out into the night, a tropical world that had the stars and moon that would never let it get as dark as it was in here. She could swear that she was running down the drive to hop the fence, moving down to the main road, already strapped into a flight back home, away from here, away from all of this...

But she hadn't opened the doors—not yet.

Her hand rested on the inner handle, the door to the night only slightly ajar, an almost undetectable bit of breeze rolling over her hands from outside. Her eyes moved back to the great glowing bulb in the middle of the darkness. The lambency seemed to refract around the edges of the pedals, shards of rainbow glinting in an aura surrounding. Its light was haunting and Jen found herself enraptured by it. Its pulsing was a signal, a sign from something outside of the physical world she stood within. She felt it every time the light grew brighter and darker, brighter and darker. In its brilliance, she glimpsed into some other facet of this dimension.

"I was so afraid of it," her uncle spoke, "that doom we all have awaiting us. I desperately tried to turn my back on it and focus on the breath of life for as long as I could, the things I could do with my time left, and to try and find some sort of grace before I left this world. But it never happened. I've had at least one eye on that darkness for as long as I can remember, maybe even my entire life. And the darkness always stays the same—thick, so oppressive and grand and aiming its inevitable momentum at me, directly at *me*. Sometimes, I could've sworn I saw it in the distance, in our actual reality, though I don't believe another soul around me could've. I saw Death, Jenny-Bear. The solution, though... The solution lay within the Midnight Baby, within the tragedies you've endured, my dear niece, and through the work I have done. We have the chance, in this glorious moment—" He sniffed as tears fell from his eyes. "I've been in here with this more times than you can imagine, yet it's never been as it is tonight. It's never been *alive* like it is now. The colors, its response to *you*… It is not only us that have prepared for this. This space, what grows within it, has prepared for this moment, too."

And as she took in what it was she stared at, the initial fight-or-flight, that rush to escape from the depths of this situation, was driven away by a warmth that slowly began to fill her. This feeling grew and spread throughout her body, starting with her chest and ending in her fingertips, only to fall back onto itself and reignite the rest of her body—a self-sustaining current. She didn't notice that her hand slid off the door handle, or that she'd turned back around completely to face the luminous flora.

"Vessel for vessel. Life into life," her uncle said.

He was right. It really was…

"Beautiful," she said.

Somewhere in the faint background of her fixed gaze, she heard her uncle Thor's voice, chanting, singing even:

Vessel for vessel.

Life into life.

She didn't remember moving from the door. She didn't remember moving to crouch in front of the thing, to bask in the lurid afterglow of the bulb, her face was mere inches from it. It was so round and, from the light of its core, her eyes saw the curvature of its base, the way its pedals wrapped gently over each other, the tips of which made a sort of crown at its zenith.

Vessel for vessel.

Life into life.

In her peripheral, her uncle moved to the other side of the oversized thing, standing behind it, his features now lit by the illumination. The old man looked like a ghoul in the diffused glow. He had something in his hand that glinted. Jen saw that it was a blade, one that curved back and forth like a snake in its form, and it seemed almost to writhe in the purple luminescence. Beyond the strange bulb, her uncle knelt down on both knees, aligned with her. His face became alight with the radiance of the magnificent flower the closer he leaned in.

He coughed into his arm, blood spatter soaking into the sleeve of his shirt at the inner arm. A gentle sob murmured from his thin lips. "It's funny," he sniffed and smiled, the stream of tears catching the light. "I've wondered about my last thoughts before Death took me, what my final words might be. I've imagined corny one-liners or great speeches... The truth is that I still hardly have any answers after all this time. What could I possibly impart onto the world around me that hasn't already been imparted upon it by someone or something else? I'm one foot in the grave and yet I still feel like the child that used to run down to the river and pet frogs, not knowing anything about the true nature of reality. I still feel like that kid who had his first kiss in his first car, that old Buick... But it's okay, because I cherish it, all of it, even if I don't have the answers I've sought, even if the memories are vague after all these years. That is the point of all of this, I think. In order to find the answers, I must be reborn. I *must* have another life."

And then he looked directly into her eyes.

"Vessel for vessel, Jenny-Bear. Life into life."

And without hesitation, the blade seemed to disappear in a pulse of darkness. When the bulb went to full glow once again, she saw that her uncle had fallen. The hilt of the knife protruded from his chest. His eyes were wide with pain and the tension of strain contorted the features of his face. His wrinkled hand grasped out at the base of the large plant's stem in one final mortal effort. With one last shudder, an unhinging release of breath, her uncle Thor went still.

Through her tears, Jen saw something then in her peripheral: beyond the pulsing bulb and her uncle's body, in the far corner, lay a shadow. Its shape was visible within the radiance, a slice of darkness attached to the inner walls of the greenhouse. Some part of her screamed and she couldn't tell if she'd actually done so. Held in stasis, she watched as the shade moved, gaining a third dimension to its bulk, toward the plant, toward her uncle's limp body. The plant slowly strobed, as did the shadow's vaporous form while it floated silently over the mulchy uneven soil below. When it reached her uncle's body, it twisted itself into a type of thin vortex, funneling its essence into a loop. It haunted over the scene like a puff a smoke and then, finally, twirled down into a point on the crown of the nocturnal bulb.

It wasn't long before the big pedals began tightening and

loosening, releasing tension and then contorting. At the base of the plant's stalk, a sliver of fiber, like a proboscis of a kind, had extended out and was half-buried into the motionless hand of her uncle. The old man's skin and musculature seemed then to deflate right in front of her eyes, as if he was a scarecrow and the straw was suddenly being pulled out of him. The thing was sucking from his corpse. The skin came to hug against his knobby bones. His lifeless eyeballs bulged and what remained of his flesh turned a pallid grey.

A ringing had built in Jen's eardrums, drowning out everything else. She took a step back, her balance shaky in the loose dirt, but when the plant suddenly shook, rippling its own mass like a dog shaking water off itself, Jen went completely still. A feeling swelled in her lungs, an amalgam of horror and astonishment.

The unfurling seemed to happen in waves down the extraordinary flora. The vibrancy of the glow intensified as each moment passed and, one by one, the pedals peeled themselves slowly away from the whole like strips of paper mache. They came to rest, outstretched and open, facing up toward the glass ceiling and the night beyond the chips in the paint, like solar panels waiting for a dark sun. When the last had fallen, the flower then lay open and exposed. Having gone still, it now resembled a bird fountain or garden piece sticking out of the ground. There was a dark aperture in the center of it, surrounded by buds of pollen that throbbed patterns of light around it like tiny LEDs.

The thing radiated, stared like an eye in the darkness. The fluctuations in the light had slowed and then came to beam steadily, instead. Jen moved to stand over it, propelled by a curiosity she'd never felt before that moment. She stared down into the darkness that lay within as the aperture of the organic hole in the center of the flower twitched, seeming to stretch and contract. Both terrified and enthralled, she watched as, out of the hole, something emerged:

It was thin slick hair matted against a blue nubile forehead. It was two closed eyes with unwrinkled eyelids resting gently over them. It was a small little nose, untarnished by clogged pores or broken veins.

It was the head of an infant.

When the rest of its body surfaced, raised by some unknown musculature within the strange budded flower, Jen could see the baby's little chest rising and falling. It was alive. Its precious eyelids slowly opened to reveal dark eyes, eyes that gazed for the first time outside of itself. It was her baby. It was Roan. The flesh was a blue color, even in the odd light, but he looked so beloved and handsome, a fuller chubbier version of the corpse that she had birthed just days earlier. Through some force beyond her perspective, from the same realm which she'd stared into through the flower's shifting brilliance earlier, she felt guided, an influence pulling her even closer. *This* was the gift it sought to give her. *This* was her son. She hadn't been able to admit before that it was her son following her from the hospital, some aspect of his short existence caged to the physical realm in an unphysical form. It would've been too much like having hope in something beyond what she'd been told was possible. Now, however, with what she had borne witness to, she'd relinquished all resistance to the process that unfolded before her.

When she saw the little thing's wandering black eyes, she knew it was him.

Jennifer reached her hands, unshaking and calm, down to the newly birthed infant and pulled it up toward her chest. The young one rose and the light from the flower grew in brightness. As she gazed down upon the infant, his skin began to change color, morphing in the throbbing glow from the pods of technicolor pollen. His complexion flowed and reverberated, then appeared to be evening out, the hue growing fairer. She could see then that her baby Roan's eyes were no longer black orbs but gorgeous irises set in white. They were normal eyes, natural and healthy. Her baby Roan was there, in her arms, this time not a leaden weight but a living being. And at this realization, she cried fiercely. The child's face scrunched and it began to cry too. As they lamented in unison, mother and child, the draw to feed the babe overwhelmed Jen and so she unbuttoned her shirt, tucked the lapel under her breast and moved her nipple to her son's mouth. As her child fed, she felt the pedals contract to gently rest upon her thighs and hips, holding her, and the whole universe seemed to rest upon her then as well. Her once wasted body felt in use again, fulfilling a purpose she thought lost forever.

The doors of the greenhouse opened. The night outside was warm and the salt breeze caressed the flesh of Jen's arms as she stepped outside. She began her steady stroll toward the main building of the complex, Roan cooing against her exposed breast. The huge leaves of the trees surrounding the path moved against each other, creating a chorus that sounded like rain. The waxing moon looked down from high in the western sky while the eastern horizon flared with a subtle grey of early morning light, the start of a new day.

The Lights on the Other Car

Daniel's hands were outstretched, the fingers spread and trembling. He stared between them to the licking tendrils of the small fire on the ground just beyond. The flames shone green, rippling across a squat mound of refuse, gnarling each piece like an old rind. Occasionally, whirls of sparks cracked and rose into the air. He couldn't remember how the fire had started, nor could he tell what the objects being eaten by the flames were. The tingling of the warmth it provided crept up through his arms like an army of slow worms under the skin. He couldn't feel the actual temperature of the heat, though, no matter how close he moved his hands to its source, or how much his skin smoked and steamed from the proximity—not in the way he used to be able to feel heat or in the way he thought he remembered being able to, before being in this place. The cracked concrete bit into the soles of his feet. He didn't know why his shoes were gone.

...the space between the...

The fire cast dim dancing shadows of Daniel against a rusted Mercedes that hunkered lifeless only inches to his right. The derelict vehicle seemed to be shielding him from some aspect of the winds, those gusts of rankness coming every so often, a product of the bizarre cosmic emptiness that hung all around.

He said, "Have you noticed that we haven't needed to eat, Dad?"

The old man sat across the fire, near the rear of the decrepit vehicle. His absent stare reflected the unearthly color of the flames, sparks in his pupils, the light of which seemed to shudder and swirl every time he blinked. The old man's mouth made the simplest attempts at a smile. It faltered, though, and the seasoned set of eyes continued to look beyond the guardrails of the floating bit of highway they were on, staring out over the green-streaked void.

...between the space between the...

Daniel wanted his father's eyes to meet his own, but they wouldn't.

He couldn't remember how long they'd been here.

"I don't feel anything in… my stomach. I'm not hungry or… or even…" He trailed off. Whatever was happening, it was more than that, a lack of hunger. The emptiness that awaited just beyond the guardrails of the highway seemed to be the same void that was growing inside of him, an entropy. How he knew that, Daniel could not say. It was there, though. He could feel it swelling inside his core, somewhere deeper than his gut.

Daniel followed his father's stare. He looked behind and over his shoulder to see for himself into the abyss that surrounded this island of reality they sat in, breathed in, experienced in. This wasn't right. The memories of life, of hunger and of energy and of sensation and aging and living…

It was all leaving him.

"Do you remember the lights on the other car?" the old man said.

Daniel turned back and looked to his father's eyes, thinking they'd be looking into his own. They weren't. They stared, instead, down into the fire, the waves of luminescence.

The lights…

The lights from the other car, the one that made the turn in front of them—that's what his father was referring to. Daniel's mind tried to grasp onto those passing images, the remembrance of those fleeting micro-moments, deep in a part of his recollection, a part that was failing and becoming detached, parting and spreading away from itself. The words to articulate the complexity of what he was experiencing, and the decay that was very apparently happening to his thoughts, faded away like tufts of smoke in a high wind. The thoughts were parting and yet the images were colorful and potent on the backs of his eyelids, the other car that drove into them. He could still see the crunching of the metal and the shattering of the glass, the bits of it raining down from the sky, ropes of blood caught in the air and on the pavement and the seats as their entire world tumbled over and over and over.

"Dad, we have to figure out what to do. I... I think I'm losing my mind. My thoughts are... they're... not staying in..." Daniel struggled listlessly with a language that seemed to be making less sense by the word. His consciousness grasped in the dimness for a familiar hand that seemed to keep retreating, taking with it the clear definitions and understanding of the reality around him, and the sense he tried to make of it. "I can't..." *I can't hold onto my thoughts.* He blinked and the images in his mind's eye flashed like single frames of a motion picture. The world turned and turned, tumbling over onto itself. "We have to find a way out of here," he said. He remembered the way his father screamed. The old man wasn't screaming now but he remembered how he did, when it all came to a point, a singularity. The echoes of those sounds broke his heart in a repetitive cycle, again and again.

"Daniel, do you remember the lights on the other car?" his father said.

The lights...

He remembered, in that final moment, the lights and their sinister glow, the lumens of a thousand rods of lightwave radiation rippling through the aether, searing the space between atoms and rolling into his pupils, burning the backs of his eyeballs and shooting pain through his skull as they came closer and into him. That pain was immediate but nothing compared to the pain that followed shortly after. He remembered the lights reflected in the raindrops that sailed in front of the car on their way down to the wet concrete below, and then the condensing began and he remembered being squished and breathless. Even this horror was fading, though, being chewed and digested by darkness around them, by the hulking hungry essence that flowed from it.

His father moved to lean back against the discarded car, the front end of which was crunched like an accordion. With the way that the thing was turned, Daniel couldn't see the front but he was certain it was the car with the lights, the one that hit them. Yet, try as he could, his limbs didn't respond when he shifted to stand up, to go look at the front of the car and see the lights once again, to see if they were still there, to see if they got swallowed up in the fading experiences as well. The memories were drifting from his fogged mind like water draining from a tub, spiraling in confusion, spiraling, spiraling...

... between the space between the space...

"Dad, how did we get here?" Daniel said. The void inside of him had grown heavier since he'd last tried to speak to the old man, how long ago he couldn't quite comprehend. Minutes, hours... Days... He felt it sag in the cavity of his gut, pushing down against his bladder and genitals. "We were driving. *You* were driving." He wrapped his arm over his stomach. "I was in the passenger seat." The weighted sensation wasn't pain but something similar, an imposter to the feeling of pain, a simulacrum to the real thing. It was a growth of nothingness, embiggening inside. It stretched at the walls of his innards and pushed them away from and then into each other, pulling and fusing the veins and tissue and the grease on an atomic level.

The very matter he consisted of was being manipulated and disintegrated.

He was being fed upon, eaten from the inside out.

Daniel glanced back to his father, watched him stare blankly into the abyss beyond the guardrails. The man had lost all persona, almost inanimate in his shock. Daniel followed his father's gaze with his own, again, this time able to lift himself slightly, to look over the barrier and out into its totality.

Out there, in the chasm, shapes swam in the endless muck: smoky emerald wisps, ghostly beings rippling to and fro. Some clashed into each other, forming different combined shapes, and others disappeared and reappeared altogether. They sailed, propelled by invisible winds so that their tattered tendrils waved in their wakes like flags of old ships as they crossed the tenebrous sea. Unspeakable things they were, like spectres of some benighted realm, and yet strangely they seemed almost human in the emotion they projected, moving in their perpetual ghoulish disorientation.

And in the blackness of the further all-encompassing, beyond the swimming beings, Daniel could see the mouths. There were more than he could ever imagine, mouths that chewed from the void, with teeth that waited to grit themselves on his soul, to turn everything he was into cud. The countless gullets gaped and screamed for sustenance, singing of their unworldly hunger. The reflections of the emerald ghosts glinted in the saliva that dripped from those countless jaws chomping in the mad dark.

"Daniel."

The horror rushed through what remained of his senses, then. The mouths were out there and now in his mind and he turned back to his father.

"Dad?"

The old man did not look into his eyes, though. Instead, he kept staring over Daniel's shoulder, to the primordial dark of Death, the mouths and those things that swam over them.

"Do you remember the lights on the other car, Daniel?"

The lights...

He remembered the lights and how they exploded into fireworks in front of him. He remembered the fire in his eyes as his sight left him to the sounds of bubbling and popping, the smells of burning gasoline. He remembered the hideous pain that scorched everything he knew, conflagrating all that existed. There had been no cleansing in the flames, only suffering. Tears fell from his tired eyes, shrouding his vision with sorrow and confusion.

...space between the space between the space between.

"Dad, I don't... I don't understand what to do. I don't understand why we are here." His breath fell short. He swallowed hard. "Are we dead?"

The ghosts floated above and around the scene in which the two of them sat. It was an aurora of alien glow, emerald radiance shimmering off of every surface of their island in the darkness. In the Mercedes behind his father, Daniel could see a shape inside the driver's seat, within the tinted windows. The head of this shape was shaking horribly, completely silent from behind the glass. It looked like a man but the features of the face and head were falling apart from the violent paroxysm. The neck twisted at odd angles and the mouth on the face gaped and stretched in a horrific inhuman way. Daniel could tell the thing, this man, was screaming and was grateful that he could not hear it.

He slumped back and leaned against the concrete below the guardrail once more.

"Daniel," his father said and, knowing exactly what the old man was going to say, Daniel couldn't help but look up to his dad, the only dad he'd ever had, the only one who'd ever said his name that way. Daniel loved him but that emotion was leaving him too, taking with it his heart. Yet, with everything he was, he looked again to his father, hoping the old man's eyes would find his just once more, so that he knew he was being seen.

Green ambient light bathed the old man's features. His eyes were catatonic, staring in senselessness, his mouth grim and quivering.

"Daniel, do you remember the lights on the other car?"

A Death to See

For in thy final moments, when thy flesh is taken with natural Death, the Most High shall ascend into thy cooling warmth; Thy soul shall be carried and His message shall be left in the wake of thine taking; Utile is thy weeping marrow and thy stilled blood, for the words of Him are present within that which remains before thou feedeth the ground and the worms and the rot; Within thy last breath and the echoes of thy last words, His glory shall paint the truths of Creation.

—Book of Divinities, Ch. 8: ver. 11-13

The razor slid over the pudgy flesh of his thigh, scraping at the stubble that had grown in since yesterday morning and catching the dim light from the bulb above the bathroom sink.

You missed a spot, Abraham. Do you think the Lord will accept you into his infinite kingdom for anything less than absolute perfection?

The raw honey tasted sweet on Abey's tongue every time he sucked it from his fingers. He shaved himself with it each and every morning, without exception, rubbing the viscous stuff onto his thick and pallid skin before dragging the blade over the meat. It was the way Mother had taught him to do it, the way that was required by scripture. Except for the hair on the top of his head, which was to be kempt and perfectly made every morning as well, he was to shave his entire body, including his privates, including his eyebrows, because, as the Lord declared, through humility came piety and through piety came faith and through faith came salvation. Abey had been taught from a very young age that to be with God was to be fulfilled beyond that which was possible elsewise. It'd been so long since she'd first demonstrated to him the methods. He could hardly remember how it was in the beginning, before he'd been shown the path of denouncing and ridding himself of the filth of his body. She'd explained to him that the signs of his inevitable manhood were the ill-begotten traces of his mortal father's seed, a man who had proven not to be worthy of her companionship or the mercy of the Most High.

Mother had made him stand naked in front of her each morning, after he'd finished his shaving, so that she could inspect the job he'd done. She would scrutinize his nudity with those same sharp eyes, eyes that Abey had looked up and into his entire life, eyes that had shaped his perception of God and molded his fears.

He remembered the look she'd given him when she'd first noticed the hair on his legs turning a much darker color. It was a look he hadn't seen much of, one of dismay rather than her usual stern righteousness. It was after they'd gone on a trip, a meeting with the other families of the congregation. He hadn't had the chance to shave for three whole days, as they were staying in the house of one of the other families. It was around that same time in his life that he'd begun to grow at a seemingly increasing rate, and eventually surpassed Mother's height by the time he was thirteen, the same time he'd noticed hair growing from his upper lip.

It was apparent from the beginning that the other families of the congregation did not share Mother's fervor for the Lord. There was a difference in respect for the scripture, and it turned out that Mother's bible wasn't the same as the other bibles. Abey remembered a particular night over dinner with two of the other families during that 'meeting trip', how she'd kept the book on her lap in the place where other folks kept their napkins. She'd rested her right hand on its worn leather cover for the entirety of the meal, fingers like a cage over the symbol engraved into it, never lifting a finger of that hand. He remembered some kind of discussion occurring, strange looks from the head of the household in which they were dining. There was an argument, and then Mother was raising her bible *at* the families, speaking the words Abey and her had read so many times together. When those in attendance shouted back at her, when they called her demon, a silence fell upon the room. Mother's furious gaze swept over all in attendance once, twice, thrice, and then she grabbed Abey's hand and they left, never to return to the homestead of who she later deemed to be those 'heretics'. Prior to this event, Mother would sometimes take Abey to learn of God in the living rooms of other families, with other children in attendance, and sometimes she would even invite those families over to their house for dinner and scripture readings. After she'd taken him from the home of the apostates in that storm of rage, though, Mother had kept him in the confines of the only house he'd ever known.

There was no need for arithmetic or the heretical fields of 'science and physics', she said, nor was there a need to learn a thing about the Lord from false worshipers. The only schooling she deemed necessary consisted of lessons and parables from the bible, from *her* bible, which grew to be his bible, too. It was one of a kind and they shared its wonders with only each other. Abey's absolute favorite parable was one that spoke of an individual who'd sought prophecy in the entrails of a dying calf, an animal that had mortally wounded itself by grazing near a slumbering viper. The book described how its muzzle swelled to a terminal state over the course of only a few moments. This new vessel of natural Death had been bestowed upon the man for his trust in the Lord. The calf was relinquished of its mortal coil and, upon giving his faith over to the flesh and organs of the animal provided, the man was able to see the lair of God, able to stare into the eye of the Great Entity, the One Who Waits Beyond the Veil.

Abey had thought it a terrifying and beautiful idea, to look creation in the face. Sometimes, scared of the thought of staring into that beautiful abyss, he would let his mind wander with the idea of him actually being the calf into which someone else's hands have plummeted, through which someone else's gaze penetrates the void into that infinite on the other side of reality. There was something strangely comforting about the thought of just lying there and watching his own stomach come apart, hands and fingertips prodding and slipping into him, baptized in his own blood. There was comfort in the idea of the grey portal from which his soul would slip out of his belly, gaping wider with each reverent churn of his worshipers' hands.

He was so young back then, when it first started, so enthralled by what was written in the book, just like Mother. They didn't need the rest of the congregation, or the rest of the world. They had the true book, the one word of God...

And they had each other.

*

Time had a way of melding into a blur when all the days Abey lived were spent in the same place, with the same one other person. The exception to this was that, once a week, Abey would walk to the local mart for Mother's medication, for bread and jam and more honey. Aside from that, though, each day, each week, was a blur into the next. Certain key events, then, stuck out in the grey of his recollections like the beacon of a lighthouse, piercing through the fog of nebulous memories.

Years ago, awakened by a *thud* against his window, Abey had opened his eyes and had been met by the gloom of daybreak through the parted curtains. Though still rubbing sleep from his eyes, curiosity in the sound pushed him out of bed, moved him through the quiet house. This same curiosity drove him to slide the back sliding glass door open, and to descend down into the backyard from the splintered old deck that sprouted from the second floor of the house like some wooden fungus. There, in the unkempt grass, lay a pigeon, alone and wrapped in the mists of morning. The bird's beak was broken, as was its neck. The head leaned limp in an irreparable way but it still moved, kept shifting and rocking back and forth as if it meant to fly away, as if it just needed to set itself right before flapping its wings and taking to the skies once more.

At the time, excitement vitalized Abey for he knew that this was a chance to get a closer look at the work of Death, to see the prophetic sight which Mother and the bible said were possible if only he had enough patience and faith. Patience... Abey was *very* patient. He thought he'd been as patient as he'd needed to be. He'd somehow known that this dying life form, the first he'd ever been so close to, was a gift from the black paradise beyond and underneath the firmament of the Earth. It was as if the Lord written of had crawled out of the void to look specifically upon their little plot of land, upon his reverent soul, and offered him a vessel required for augury.

Ravenous had Abey's hunger been for the feeling of the glory of God.

He'd knelt down in the grass, then, the blades of which tickled his stubbled knees and shins. He'd squeezed underneath the bird's head. The eyes of the little thing bulged the tighter Abey squeezed. Finally, when it stopped moving, Abey breathed deep of the cold surrounding and then dug into the avian corpse, parting the down and severing the tissue with his fingernails. He'd felt like a creature had risen within himself, some animal left dormant for all his childhood life until that moment. When he'd finally broken into the cavity of innards and slid his fingers in, though, rather than revelation, he was met by hesitation, and that beast he'd felt he'd been becoming put its tail between its legs and held itself in a kind of defeated hush. Those bizarre textures the guts provided captured him through the sensory of his fingertips, and the miasma of the thing's hot blood and excrement seemed to spellbind him.

A familiar presence stood over and behind him during those moments that he looked, wide-eyed and short of breath, down upon the bird. He didn't need to turn around to know that this presence wore the skin of his mother. It was a presence he'd always known, the amalgam of his mother and the thing that spoke the word of God from her lips. He felt it inch closer, heard it crane its neck down slowly, to hover its hot mouth next to his head. And then it whispered words of oblivion into his ears using his mother's voice:

Abey, you haven't been patient, and your faith trembles so.

The thing that wore Mother's body, the thing that *was* her body, used the wooden spoon on him after that, chastising the meat of his rump and testicles, over and over again, for each of his transgressions: his impatience, his greed, his lack of humility.

At that time, he hadn't really understood what it meant to be patient, not like the way he understood it now. He hadn't known how to be discreet in a world of ogling charlatans. This, too, had changed with time. The memories of those beatings seemed so distant from his current state, from the mindset of tempered piety out of which he worshipped nowadays. He didn't realize how much he needed that punishment back then, how it would shape him and how often he would think about it as he grew through the years, how he would reflect upon it any time his lack of faith would threaten to get the best of him. In those rare times that his rebellious nature took hold now, the occasional fleeting moment of anguish at how long it was taking for the prophecy to be fulfilled, he would punish himself in the sight of Mother and in the infinite presence of the Almighty Lord, for Mother's body had decayed but the fire in her eyes still remained, and the Most High was in all things of flesh and memory and mind.

Ravenous Abey's hunger still was for the feeling of the glory of God.

*

A few years after the morning with the bird, sometime later in Abey's slow but steady exodus toward what lay beyond puberty, another incident occurred. Again, the Lord's hand was seen, blatant and clear, at the tail end of an interaction in which he'd come into contact with a neighborhood boy.

It had been on his way home from the corner-store, a place called *Gas N' Goods* that squatted at the four-way stop kitty-corner to the Mormon church, just beyond the end of Shaw Road. Cashing the check that showed up in the mail each week for Mother, grabbing whole milk and honey among a few other groceries, and making sure to pick up Mother's medicine had been Abey's only responsibilities back then. Two of these tasks could be done at the corner-store (Mother's medicine had to be picked up from a pharmacy down the hill, beyond the borders of the neighborhood and further into town). On the return of one of these trips, as he was just rounding the lip of their driveway, Abey stopped when he heard shouting from the playground at the school, Bridgeton Elementary, the one that could be seen from his backyard. It was early afternoon and, judging by the sounds of roaring school bus engines dispersing from the direction of the school, class was out for the day.

The boy had been slowly riding a bike in the opposite direction as Abey, coming toward him on the same side of the road, about to pass right in front of Abey's house. The kid stared down at his video device held in one hand, the other hand wobbly steering the handlebars, and almost rode right into Abey. The boy hardly glanced up, veering to the side and continuing on.

As he passed, Abey stared after him and then, on a whim, said, "Hello."

The kid stopped pedaling and slowed to a halt. He turned. "Yeah?"

"My name's Abey."

The kid stared at him. "Okay?"

"What's yours?" Abey said.

"My what?"

"Your name."

The boy's eyes wandered to the areas where Abey's eyebrows ought to have been. He regarded Abey as the children from the other families had, the same way that even adults looked at him.

"Travis," the boy finally said. He had a look of apparent discomfort.

Abey had just wanted to talk with someone more his age.

"Travis," Abey said.

"Yeah," the boy affirmed.

Abey nodded. "What're you doing?" he said, motioning toward the boy's video device.

The boy rolled the bike backwards to come within a couple feet of Abey, then angled the thing toward him. Abey took a step toward the kid, standing over him by at least a foot in height, to look at the thing. The black brick of a device had a small lit up screen, surrounded on either side by the phrases GAME GEAR and SEGA. "It's a game called Mortal Kombat," the kid said. The images on the screen, even in the daylight, were bright, the colors vivid. Characters punched and kicked at each other, summoned flaming skulls and floating shards of ice amidst the fighting, and digital blood splattered over the screen in congruence with the boy's button-mashing. *Mortal Kombat...* Abey's thoughts floated around the words, and then his eyes drifted from the screen to the kid's hand. He stared down the kid's thin arms, to his bony shoulders. Prepubescence still rang like a bell throughout this boy's demeanor and it was standing this near to him that Abey's growth had felt all the more apparent, how tall he'd grown compared to the other boys of the neighborhood. The kid's arms were covered in that child-borne hair, soft as down, a strand here or there glinting in the afternoon sunlight. How brutally *primal* this image appeared to Abey, his own shaved arms bearing gooseflesh in the afternoon breeze, his hands buried in his shorts pockets. He'd made fists inside the pockets and, without realizing it, squeezed them harshly in their tight dark environments. The blood on the little video screen pulled his thoughts to ideas of how easily the skin could be pulled from the boy's arms, like paper, and how easily the same thin skin of the boy's stomach could be opened, if only the kid could somehow fall flat right now, struck from some divine force—a natural *mortal* death. Abey imagined biting and gnashing to get himself further into the boy's flesh, imagined finally unlocking the stomach and seeing inside, to finally feel the—

"Ew, what the heck!"

By the time Abey realized his thinly-made khaki shorts were making way to his stiffening bulge, the kid had sat fully back onto his bike and pedaled out into the street, slinging his backpack over his shoulder—

And then there was a loud skidding noise. It was a screech like nothing Abey had ever heard, seeming even more strange as occurring in broad daylight, for it was a sound like some creature of his nightmares. At first, Travis had been upright on his bike, pedaling away while staring back at him with a look of blatant disgust, as so many others had looked at Abey in the past, and, in the next moment, the boy was roughly fifteen feet further ahead, crushed under his own bike and the front passenger-side wheel of a dirty black sedan. The vehicle was only stopped a few seconds before it lurched a couple times, then drove off, dragging the boy for another five feet before its tire ungripped from the body and sped away. During those few seconds the vehicle had been stopped, the driver's head had been turning in all directions. The windows were dark but, in that fleeting instant, Abey had seen the head turn to face him and knew whoever was beyond the tint was staring right at him.

After the car had gone, everything else had greyed out save for the central point of Abey's vision, which was focused directly on the hole in the boy's skull, already leaking curdled matter to the concrete below.

A child screamed from down the street. Abey glanced in shock toward the source: a girl, who was probably walking home from school when it all happened, who was running away in the opposite direction. And it was in this moment, as Abey looked to either end of the street, to the windows in the homes across the way, scanning for prying eyes, much like the driver in the vehicle had, that he realized he now had the mangled boy all to himself.

The kid Travis lay coughing and twitching, trying to breathe through a clearly crushed trachea. His eyes were wide in confusion and searching while matter continued to drip from his head. His shirt had ridden up on his body, displaying that blood was already pooling somewhere in his stomach, for it swelled and bulged with brilliant lividity, shades of purple and red, just under the surface of the skin.

Abey's fingernails dug into the palms of his fists inside his shorts, the pain sharp and turning almost immediately into a sensation of ecstasy. Adrenaline cracked within his limbs and lungs and his very animus felt caressed by the possibilities of what lay in front of him. He need only act to obtain them, need only take the opportunity and seize what had been given by God for everything was within His design. Hesitation in this would wrought Abey the same as it had before, and these few years of contemplation may as well have been eons for all the time he'd spent thinking upon his failures of the gift previous.

Abey licked his dry lips, tasted the salt of his insistent mustache stubble upon his tongue, and took a step toward the dying boy.

Heavy footfalls came quickly, followed immediately by a man skidding into the scene to kneel down. "Oh, fuck," the man said. "Oh, fuck." He searched the vicinity briefly, as if he hadn't seen Abey standing there, and then his eyes found Abey and he shouted to go call 911. Abey stepped back, his attention still held in a kind of sabbatical from reality, staring at the gurgling boy, bewitched. The man glanced down to Abey's groin, then said "Jesus Christ" in disgust, turning to a woman who'd rushed from one of the houses on the opposite side of the street. The two adults exchanged words about needing an ambulance, and then the woman ran off.

In the dusty curb next to the crushed boy's twitching feet, the Game Gear was lying broken. The video was flickering behind a web of cracks in the display.

More shapes approached from all sides, more voices…

Abey saw all of the incoming faces. There were too many of them.

He ran up the driveway, then, propelled by his erection and by a flooding anxiety. The sun's warmth fell upon him, the stripes of its beams falling through the trees across the driveway in front of him yet he did not notice it, did not feel any of it. By the time he reached the front door, his limbs were shaking and tears burned to drip from the corners of his eyes.

Abey's erection had died by the time he'd entered the darkness of the house, where a tittering shred of what felt like safety caressed him, yet there was a still a throbbing disappointment in his gut, a need left unsatisfied. He peeked through an opening between the nails that held the black curtains taut against the windows, a sliver large enough to see out to the road below. Through the watery tears, he could no longer see the boy Travis due to the clutter of the dozen or so people that crowded the scene. Shortly thereafter, as a feeble sob escaped Abey's lips, swirling red lights came to a halt a few feet from the circle of pedestrians. Two EMTs made their way quickly out of the ambulance to disappear into the throng. Abey stepped back from the window, retreating into the darkness.

He'd gone to Mother and had told her everything, then. He knelt in front her and she cradled his head, and beyond her pallid tight skin and sour breath, there still lay the sweet maternal voice of guidance that had always forged the path down which he followed. She wiped the sweat from his forehead with the backs of her bony hands and plucked the tears from his cheeks with her frayed fingertips, and she'd said, "Perhaps, my child, the Lord found you wanting today." She smiled that smile of hers, the skin stretching back from her dying teeth and grey gums, and told him to go get the wooden spoon, as she had so many times before. He did, of course, as he did anything Mother asked of him. At that time, she hardly had control of her limbs, being fed and hand-bathed by her son on an almost daily basis, but she made his skin cry streams of blood, for though her body was rotting, Mother's faith was as strong and boundless as the tides of the sea and, through the Lord, all that was required was possible. And, for answering his chastisement with the devotion of a lamb, she massaged his bruised and bloodied skin and, afterward, sent him for the second time that day to shave himself, for reflection and good measure.

*

Weeks blended into months. Months blended into years.

This desire of prophecy left insatiate, in that time after the incident with the boy, Travis, grew into something of an entity of its own within Abey's mind and heart as time went on. It jabbered madly at him in the darkness of his dreams, showing him thoughts of what could've been if only he'd had some time with the boy's body. It spoke to him with distant fiendish whispers when he'd submerge his head in the bath, chanting at him drowned songs he could've sung if only he could've seen a mere glimpse into the prophetic space within the kid's flesh. This entity squawked at Abey from the beaks of crows while he walked alone on his weekly trips to the store, yattering at him from the branches of the trees that lined Shaw Road, as if, through the small black crow eyes, the thing witnessed his failure and would be there to remind him of his regret for all time.

Years passed. Abey had given up trying to deter the feelings that had arisen out of his failure and, instead, allowed himself to surrender to the humility befit a true worshiper of the Most High. He gave himself to the images of flesh that flooded his thoughts daily, relinquished his very essence over to it, fell *into* it those hypothetical scenarios of blood and prophecy that seemed to grow somewhere inside of him. All the while, he brooded on how best to remain with such patience while the Lord plotted out the inevitable reward for his tested but true faith in the divine plan.

Opportunities didn't give themselves often for Abey, chances in which to covet unimpeded witness to bodies freshly visited by Death. He played with the idea often of searching for employment in some place with exposure to the public, to maximize his chances of being present for such a moment for, even with his weekly treks outside, the house, his home, was all he felt he knew, with its dark innards and dusty rooms like long dead organs. Mother didn't think it appropriate for him to have a job at some place external of the home, though, for each and every job he could possibly take would keep him away from her ever-watchful eyes and, instead, bury him under the heavy weight of the sin of the outside world and the heretics it harbored. And, oh, was there still so much life in this home, so much still to be learned and to experience in this darkness...

Sometimes, Abey would sit in front of the curtained window and watch the cars and pedestrians that would occasionally pass by the front yard. Other times, when Mother would give him leave, he would go out to the backyard and peer over the fence to the elementary school and observe, through the copse of trees, the children at the playground, bearing witness to their ruckus into the late evening, as night fell upon the world. Mother forbade him of ever approaching the school building or any portion of its property but, even in the summer, there were kids playing on the slides and swings and climbing up and down the ladders, laughing and shouting and screaming from a perspective Abey never knew, one of camaraderie and friendship. In the clamor of children outside himself, he seemed to always find a bit of solace.

He continued to watch over the years, tempering his impatience and biding the time. Rather than believing the accumulation of days of watching and waiting to be some sort of sign of divine ignorance, that God had abandoned him, something in Abey knew that one day, one inevitable day, indeed the Lord would provide for him. Mother had shown him the verses, spoke in unison with him to help him learn and retain them early on. Even after she'd stopped breathing, her voice remained angelic. Even after her body decayed and her fetor grew oppressive, Abey would still sit with her each night and place his hand under hers in her lap. He would listen to her tell stories about the trails that the dead tread upon, and absorb the lessons she would teach him from the black bible, the word of the Most High, and all it bore.

*

It was a large neighborhood but there was only one elementary school for the surrounding areas as well, so Bridgeton was almost always occupied by at least a few wandering souls. Kids leaving in the evenings and nights would run off in all directions toward their homes, disappearing into the darkness like phantoms. Abey would watch, and wait, and still, throughout all that time, he would toy with that little something inside of himself that *knew* he could be pious, that he could show the Lord how patient and worthy of a proper vessel he was, one through which he could see the All. Abey would stare into the roiling of children's bodies that moved around the gravel playground, or gaze upon the men and women that used the track for nighttime jogging, and could almost *feel* that moment when one of them might fling themselves headlong from a set of monkey-bars to break their neck, or get caught in asphyxiation within one of the slides, or trip over the gravel of the track to fall unconscious in the grass. Then, he would have his moment, no matter if the vessel was man, woman, child or elder, animal even. He played the scenarios over and over in his thoughts, whether there would be other people around, if good-natured help would seemingly manifest out of nowhere to assist the downed body and ruin his ritual. He'd decided that, if so, he would fend them all off from his moment to see, terrorizing the encroachers like a stray rabid beast.

Sometimes, when he'd hear shouts and laughter coming from the playground in the early A.M., he'd creep outside, moving silently through the grass of the backyard to stand upon the old dresser set against the fence. He'd then raise his head so that his eyes were just above the fence top. Sometimes, he'd see older teenagers messing around on the swings, cherry tips of cigarettes dancing in the dark like fireflies. Other times, there'd be a couple, snuggling together at the top of the slide, two shadows intertwining in the night, all the while his eyes gazing through the distance and upon them. They would giggle or howl in their secret private glee...

And it was a sound just like this that had awoken Abey this very night.

He'd gone to bed earlier than usual tonight as there'd been a queasy sort of anxiety with him all day today, accompanying his walk to the store around lunch time for the usual supplies. It was there when he'd done his verses and all the while through his mother's inspection of his morning shave. With his skin glistening under the single lamp in the living room, and Mother's eyes showing a mirrored light from the reflection off of Abey's paleness, a creeping edge of worry had nibbled at his nerves in a most disquieting way. He'd reasoned that getting a couple extra hours of sleep in the only bed he'd ever known might just alleviate whatever it was that was elevating his heartrate at frighteningly random intervals throughout the day, making him sweat and his mouth feel dry and dehydrated. Perhaps this had been only wishful thinking for, as he awoke, he immediately recognized that same feeling in his stomach, its presence having not left him but seeming to have actually extended somehow.

A voice had pulled him from a dream he was already forgetting, a dream in which he'd crawled into a rusted old car in the woods, fumbling over the rotted seat springs inside the thing, and came out on the other side of it to a completely different forest. The details of that forest dripped from his mind like water down a drain, and any sort of sense in these fleeting images could not be made. And it was a shallow sort of sleep he'd been awoken from. Groggy as he felt, when he'd heard the sound, his eyes had almost immediately opened to stare at the nightstand, his sights meeting the half empty glass of water that stood there. Why his focus had seemed to pinpoint that object, he couldn't say.

Most nights, Abey would fall asleep to the sounds of the occasional shout out on the road, or from the school beyond the fence. Some extra facet of this very night called to him beyond the sound that had awoken him, though, like a stench behind the smell of roses. For this reason, there was no other remedy except to follow the pull to investigate.

Abey crept out of the old blankets of his bed, blankets his mother had given to him before he could remember, then slid the covers back into their place. He moved out into the dark hallway, finishing the last of the water in the glass. The fourth stair of the staircase creaked under his step, as it always did. The darkness down here seemed more corpulent than that of upstairs, spreading itself like a black fog. Abey stepped lightly through the living room, even though Mother never slept anymore. He walked right by her couch, the one she was always sitting on, and he could feel her burning stare upon him. He could hear the buzzing wings of the flies that moved in and out of her mouth and nose. The living room was dark but he could see the way her face had remained for quite some time now, a grin pulled outward by the stretching discolored skin, a grin not of happiness or of humor but of perpetuity, accentuated by the gaunt blackness of her eye sockets.

There was no moon and there hadn't been in months thanks to the oncoming winter, save for an occasional clear night here and there. Abey found it comforting, the way the overcast seemed to always blanket the skies this time of year, smearing everything during the day with a grey tint as well as suffocating the nights with an almost inescapable darkness. The kitchen, though, was gloomily lit from afar by the bright orange floodlight attached to the closest wing of Bridgeton Elementary. The low brick building squatted silent in the distance, glaring its one eye through the trees to come through the window above the sink. It was the only window in the house that Mother had kept uncovered, so that she could look down into the backyard and into the playground of the school, as Abey had taken to doing. Abey went to pass by this window and could feel that orange light sliding over him, as if the distant glow lent a specific type of sensation when it met his skin. Sometime during this specific sensation of distant light, the mounting queasiness he'd awoken with had gone through a metamorphosis, for it was no longer a queasiness he felt, no longer an anxiety, but a different kind of building-up, an evolution into something like excitement. Abey could feel it in his stomach and in the marrow of his bones: something was different about tonight.

And then he heard that muffled distant sound again.

Laughter…

The sliding glass door silently slid open on its track and then glided closed just as quietly. The copper brackets of the curtains rattled against the inside of the glass a couple times and then came to a still. Otherwise, the chilled night was silent save for the soundless stifled moaning of the fog. Abey breathed in the cool air and glanced over into the darkness of the neighbor's backyard, half-expecting to see someone or something there, watching him, like how the eyes of the hit-and-run driver had watched him, glinting in the darkness. Yet, there was no one.

Ahead and beyond the fence and trees, the school track field was orange-lit and flaring in the misty shroud. The playground was huddled up against the track's northmost bank and, on one of the swings, a shape rocked back and forth. From it, another sound came, one like that which had awoken Abey. It was a laugh, an exhausted breathy laugh. There was another sound accompanying this laughter, too, like the constant mumbling of a television—sharp, small and tinny.

The wooden steps of the deck leading into the yard below were damp with an earlier rain and soaked the soles of Abey's feet as he crept down them. His toes met the grass and then he moved through the night dew, avoiding each lump and hole in the ground and following the same path to the fence he'd taken countless times in the past. He came to stand within the fence's shadow, directly in front of that old rotten dresser, and peered up at the dreamy glow coming from beyond. It looked like a fire blazed just on the other side. Abey climbed up the dresser and, from a kneeling position, clasped his hands over the rough top edges of the wet planks of fence and pulled his head up to see.

Beyond the trees, the track field was empty, as was the parking lot further on. The school's floodlight dissolved into the night's ripe darkness in all directions. There was no sign of anyone else as far as he could see, and all was quiet and inanimate, save for the shape slowly draping back and forth on the swing. A blue little brightness hovered next to the shape on the swing, shifting occasionally or changing angles this way and that. It illuminated the profile of the one holding it, this person being the source of another small mewling of laughter. Long hair played in the simultaneous lighting from the device in hand and the orange floodlight from the school behind. A slender shape of a bottle hung in the thin hand that dangled below, the one not holding the lighted device. Abey couldn't tell from here if she was a child or a woman grown. She was alone, though, much later in the night than most children hung around the school, and the presence of what looked like a bottle of alcoholic beverage gave hint to an age beyond those that he usually spotted in the playground. Who knew what had driven her out here this late—perhaps an abusive perverted parent or maybe a shameful drunk for a partner. Maybe *she* was the shameful drunk.

She was alone, either way, and this apparent aloneness drove Abey's thoughts in a direction they'd gone so many times before: if something would happen to bring this one to the brink of Death, with no one else around, maybe then there'd be a chance to finally have a moment with the divine. All humans were potential vessels, all situations a potential for Death. *Could her body hold the sight promised by the prophecy?* Abey found himself getting caught in thought-loops asking the question over and over, and wishing for something, *anything*, to make this woman, out here in this chilled nightfall, become the vessel for him, to finally have his answers amidst fleeting life essence. He imagined things as ridiculous as an errant bird corpse tumbling down from the dark skies to land directly on top of her, or a falling piece of plane fuselage obliterating her under its weight...

A sludgy feeling, envisioned in Abey's mind as concrete moving through his veins, settled over him then, pumping slowly through the muscles beneath his chubby shaved bulk. This feeling wavered the edges of his vision, caused the lone bright eye of the school building to wax. He had the faith. He'd kept and held it and cultivated it all this time, right alongside his evolved sense of patience. Mother had made sure of it, and her voice was always speaking inside his head, even in this very moment.

Just you wait, son. Patience always gets the prize.

But even the most stoic of the faithful must have had an end or cap to their waiting, and even though he'd tried, Abey knew he was not the most stoic, knew he didn't even come close to Mother's righteousness, and he could no longer hold onto the promises left empty.

It seemed an inhuman thing at first, this overwhelming fight-or-flight heat of aggravation that boiled in him. The knuckles in his hands popped as he clenched his defiant fists. He wanted to climb over the fence, taking with him a rock or tool from the garden shed, or even use his own hands to bash this potential vessel's brains in, to choke her like he choked the pigeon, and then to search her intestines for the glimpse he sought, all the while watching the life dissolve from her eyes.

Wait it out, Abraham. We are all slaves to the consequences of our virtues, or lack thereof.

Abey knew that the knowledge existed there for him within the patterns of the small intestines, within the organs surrounding or buried deep in the stomach or kidneys. This thirst for the knowledge overwhelmed him, snaked through his nervous system, a haunting future promised to him but never given, a bestowment that would remain just out of reach and unfulfilled forever.

Stacking together like the bricks of a mad house, this feeling built upon itself. It had driven him further into that solitary feeling of confinement within his own stagnant frustrations and the manifestations thereof. This feeling came into being within the recesses of his mind as that strange beast that had always waited inside of him, the beast he was supposed to become. The images it showed Abey, the plunging of hands slipping into a stomach, whether his own or someone else's, were tempests in his mind alongside Mother's voice repeating her mantras of patience over and over. It all combined to create a throbbing lurid ache for the final sight, that last look of this world and the first look into the next. *This* was the time. It had to be.

That companion of letdown, fast congealing inside like a wretched inhuman fetus, pushed at his resolve and tears began to fill his eyes. If this wasn't it, if this wasn't the time, then he didn't want to know any more of the supposed truth of the Black Gospel. Either this one ahead of him, the one that took swigs from the bottle, whose feet dragged in the groove of gravel below her, was to be the vessel, or he, himself, Abey, wanted to be it. In any way possible, the actualization of the prophecy was what he wanted most, to know that his entire life of belief hadn't been a lie. The anxiety had reached its threshold within him, and why had it come in the first place, he asked himself. If it was all a test of faith, a riddle amounting only to a window through which to see his own unworthiness, and that nothing was actually going to happen on this dreary night, then all was lost: everything Mother had ever taught him, each night he'd laid awake praying and hoping and reflecting, trying to understand the message, the path...

A decision, as sharp and swift as a blade through flesh, came to him, then: he was either going to kill this woman or kill himself. The concepts of murder and suicide melded together as one solution in his mind, and the actual exactment of this decision, though unclear, whatever the outcome, was going to happen. And as this blatant thought, reeking of apostasy, came to be within his mind, he heard the brackets of the curtains back and above rattle against the inside of the glass, and then that sleek sliding sound of the door opening and shutting once again. Then came the sound of distinct creaking on the wooden steps leading from the deck down to the yard behind him.

It had been a long time since Mother had left her couch in the living room, but he knew she'd felt the sensation, too, that inevitability that had come with him from his dreams, that something *had* to happen tonight, the hope that turned into despair that then, through some strange alchemy in these last few moments, evolved into a certainty, whether self-destructive or otherwise. Just like before, he didn't need to turn around to know that the shuffling of the grass behind him was her approach and he didn't need to see to know that it was her breath that caressed the skin of his nape once again. The warmth of it pulled on the boundaries of the peripheral around him, and he smelled inklings of that other world, the place for him to see, like some sort of fetid smoke humming and waning from just beyond her whispers. It was not her ire he felt in that moment, though, punishment for his thoughts of action rather than patience. Instead, he felt her deathly embrace and she spoke lyrics into his ears, producing memories of the way she used to do the same when he was only a baby, moments lost in time now retrieved through this moment of feverish determination.

And as if the spaces between thought and will, between reality and fate, opened up then, bloomed out, Abey could've sworn that he saw it before it happened: the woman out on the swing let fall the bottle held in her hand and it made a *clink* noise as it hit the ground. She pocketed the bright-screened device and then, with a drunken giggle, swung her feet high once, swung them high twice—

And then she fell.

There was no cry or a yell as the silhouette descended in that brief moment, hands grasping up into the air for purchase that didn't exist. There was only a *thud* as her head hit the gravel first, followed by the rest of her body sliding from the swing seat, slumping into a perfectly still position below.

The burning orange floodlight lit a stationary scene, with no movement anywhere and only the quiet night meeting Abey's ears. The seconds filled with silence and, as these seconds passed, blood and nausea pumped through his veins. He could hardly believe what he'd seen. He blinked and blinked, expecting this image to disappear as an illusion would. Mother was silent behind him, as if not even there, but he knew she was for he could feel her presence arching over him, could hear her whispered words:

You've been so patient, Abraham. You've accepted your punishment when you needed it most, and now you've made your mother proud.

It's time for your turn, son.

His vision flooded with tears. The most direct path to the playground was over the fence, through the clutch of trees, and over the short chain-link into the school's track field. From there, it would be a short run to the low wooden barrier where the gravel of the playground started.

The tops of the fence planks bit into his pudgy palms as he hoisted his bulk up and over, a feat made almost easy by the endorphins fueling his ascent. The nettles in the small forested area between he and the field stuck to his socks as he passed through them, scraping at his smooth calves, but he hardly felt them. Within seconds, he'd exited the underbrush, hopped the chain-link fence and stepped out onto the field. The mowed grass glinted with dew like stars in the orange glow. Again, he looked to the far corners of property, to make certain there were no other eyes staring upon him. Abey searched the fence line, the shadowed school beyond the floodlights.

No one else was coming. Nobody else had witnessed this moment of Death, this radiating jewel of chance.

There was a moment in which Abey thought that he was only moments from being caught out here, or that he was imagining all of it, that he was actually still up in his home, dreaming in bed under the sheets. It was the crunching sound his steps made when he moved into the gravel pit, on which was built the kid's playground big-toy, that brought him back to the reality of the gift in front of him.

With a breath held in suspension, Abey approached.

As he came to stand over the woman, it was a choking sound that came from her throat. In the orange light, her shape appeared to warble with the erratic intakes of her heaving chest. Her eyes were open, and a glassy look of confusion accompanied the breathless words spelled by her mouth. Every few seconds, her facial features would contort from the confusion into a look of agony, of terror, and then her expression would return to that bizarre gloss of misunderstanding. Blood poured awkwardly from a place behind her ear, gushing into the countless small rocks that held her up like a million tiny worshipers.

Abey knelt down.

Ravenous was his desire to feel the glory of God.

Mother hunched right over his shoulder, marking her presence not only by her warm stinking breath but by the extra shadow next to Abey's own, stretched long over the gravel and the lawn to his right leading up to the school's perimeter fence.

He saw the woman's eyes turned again to confusion as she looked up to him, tears running down her cheeks. The pressure released with a warmth in Abey's stomach as he found himself already lifting the woman's shirt, whose neck was bent at a bizarre angle now that Abey was staring right at it. She mouthed the word "please" but no voice came out. A sliver of her underwear's seam met his shadow, as did the base of her bra, but these were not enough to distract him from his path. The anticipation of being able to finally see the other side overtook any sense of sexual advantage, for he was chaste in the face of all that tried to distract him from what God had provided for him.

Fixated were Abey's intentions onto the sights that he knew awaited within.

His fingernails were short, just as Mother always liked them, and they proved insufficient when he tried to separate the tissue of this vessel's pale stomach. She'd always wanted them short and trimmed and a part of him wished, just this once, he'd disobeyed her command and kept some to aid him in his digging. But then Mother whispered:

You've waited so long, my sweet son. Do not let all of your patience dwindle in these last moments. Delayed gratification is all the sweeter...

Abey wanted no delay, though. And so he pulled the flesh of the woman's stomach, gripping a roll of it and leaning over to put it in his mouth. Her soft skin smelled like something flowery and tasted slightly salted. He chomped and gnawed, sinking his teeth into the fatty tissue. Only a few bites were required, pressured by the years he'd waited for this moment, for the layer to be torn and exposed. He pulled then at the muscles of the abdominal wall, ripping into the sinew. The vessel's fingers went rigid, one last action before the final exhale, and then the serenity of lifelessness washed over her face. The rest of her body went limp. Her bowels released.

With his mouth and finger, Abey dug and scooped and tore at the innards. Wrapped in the smells of shit and blood, he pulled the heaps of entrails steaming out into the wintry night air.

You see? Mother said. *At long last, your patience rewards you, my Abraham. Now, gaze into the darkness and accept your communion.*

And when he knew he'd dug far enough, Abey sat back on his calves and stared at the hole in the body beset in front of him. His tired eyes leaked hot tears. He sat in that moment, smelling the aromas of what was to come. And then he placed his hands on the grass near the body, positioning his head above the hole, and lowered his blood-slathered face down into it.

The frayed flesh of the aperture tickled the sides of his head, and when the gory black fully enveloped his sight and all trace of the orange eye looking upon him from the building behind disappeared, the darkness then showed him things: it showed him the unearthly colors of a realm beyond, geometry of an eldritch design far beyond the scope and boundaries of the human mind. It showed him the slithering appendages of the void, and these things drew circles and transcribed runes in the very space of what he saw, shredding the fabric of reality and alighting the slits into the after with a mirrored psychedelic emptiness Abey had never witnessed before but always knew existed. The wonders that spiraled into his senses drew him with bloody hands from his earthly perspective out of his physical body. They swam like ghosts with him in the aether sea of the Old Knowledge. They shared with him the cryptic songs of the One Who Waits Beyond the Veil, the great annihilator holding court in the black depths of Sheol. And they finally chanted the verses that the angels would sing when that moment came for him, the moment in which Death would guide him in his fall from life down into that inevitable cold embrace of an eternity without breath.

Eyes Out

Someone was talking in one of the other suites when the office door, labeled with black letters spelling out *Tanner Redding LMHC, Psychotherapy* across its warbled glass, opened. A draft from the hallway followed a man into the lobby, rustling some of the magazines spread over the end table in the center of the seating area. The leaves of the tall potted plant in the corner did their own little brief dance, too, as if they'd been waiting to jig all morning. The door swung closed on its own and stifled the voices beyond.

The reception desk was tucked into the corner along the northern section of the suite, underneath a generic painted mural of some unnamed lake and shore, and sat squat just in front of the only window in the place. The man that had entered came toward said reception desk. He was average looking, of an average build and stature, but exhibited a strangeness in which his stare played with the slatted light from the window. That's the first thing that caught the attention of the receptionist, Elizabeth—the strange interaction between the man's eyes and the office light. She wasn't sure how to pinpoint what exactly it was she was noticing but, by the time he'd come to stand in front of her desk, before she'd been able to figure it out, he'd already begun speaking.

"Hello."

"Hello," Elizabeth said.

"I'm Jake Harborough. Here for my appointment with Dr. Redding. Supposed to start at ten."

Elizabeth put on a smile as best as she could, said, "Okay, Jake," but her voice cracked in a way that must've given away her discomfort, for there was a slight twitch in the man's grin in response. Though most patients the doctor saw were, in some way or another, a little off, there was an intensity in this one's demeanor that set off a few red flags from the get-go, separating him from the others Elizabeth had met. When he'd greeted her, it seemed that only his mouth had spoken but his eyes and the rest of his face remained in their almost artificial state. She'd been warned when she'd first taken the job that some patients were 'healthier' than others, and that the interactions with them weren't always going to be 'by the books'. She'd never really dealt with anyone she thought too weird, but this sudden flush of anxiety seemed out of the ordinary. She doubted the caffeine from the two cups of coffee this morning was helping, either.

The doctor's first patient of the day had come in at nine-thirty for an appointment that was supposed to last an hour, or so she thought she remembered from her cursory glances at the schedule. To verify was an excuse to look away from the gaze of the man standing before her, so she looked to her scheduling book and ran a finger down the first few appointments.

7/17/2019 – 9:30AM — Kyoko Tanaka
7/17/2019 - 10:45AM — Jake Harborough
7/17/2019 – 12:00PM — Janston Cordell

"Well," Elizabeth said. "We definitely have you in the books but it looks like you're scheduled for ten forty-five, not ten."

The look the man gave upon hearing this information was one of almost fake disappointment, too animated, like someone trying to act upset, as strange as that reasoning sounded in her head. Disquieting as it was, Elizabeth tried to keep a light expression on her face while he *hmmm*'d a bit, turned to look toward the door into the Tanner's office, as if he'd given thought to simply walking in anyway, then looked back to her.

"That's no problem. I'll just wait."

And at that he moved, without waiting for her to respond, to one of the chairs against the wall near the door. He stood in front of the seat for a good five or six silent seconds, staring down into the well of it and rubbing at the corner of his eye, before finally sitting. He looked toward her, smiled, then returned his attention to the doctor's closed office door.

The man's presence did something to the space they now both

inhabited, that much was apparent. Elizabeth wasn't certain of the qualities by which Harborough, in his silence, continued to interrupt her ability to focus on the reports she'd been typing before he'd arrived, but the agitation was very real, as if it were a third occupant of the room, squatting invisibly in the middle of the lobby between the two of them. The music hadn't been running, that forgettable jazz station Tanner had her tune the radio to every day, which was usually played at a low volume to keep the monotony at bay. Some mornings, she worked in quiet. Now, though, those noodling chords seemed a welcome respite from the hulking silence, so she turned the music on. Eventually, after about ten minutes, her attention settled back into her work, finally able to get right with the groove of typing. She filled out subtexts, printed and filed documentation and ignored the man sitting only fifteen feet from her own seat, who remained statue-esque in his fixation on the doctor's door, only moving every so often to rub at his eye.

The light from the window seemed to grow sharper as another few minutes passed, as the morning swelled and climbed into early day beyond the blinds.

The analyzing, copying and editing that crowded Elizabeth's headspace was interrupted when the man in the chair spoke.

She looked up, wasn't sure what she'd heard. "Hm?"

He had that same grin on again, the one that didn't touch the rest of his face, that one that hinted at odd thought patterns.

"I asked does he ever share things about his patients with you," Harborough said.

The truth was that Tanner did talk about his patients with her, when they were snaked around each other, wrapped in the cool sheets of his bed after fucking late into the occasional night after work. *You wouldn't believe the story I got from my patient today*, he'd say about one or *I wish you could've been there to hear this one* about another. This man sitting in front of her, though, she didn't know anything about except for, after his first appointment with the doctor last week, Tanner had said that he was *definitely a strange one*. The doctor had been contemplative but unwilling to go further into detail at the time, so she'd shrugged it off and simply touched him into arousal once more. That little bit of info, however, added onto the behavior she'd already witnessed from this man, and she found it reason enough to keep dialogue with him to a minimum.

Elizabeth cleared her throat and put on her smile again.

"I can assure you, Jake, that the doctor-patient privacy is well in effect here."

He only smiled for a moment back at her, causing her own to falter. She looked back to her screen. In her peripheral, she could see him still staring at her and, a moment later, he spoke once more.

Again she didn't hear him, so she looked up from her computer.

"What was that?"

"I said dreams are funny, you know?"

She cleared her throat. "What do you mean?"

"Dreams," he said. "The nature of them. They're... funny."

Elizabeth didn't want to respond. In fact, she had the feeling he'd simply made a statement vague enough to get her to inquire into it, in order to open dialogue again.

Against her better judgement, she said, "How so?"

Harborough stood, slid his hands into his pockets and approached the reception desk. He stood only a foot or two from it, close enough that Elizabeth could smell whatever cologne he was wearing, a tangy musk.

"You ever dream, Elizabeth?"

She was taken aback by the question, a question she hadn't expected, and opened her mouth to ask how he knew her name, but then remembered her nameplate at the head of the desk. Instead, she said, "Well... I think everyone does at some point or another. Right?"

"Hmm. Yes, I suppose you're right. I mean, do you ever *dream* dream? Like, do you ever dream of things that stick with you for hours, days, maybe even months or years later?" He rubbed at his eye, the corner of which was taking on a blushed shade of skin irritation.

"Uh, well, I had a dream or two when I was a girl, ones that I can still somewhat remember."

He said, "Hmm," again and then did a slow walk around the coffee table on which Tanner kept the majority of the self-help and therapy magazines for the patients to read. When Harborough had made a full circumference of it, Elizabeth watching him discerningly the entire time, he stopped and looked back at her.

"You ever have dreams recommended to you by someone else?"

The question confused her.

"What? What do you mean?"

"Oh, I mean just that: recommended, implanted, *suggested.* Do you ever have dreams *suggested* to you?"

"I'm not sure I follow," she said.

He stood in silence, staring at her for a few moments too long and, just as Elizabeth was beginning to feel like prey in the sights of a predator, the slight hint of agitation beginning to color his expression, he spoke:

"This woman I met on the bus. She was rubbing at her face and talking aloud while we sat waiting for the circuit through downtown the other day, sometime late last week. It was busy and the only seat really available was the one next to her. At first, she was talking gibberish," he said. "Absolute nonsense. Not even sentence structure involved at one point. I ignored it as one ignores all degenerate passengers seemingly present on any trip involving public transportation. Then she leaned toward me, just a hair closer than how she'd been sitting previously, a barely noticeable movement, but definitely toward me, and then began whispering from the side of her mouth, this too toward me. For some reason, in that particular moment, rather than scoot away from this deranged woman, I listened to what she had to say to me.

"She told me about her dreams, strange sad things, things I'd never imagine, even if given a thousand years to think of nothing else. All the while, she kept moving her hands to her face and I didn't understand until much later."

There was a longer pause, as if he was waiting for Elizabeth to say something. So she said, "Understand what?"

He stared at her. "I had a dream last night, very similar to the one she described to me. May I tell you about my dream, Elizabeth? I wasn't going to share it with anyone other than Doctor Redding. I am going to be telling him about it today, actually. Seeing as you're so friendly, though, I think it might be fun. It's been a recurring dream each night since, well, since I met that woman on the bus."

"Um," she started. "I think it's probably—"

But before she could finish, he half-sat on the edge of the reception desk, staring off at the wall, and said, "I'm in a waiting room of some kind. Not sure where or what company owns it, or why I'm even there. I don't remember when I arrived but I know that I must leave. Funny, it kind of looks like this one, only a bit brighter, and there's no window." He nodded toward the blinds behind Elizabeth, through which unobstructed rays of sun were beaming.

"There is a clock on the far wall ahead of me," he continued. "The wall is a bland white, and on it is this clock that is white. The circle of its frame is polished wood. Its time is indiscernible. The hands keep spinning and spinning, blurring into a whir of grey over the face of the thing. There is a potted plant underneath the clock and, behind the glazed wood of a reception counter to the left of this plant, there is a woman that sits and stares at me. At least, I think she's staring at me. The truth is that she has no eyes. I know it makes no sense that I say she was staring at me, but I could just tell she was. Somehow, it was possible, even without eyes. Her head is facing toward me. You see, she keeps pulling them in and out of their sockets. Her eyeballs, I mean. You'd think there would be tendons or capillaries attached to them, something to prevent them from being so easily taken out and then put back. But nope. They just keep slipping back into their sockets to return their attention to me. She takes them in and out of her head, all the while looking at me. I can still feel her empty gaze, even as I sit here talking to you." He smiled and looked back to her. "It isn't actually so empty. There's a fullness to her staring, a contemplation, that I can see even during the moments that her eyes aren't in. She isn't moving at all, though, save for her prodding hands and the eyes."

Elizabeth, stuck somewhere between anxiety and curiosity, wasn't moving either.

"The lights in the ceiling above where I sit are too bright to look at." He rubbed at the corner of his eye again. "The chair I was sitting in is comfortable I think but, truth be told, I couldn't feel it either way. I couldn't move my head or my neck at that moment so there really wasn't any way for me to know if I was all there or if I was just a head without a body. I try to move my hands, to flex my fingers and forearms, but I don't feel anything happen."

Harborough clenched and unclenched his fingers, staring

down at them. Elizabeth shifted her crossed legs around under the desk, thanking God for the sensations proving to herself that she wasn't numbly locked in the way this man was describing he'd been in his dream.

"My eyes, though, must be working still in the dream because I can see the room, the woman and the clock. I can also see fingers, a bunch of fingers, wriggling out of the two corners of the room visible from where I'm sitting, where the wall intersections meet the floor. It's as if the fingers are extending from within those angles of wall and carpet. I get this feeling that they are entities unto themselves, these clusters of fingers, and that they're being fed by some unknowable nutrition making its way through the tough cheap carpet, to the root of the growth somewhere underneath. Maybe in the foundation somewhere. In these clusters, there are at least a dozen fingers but no thumbs. And they're not constantly wriggling. They move in a strange spastic manner for a few seconds, blooming out like a flower of digits, then completely stop. They look almost petrified when they go rigid, only to continue another bout of movement moments later. I think they are trying to keep my focus somehow, or they are speaking to me in some mimetic language I can't decipher. I never learned Sign Language, and that I only know a few of the letters of that alphabet doesn't seem to be helping. There's… a *feeling* I'm getting from them, though. It's hard to describe.

"I have the ability to smell, also, in this place, but only a specific smell, like the sterility of a hospital. I can hear, as well. There's a purring sound that I can't locate the source of. At first, I thought it was the central air-conditioning running through the ducts of the room or something.

"Directly above the reception desk and the staring woman, a plyboard ceiling tile shifts in its bracket. There is a scratching sound, a dragging of sorts, and the tile slides back, revealing a sliver of the darkness in the utility rafters beyond. In that darkness is a pair of eyes. They are yellow and they bulge, reflecting light not unlike the corneas of a cat, but the pupils are horizontal and strangely jagged, reminding me more of a goat's eyes. Two dozen or so human fingers creep out of the darkness around those eyes to grip and flutter against the plyboard aperture, signaling that same message the clusters of fingers below are. The eyes are staring directly down into my own."

A shiver rippled its way up Elizabeth's spine.

"It's then that I realize," he continued, "that I really have to find an exit. I have to get out because the more I see the receptionist pull her eyes in and out, in and out, the more I want to do the same with my own. I stood up and felt that I was standing and that I had a body, and that I could move my head and neck."

"Um," Elizabeth shifted in her seat and reached for her water bottle. A coarse dryness had overtaken her throat and tongue. "It's probably not necessary to finish." She took a swig of the water. "I mean, I'd actually prefer if—"

"A door, one that I could swear wasn't there moments ago, stands to my left." There was a rising intensity in Harborough's stare, accompanying the growing levels of his vocal tone. "Its wood is dark against the white contrast of the wall its embedded in. I turn and approach it, trying not to look at the receptionist. She has her eyes in at the moment. Nor do I look to the open ceiling tile, even though the fingers still wriggle above in my peripheral and it's hard not to glance up to them. I can hear them shuffling and twitching."

Harborough's finger traced under his right eye unconsciously, rubbing at the corner. Elizabeth could see the skin beginning to dry and chafe. She couldn't take her eyes off of his probing fingers, the swelling redness.

"The door handle is cold in my hand when I reach for it. I turn it fully clockwise, pull it open. And inside... Inside is another lobby, like the one I was already standing in. So I step through."

Elizabeth's breathing had diminished to rapid short inhales, even shorter exhales. A slow tingling crackled under the skin of her hands and in her chest, concomitant with the beginning of a suspension of action or something like hyperventilation. Half of her mind screamed for Tanner to come out of his office, hoping and praying he would, because this man, though not harming her advertently, was between her and the door to the doctor's office as well as between her and the exit. The other half of her mind had fallen into the story Harborough was telling and was only getting sucked deeper into it the more he spoke. And it was during this reflection, of the two dissonant halves of her psyche, that Harborough continued his story.

"The door closes at my back. It's at this point that I realize that it isn't a similar room that I'm in. It's actually the very *same* room. The woman with the removeable eyes sits behind a reception desk cut out of the far wall ahead of me... To the right, there's the potted plant, the leaves of which are slightly more wilted than I remember them being from the first rendition of the room... The clock still hangs on the wall, its arms spinning into obscurity... And those human fingers, they still scream their silent frantic messages from the corners of the room.

"When I turn around, there is only bland wall. I run my fingers along the surface, to try and find the seams of the door I just came through, but I don't find anything of the sort."

Harborough smiled, picked at something on the knee of his left pant leg.

Elizabeth glanced to the spot on his knee, then to clock on her computer desktop.

10:18AM.

Jesus Christ, she thought.

"A sound of a door closing comes from somewhere in the room and I turn back toward the reception desk. At the very same time, the woman returned her gaze to me from somewhere off to the side, and her eyes are in now, wide and glaring. I didn't notice it at first but then I see stains on her shirt, pockmarks in her skin. That same wood door stands embedded in the wall to my left. I can almost *feel* that someone else was just inside the room with me, with *us*, me and the receptionist, not to mention the sound I'd just heard of the door closing and the fact of the receptionist having looked toward that direction briefly, to someone or something else having just left."

Out of sheer instinct, Elizabeth glanced to the entrance door of the suite, the door through which the man speaking to her had entered. It was still dormant and unmoving, though she expected something to happen, something she couldn't rightly identify.

"That same scraping sound from before," Harborough continued, "comes from the plyboard ceiling tile above me. The rattling beyond is louder this time. My eyes are starting to itch for some reason, too, like my contacts are dry." His voice took on a sudden rambling quality. "I remember thinking to myself whether or not it was possible that I even had contacts on in my dreams. I figure you can apply any facet of reality to the dream world if you focus on it enough. I remember even wondering if it was possible to manifest aspects of the dream world into real life, if I gave them enough... attention, enough thought..."

The images Harborough was espousing had begun to take shape in Elizabeth's mind. It was without conscious effort that she imagined the lobby he was describing to be the very lobby she was sitting in, where she'd worked for the last three years, but in this small daydream, she was standing near the door leading out into the hall and, behind her desk, sitting in *her* chair, was this eyeless receptionist. A type of spiraling wooziness wavered on the edges of her vision, caused her stomach to ache as she imagined it. The thought sickened her. She looked up to the ceiling. The plyboard tiles appeared stationary and clean. And then Elizabeth realized Harborough was silent.

As if he'd been waiting for her attention to come back to him, Harborough smiled when she looked again to his eyes. Then, he continued:

"I move to the door in the left wall before the plyboard above finishes its shifting, before the thing beyond can peer its weird eyes down into the lobby at me again. When my hand touches the doorknob, I notice it's chilled but doesn't seem as cold as the last door had been coming into this version of the lobby. Seems warmer, like somebody's hand had just used it. So I open it.

"Beyond, it's the same waiting room. And as I recognize this, I see a shape slide through the door on the left of this new room, shutting the door immediately behind them. I'm stunned, not only by the surprise of the sound of the door slamming shut, and from having seen the door-opener, even though I didn't get a good look at the face, but also because I am seeing that this third version of the lobby is noticeably different. It's grimy. Dirt and other shit fills the cracks and creases throughout, like along where the carpet meets the wall, over the cushions of the chairs on either side of me, as if the place had been leaking water in somehow. The place seemed as if it'd been left to mold. The plyboard tiles that make up the ceiling above look damp, turned green and brown in their corners from mildew and moisture. The woman behind the receptionist desk looks even dirtier than she had before, her clothes and her hair... And before I can look away, that same tile above shifts. I see the eyes, those fucking goat eyes, but they're bleeding this time, as if they're crying blood. It's black blood. So I run to go through the door again, to find the one who fled before me, and so that I don't have to keep seeing those weird bleeding eyes from behind the ceiling tile."

Elizabeth's ability to listen to the words Harborough spoke competed with her focused attention on his constant rubbing of his eye, and the now spot of open skin that his fingertips scratched at and seemed to expand every few seconds. He continued his explanation, how with each subsequent entry through the doorway, a temporal plaque of some kind had been layered over all he'd seen. A decay or dissimilation of the flesh around his eye was seeming to follow in congruence.

"By now, I've started to figure out at least, through some intuition, that this process could potentially continue forever: I enter into the next version of the room, the one ahead of me barely escapes my gaze, the woman behind the desk growing more sickly and dirty, the room falls further into ruin… Yet, as I continue, from the next room to the next to the next, I see a longer glimpse of the one who passes through the next door before me. I even tested out the timing of it by waiting a few moments in the fifth or sixth version of the room, before opening the door to the next. And still, I saw just a hair more of the one who came before. I determined that his passage through, and it was a man, that much I knew by then, was dependent upon my entering the room right behind him.

"It's the same routine each time, though: I move into the room, see the receptionist, those fingers rummaging in the corners of the room, the scratching sounds above and beyond the grotesque ceiling tiles. I move to the door on the left. The handle is warmer each time...

"Eventually, I reach a version of this lobby in which I catch sight of the face of the one ahead of me, looking back at me. It was… Well, it was *me*."

Elizabeth said nothing but simply stared, caught in a stasis of confoundedness.

"I followed him once more into the next version of the room and he was standing right inside, about a foot to the left of the potted plant, between it and the receptionist's desk embedded in the wall. He pulled his eyes out right in front of me, just as she had been doing. There were tendons attached, though, and blood flowed from his sockets like faucets. It was when my forearms were covered in it that I realized I had been the one that was removing his eyes. My hands were out in front of me, performing this horror on their own. This other version of me was screaming and batting at my hands. I still feel that urge to grip with my fingertips, the gelatinous... *texture* of those things, you know? I mean, I got my own and—" He raised his hands, fingers extended in a beak shape on both hands, pointing them toward his eyes. "—I could just..."

Thinking she was about to witness this man exact some sort of ocular amputation on himself, Elizabeth stood, shoving her chair back, shaking her head. "No. NO. I am not going to listen to this anymore. You've—"

The door to Tanner's office opened and Elizabeth jumped. The 9:45 client, Kyoko Tanaka, walked out and toward the door out of the suite. She looked back to Tanner, who was standing in the doorway to his office, and said, "Thanks, Doctor Redding," in her quiet reserved voice.

The doctor nodded, then turned toward the man still sitting against the reception desk. "Alright, Jacob. You ready, my friend?" When he noticed Elizabeth, he gave her a peculiar look of curiosity, maybe concern.

Elizabeth glanced at the clock on the wall.

10:43AM.

Jacob stood from the desk, still smiling. He looked to the doctor and said, "Definitely." As he walked toward the office door, he stared back to Elizabeth. An eerie tickle crept into her skin as she watched the man, Jacob, enter Tanner's office. She could swear he was lifting his hand to rub the corner of his eye again.

Tanner glanced briefly toward her and winked before disappearing into the office and shutting the door.

*

Lost as she was in her mind's capers through the visions Harborough's story had given her, Elizabeth hadn't been able to wrangle her thoughts back into her work before Tanner had erupted from the office, screaming to call 911 and that something terrible had happened. The sound of him bursting into the lobby had almost given her a heart attack.

The ambulance arrived within minutes of Elizabeth dialing 9-1-1.

Turned out that just about twenty-seven minutes exactly into the session, Harborough had stood from the couch that Tanner's clients usually lounged on during their sessions, reached his hands up and buried his fingers into the space between his eyeballs and their eyelids. In a swift tearing motion, he'd ripped his eyes from their homes, separating them from their umbilicals, and passed out in a pool of his own blood, gushing from his empty sockets.

Jacob Harborough did not survive this event.

*

With a sharp intake of breath, Elizabeth woke.

She could still feel the gore in her hands, the snapping of the tentacle-like capillaries from the dream. She could still feel the sensations of pulling and twisting.

"Jesus Christ," she said.

Beside her, Tanner was partially propped up with his pillow against the headboard. His hands were on his face, moving in gentle patterns down his jaw, up and over his lips, then encircling his eyes.

"Babe, you okay?" she said.

Tanner's hands stopped. He looked at her. "Yeah. I... had a nightmare."

"Goddamnit," she cursed. "Me, too. It was... It was *visceral*, like I could feel the... *Ugh*."

The sensations seemed to still crawl and slide over the webbing between her fingers. The sense-memories of that slickness, of the snapping and tearing...

"Jesus Christ is right," Tanner said. He slid back down from the headboard to lay on his pillow and wrapped his arm around her. The two lay entangled in the bed sheets, which were sweat soaked and wrapped around their legs like sleeping pythons.

"I'm surprised you were able to sleep, with what you saw today," she said.

He was silent for a moment, then said, "Yeah."

Traffic seared over the wet pavement outside the window of the bedroom. The sounds of the city never ceased. It was something that had grown to comfort her since starting to crash here on some nights. Tonight, though, something was different. She didn't feel comfort, only tension and exhaustion.

"He told me about his dream today," Elizabeth finally said, as her fingers stroked their way through her lover's chest hair.

"His dream?" he asked.

"Yeah."

"When?"

"When he was in the lobby, waiting on Ms. Tanaka to finish with you. He said... He said one of the strangest things I've heard in a while. He said that a dream can be *recommended*."

"Yeah. He touched upon the same thing with me in our session before he..."

They lay silent together in the darkness, the glow from the streetlights outside slicing through the parted curtains over the window.

After a moment, he said, "What did you make of it?"

"Of what?"

"Of the dream."

She said, "It creeped me the fuck out. It creeped the police officer out, too, when I told him about it. You were busy with the other one when he took my statement."

"I didn't know that you'd talked to them about it."

"Yeah. I didn't want to add onto what you were dealing with. I'm sorry I didn't mention it."

"It's okay," he said.

She put her mouth on his chest, felt him shift his arm at the same time, moving a hand up to his face.

"Why were you two discussing his dreams to begin with?" he asked.

She circled her tongue around his nipple, wanting to forget the images boiling inside her psyche, to focus rather on her lover's flesh. "I didn't bring it up. He did."

"Strange..." Tanner said.

She rested her hand on his chest, and then her chin on her hand and looked up to him. He was rubbing at the corner of his eye.

"And just earlier, I—" She paused. "I was having a dream, before I woke up. A nightmare. Reminded me of what he'd told me."

"Me, too," Tanner said.

After a minute of silence, save for the sounds of her lips and mouth kissing his chest, Elizabeth said, "I have to pee."

She got up from the bed and heard the man she thought she might love sigh before she stepped away and into the dark bathroom, her bare feet slapping onto the linoleum as she entered. For a moment, she thought she saw Harborough standing in the shower, eye sockets dark and empty but, when she flicked the light switch on, he was gone.

After she finished peeing, she took a deep breath and washed her hands. As she dried them on the little towel hanging next to the sink, she looked into the mirror. She stared into her own pupils. In her peripheral, her right hand, as if alive in its own right, rose to absently rub at the reddening corner of her eye.

The Harem Within

My father told me once, during a not so peculiar night—one in which we'd been sitting around the folding dinner table in the small kitchen of his inner-city apartment, eating macaroni and cheese that came from a cardboard box while he smoked his umpteenth meal cigarette—, that I was going to do great things with my life. He said that no son of his was going to be left squabbling, refusing to contribute to The Country, choosing instead to be another part of the petty victim generations that'd grown out of the wake of the Great War (this new breed of, as he called them, *socialist millennials* being the worst of the bunch). He said that his own blood was worth more than that, that it was meant for something like glory. There may have been times in which this bolstering of my heritage left me feeling prideful in my youth, because my father often liked to tell me this same thing as if it were some sort of family motto. I practically worshipped him when I was that young. I suppose it makes sense, then, that the slow creep into adulthood without having had the experience of a relationship, of knowing what it felt to kiss a girl more than just a quick peck on the cheek, had made me jaded to the idea of any sort of intimacy involving another, and made me question heavily this supposed efficacy of our bloodline.

As I grew into my late teens, it wasn't so much that I hadn't had full-on sex that bothered me, even though my 'friends' ribbed me for it pretty frequently. Everybody in high school had fucked, it seemed, except for me. No, the issue was more than that. The issue was that I didn't know what it was like to just *touch* someone, in an environment and a way that let me explore through the insecurities that had built up like bricks to form a nigh impregnable wall around myself, something that felt almost plastered over the surface of my skin like concrete.

I didn't have the innate jingoism my father seemed to be made of. My fight wasn't a battle of patriotism but one against myself in the trenches of human contact. I was supposed to do something great, to be something great, yet, as time moved on past high school, I'd constructed my own little Hell out of my inability to make the right moves, or to become a person desirable for a partner, or any other excuse I thought I could come up with for the reasons why. Years rolled over into each other and, by the time I was in my early twenties, I was still a virgin, still had not known love in a way that so many others say they'd known it, with only a three-month-long pseudo relationship with the foreign exchange student I took to prom back in my senior year (I'd even tried to kiss her once at the end of the entire event but she refused, albeit politely) to notch onto my belt, so to speak. By the age of twenty-three, I had fallen deep into the depths of self-service and carnal gratification in the form of regular masturbation and resignation to the life of an emotional and sexual hermit. By then, I could hardly keep my dick hard when I masturbated and, even then, only when I was watching something I'd be ashamed of if someone found out about it, or had some rod shoved into my urethra or an object up my ass, anything to feel like I wasn't so goddamned empty, bloated with a vacuity that had grown with me over that span of loneliness in post-pubescence. Sex had turned into an obsession, though I'd never experienced it. So when I had my first intimate encounter, one night after a company party, you could say I could've expected things to get a bit... strange. However, nothing could've prepared me for what was to come—no pun intended.

Her name was Brenna, or *is* Brenna, because I'd thought her dead or missing for years after that first and only night I'd had with her physical body. You see, I make that distinction—*physical* body versus whatever else—because a part of me has always known that I'd kept her within me, truly *kept* her, as I'd tasted her many times after that singular romp in her bedroom.

Though she'd disappeared, I'm not so sure she'd ever been completely gone, dead or only hibernating. Really, these last thoughts before the great end has allowed me to see much and recall what led me to this place, a place in which my body is being rocked side-to-side from that which is currently crawling out of me, escaping my open steaming stomach. Clarity, though, or at least a meager understanding of it all, isn't really what is being offered in this life-flashing-before-my-eyes point within the process of my dying. No, it's not like they'd said it would be.

Brenna was the first, and I mean that in more ways than you might imagine. She'd been a coworker of mine at a publishing studio that held its headquarters near the docks in downtown Seattle. It was this very corporate enterprise that was throwing an "all-hands party" in the wake of a slew of layoffs, a pretty shitty condolence considering none of those who were laid off were allowed at the party for "safety and security reasons". It was held at one of the theatres along 2nd Avenue near a tiki bar I'd frequented with coworkers, and I'd originally weighed out the options of either just avoiding the gathering all together and going to the place of hula skirts and karaoke, or actually making an appearance at this shindig. Against my antisocial nature, I ultimately decided on the company party, though I'm not certain exactly what led me to the decision. Fate has a funny way of nudging you this way or that, I guess.

I'd arrived stag, naturally, to find the place decked out in a *Baton Rouge* theme: gaming tables were scattered about, harboring card games and roulette wheels in which guests could gamble for fake money that could be later redeemed for beaded necklaces, gaudy plastic sunglasses, foam hands, silly-straws and other useless party favors. Multiple bars lined the curtained walls, lit low and tended by attractive women in miniskirts that glittered with the strobe of the stage lights, serving stronger-than-usual drinks and thus filling fish jars full of tips. Picture booths hid in opposite corners of the hall behind makeshift barriers of cloth drapes, with chests of silly props to be used during the picture taking.

I was more than a little buzzed when Brenna approached me, and it was pretty apparent that she was too when she asked in a sultry but somewhat slurred tone, "Why didn't you ever hit on me when we worked on the same floor?" I'd moved last year from the second floor to the third floor, from third-party support to studio support, essentially working on the same styles of software but for the company rather than the Ukrainian multitudes of shitty contract developers. I'd been given more money, my own cubicle (as if that would somehow fulfill me) and enough of a view out of the window to see the waves of the Puget Sound as I worked, so long as Chet from QA wasn't in his chair. If he was, all I got was the profile of his back, so brightly backlit by the sun shimmering off the waves outside that, when I blinked or closed my eyes against the typical afternoon headache, I'd see the negative of his silhouette in the space behind my eyelids.

My response to Brenna, as to why I hadn't hit on her, was truthful but did not contain the whole truth. "You weren't single at the time," I said. "You were with Stanley, remember?" The whole truth was that, even if she'd been single, I'd been too much of a chicken-shit at the time to do anything about it.

"Oh yeah," she'd said, laughing bashfully.

As I said, by this point I was already a few beers in and was feeling the liquid courage so, almost without thought, I said, "Are you single now? Maybe we should get a beer sometime." Immediately after realizing the words had left my mouth, and that we were both in fact already holding beers, heat flushed my neck and face and so I took another gulp of said beer, part of me almost wishing she hadn't even heard me speak.

She laughed, though, and touch my arm with her hand.

"I'd love to," she said.

The company event was supposed to last until one in the morning though by ten-thirty, many of the work-tired employees were already drunk and stumbling around the dance floor, including the CEO. Somewhere around midnight, the rich buffoon approached the microphone, as he'd already done multiple times that evening, and made an ass of himself by giving a drunken impromptu pep-talk to the crowd of employees, referring to them as *the ones that made the cut*, and then proceeding to puke all over himself, the microphone and the people standing closest to the stage. I remember seeing it spatter against one of the receptionist gals whose name I couldn't remember, but whose ass I'd stared at no less than a few times a week for as long as I'd worked there, and then I remember her screaming and running to the bathroom while a couple of the CEO's handlers came and got him off stage, moving him toward a table somewhere in the back to clean up and probably get chastised for misrepresenting the company image or something of that nature. After this explosion of vomit, the property management decided to usher everyone still within the party hall, only a couple dozen of us left by that point, out and into the foyer for more drinks, bottles of water. The remaining platters of finger foods had been wheeled out just a few moments prior, as well. Most bypassed the leftovers and went outside to the curb for cigarettes and weed, some beginning the mass exodus to the strip one block over, along which multiple bars huddled together like squat lambs caught in the rain, all open until 2AM.

As the remaining guests shuffled their way out ahead of me, Brenna approached from the coat checkout desk and slipped her hand into mine, interlocking her fingers with my own. The contact had been more than I'd expected in that moment and I couldn't remember the last time I'd touched someone like that. That's not true, actually. I could remember. On a first and only date with a gal I met online, one whom I hadn't been attracted to but, through cowardice and a general shock of inexperience, had said nothing to decline her hand-intimacy advances when she'd grabbed for fingers during our fancy dinner at Denny's… That had been the only time prior to this night in question with Brenna. I felt the heat of her palm warm me through my own, up my arm and into my chest like electricity.

We left the place in a pack of coworkers, her stumbling a little once we'd reached the concrete steps leading down to the sidewalk outside. She leaned her small frame against me for support. I'd gotten a whiff of her hair then and hoped that I'd get to walk like that and smell her scent for hours. Her perfume seemed to add a slightly psychedelic waver to the neon lights and signs of the bars I spied as we rounded the corner of the block. I was filled to the brim with an excitement I hadn't ever known before. Her arm around mine, the smell of her conditioner and her scent filling my nostrils… It was heavenly, to say the least. Though I hadn't smoked weed yet, the phrase *the ultimate high* kept repeating in my mind during those moments.

For lack of a better way of putting it, I felt elevated.

"Want to get a drink?" She nodded toward the bar closest to us, a place called *The Cliff Dive*. Brilliant neon shined through its front windows, advertising the different brews they stocked and obscuring the dark interior within. My heart thumped like a drum and I hoped that she couldn't feel the quickened pulse through my hand and arm. My voice cracked when I responded with, "Definitely," and she laughed and pulled me across the road.

The avenue was empty of car traffic. Employees and other patrons of the bar stood in clusters outside the front door, groups bleeding out onto the street and emitting collective clouds of cigarette smoke that glowed blue from the streetlamps as well as from the myriad of smart phones gazing up into their owners' eyes through the haze. Light from the other block over flared up into the night above, making it appear as if there were fires just beyond the wall of silhouetted buildings to either side of *The Cliff Dive*.

Inside the joint, under the seedy radiance of the arcade games along the walls, and partially lit from the lamps hung low over the frayed pool tables, Brenna's eyes were glazed with lax amusement. We found a place in the back near the ATM, joked and bitched about work, briefly falling upon politics though we both agreed quickly that it wasn't a topic that ought to be broached on the first date. Her cleavage kept my attention, though I did my damnedest not to make it obvious. When we'd had another two drinks each, she laughed especially hard at something I'd said, then excused herself to the bathroom with a look as if she were going to vomit. I stared at her ass as she walked away, sight being driven by obsession. Ten minutes later, she'd emerged from the women's restroom, wavering a bit in her gait walking back to me. She'd put lip gloss on, I could see, glistening under the dim setting in which we stood.

"You want to come back to my place for a bit? Watch a movie?"

She was smiling something mischievous and, even without experience, I had an idea what she was hinting at, especially with the way she was looking into my eyes.

This was going to be it.

"Definitely," I said.

She'd elected to drive and, in hindsight, it was a dumb move considering how much she'd had to drink. Luckily, we made it to her apartment unscathed, though I did almost pass out on the drive there. I was exhausted by the alcohol, the passing out being an inevitability she managed to thwart by continuing to talk to me about music, about how good I looked that night. I didn't feel any different than usual at the time but perhaps the beer-goggles were working in my favor.

We entered the apartment. There was a sharp bark from some room off to the right down the hall. A scurrying sound followed immediately after as a little terrier rushed into the entryway and started yapping at me as if I'd been breaking and entering. Brenna crouched over the little beast and petted him, scratching behind his ears while smooching his bug-eyed face.

"This is Badger. He's harmless," she said with a smirk. "Aren't you boy?" Brenna's shirt had ridden up in the back when she'd crouched to pet the cretin and the light above the coat rack kissed the tattoo spanning her lower back. I wondered what her underwear looked like and how it would smell, what her fluids would taste like in my mouth.

The dog quieted and continued mouth-breathing with each scratch of his neck, licked Brenna's hand, all the while maintaining a sideways glance at me. I'd read somewhere that dogs like this one had breathing and sinus issues from so much inbreeding, that they hardly lived beyond a decade due to the physiological shortcomings shaped and formed by the humans that had tampered with their lineage, all in the name of trying to squeeze every ounce of cuteness out of the things. Poor little bastards.

Brenna stood. "This is the place. Nothing too fancy," she said.

It was homely but cramped, a bit of a hovel, with stacks of books in the corners of the living room amidst clusters of cardboard boxes, as if she'd not yet fully unpacked from moving in, whenever that had been. The mantel over the fireplace and the two window sills were cluttered with pictures and small various belongings, though, so I imagined she'd been there for at least a while.

"I like it," I said.

She moved past me, her chest brushing against mine. "This is the kitchen. Over here," she continued as she rounded the corner, "is the living room, which you already saw. The bathroom is the door on the right down here."

I followed her down the hall.

She flicked the light inside the bathroom, illuminating a small stained sink, a low toilet and a shower hardly large enough for a full-sized adult. Towels and clothes hung everywhere they could, drying in the breeze of the groaning ceiling fan. The light above the dirty mirror shone a murky yellow.

"Feel free," she said, nodding at the toilet. "And this is my room." She opened the door opposite the bathroom and walked into its darkness before switching a light on from the wall on the right. "Come on in."

I followed her in. Badger was right behind me, breathing loudly and sniffing at my shoes.

"There's another bathroom in here, though no shower in this one." She pointed to the corner of the room where a door stood ajar, only darkness beyond. "I have to pee," she laughed. "Had like seven drinks tonight," then slipped into said darkness, turned the light on and pushed the door closed, though it didn't shut all the way. "Go ahead and sit," she called from inside. "Badger won't bug you too much."

"No problem," I said.

The walls were a muted pink and the aroma in here was a stronger version of what Brenna's hair had smelled like earlier. A cursory look around the room didn't yield much for me to sit on, save for her bed and a stool against the wall near the mirrored dresser. An array of various make-up, nail polish and lotion capsules cluttered the surface of the dresser. The bed was small but full of pillows and covered by a comforter that looked billowy and soft, a patchwork of pink and blue and purple fabrics. I opted for the stool, so as not to assume a place on her bed quite yet.

While she was in the bathroom, it seemed the perfect time to remove the small blue pill from my pocket. It was an unmarked knock-off brand 'male enhancement supplement' I'd been saving for a night just like this. I swallowed it dry and then moved to sit on her bed. I'd taken the supplement in the past, to enjoy on my own in front of a computer screen of saved porn videos, and knew the effects took somewhere between fifteen and twenty minutes to begin kicking in. I had no idea when or how Brenna and I were going to get into it. Sitting there, practically melting into her comforter, engulfed by her scent, listening to the sound of her piss echoing out into the room, I contemplated ways to hide the artificial erection should it choose to make its debut too early in this dance.

The dog had come further into the room and was approaching me warily. I put my hand out and said, "It's alright, buddy. Come on." He stopped about a foot from my hand, continued to stare at me. I could see the musculature under his scrawny legs quivering with tension, the same anxiety most dogs that size seemed to carry with them at all times, ready to flee without a moment's hesitation. I could still hear the stream of piss from inside the bathroom, the sound beginning to finally diminish in strength after what seemed like an hour. A few seconds of silence followed the cessation of the noise and, as if on cue, the dog yapped so suddenly that I jumped. Then it yapped again.

There was a flush inside the bathroom and Brenna said, "Come on, Badger. Stop it."

The dog went full on into barking at me. I retracted my hand and just sat there, staring into the creature's scared little eyes. It reminded me of those bulge-eyed deep-sea fish they show in the nature documentaries, or of shark's eyes before the kill—all black, all instinct.

The bathroom door swung open. Brenna stepped out, switching the light off behind her. Her hair was down and she was smiling hazily. She'd removed the long-sleeve shirt that she'd worn that evening, leaving only a tube top on over her bra, which I could see through the thin cotton was a hot pink color.

"Badger!"

The dog didn't stop barking.

"Alright. You're going out."

She picked him up, still yapping, and set him into the hall and shut the door.

"Sorry about that," she said.

I tried to insist that it was fine, "It's no probl—", but before I could finish, she'd approached and straddled my lap, wrapped her arms around my shoulders and put her mouth to mine.

Her tongue slipped between my lips and smashed against my own, and I felt her saliva drip into my mouth. It tasted like beer, wine and a hint of vomit. The sensation of it overwhelmed my initial aversion to its flavor, overtaking me in a feeling not unlike a rapture of some sort. I was stuck in a stasis, as if my mind hadn't yet caught up with what was happening, still bogged down in that time a moment ago with strained thoughts of the pill I'd just ingested, my impotency, the yapping dog and the subtle irritation it had produced. After moments that seemed like eons, my mind finally did catch up, accompanied by an increasing vacillation of shock and anxiety rising within me, only to then be swept away by the feeling of her beginning to rock herself against me. She reached down to grab both my hands and moved them to her ass. She'd slid her jeans down a bit, exposing her underwear, her flesh. My hands, as if driven by their own accord, kneaded at the supple weight of her butt cheeks. The fingers gripped deeply like animal's claws and I fell into that moment as she moaned into my mouth.

I lost all thought, all will outside of this experience.

I didn't remember removing my clothes but, at some point, the pill had kicked in and, when she'd slipped my erection inside of her, the heat from her cunt flooded my nerves with a sensation of conductivity, an electric maelstrom. Within moments, I was thrusting fast and hard and pulling her down onto me, her ass still subjugate to my hands. She wore nothing but her bra, that hot pink color somehow defining these moments, solidifying them into my memories. Her alcoholic breath poured over me in waves with each exhale and I breathed it in like oxygen, swallowed her saliva, lapping it off of her lips like a dog. I pulled her down onto me again and again, losing feeling throughout my body, losing my sense of touch, of taste and sight, save for a growing tightness in my groin. Proprioception had slipped away and I'd lost track of my own body as we pushed against each other. I felt weightless. I was floating.

In congruence with this release of sensory, I'd closed my eyes and in the black behind my eyelids, I saw a gaping chasm, blooming from somewhere within that darkness. I witnessed its psychedelic glory through my third eye, manifesting as a great and terrifying aperture, burgundy and bloody. In the landscape of my imagination, it stretched out to the size of a canyon, expanding out in front of my mind, quivering around its edges like an orifice at the anticipation of being filled with a satisfaction I'd waited for so long to feel. My hearing went numb, too, and I was left with only the smell of her skin as I stood on the edge of that vast internal darkness, sight of the bedroom around me completely gone, on the verge of an orgasm that threatened to pull me down into nothingness. Fear and pleasure mounted in me, as did the tension in my body left so far behind.

When everything culminated, finalizing that crescendo into a colossal moment, I could hear Brenna moaning again, piercing through the veil, and then I slipped on the greasy edge of that void I'd been staring down into, and fell into the sound and sensations of my first lover screaming in horror.

*

I couldn't tell how long it had been when I came to. The dog was out in the hallway, I could hear, still yapping at the other side of the door and sniffing at the carpet underneath it. I lay there, staring into the backs of my eyelids for a long while, the colors and shapes replaced with a blank dark grey, listening to my breaths between the barking. My lungs felt sore with each inhale, as did the musculature of my chest and stomach and arms. Inside, I felt like I'd been punched in the gut half a dozen times while unconscious. Finally, after waiting for the dog to calm down, which it never did, I let my eyes open.

For a moment I thought Brenna might've hidden under the bed or in the dark bathroom, the partially open door of which gaped at me like a strange toothless grin cocked sideways.

"Brenna?" I said to the emptiness of the room. My voice was hoarse, strained as if I'd been screaming.

Only silence answered me, save for the sniffing at the base of the door from out in the hall. The smell of Brenna's cunt lingered, was plastered against my skin, her perfume all over my hands and arms, the slather of our copulation still a slime over my cock. The hot pink bra lay sprawled over my chest, still clasped.

Otherwise, the room was vacant.

I knew I should've stood from the bed, made my way out into the living room, to wherever she had gone but, instead, I lay there a moment longer and draped my hands down my chest, over my stomach. My own cum lay smeared over my belly and groin, having gone cold in the still air of the room while I'd been out. My fingers skied through the muck and met the tuft of my pubic hair and I could've sworn then, in a weird awareness that seemed to manifest in that sensitivity, that I could feel someone else's skin under my fingertips. The bizarre quality of the sensation sent my blood running cold. It felt like *her* skin, but I was touching my own body. It was in this strange confusion of perception that I realized I could hear Brenna's voice. She spoke from somewhere, maybe out in the living room, but I couldn't be certain, as it seemed somehow closer than the sniffling of the dog out in the hall. It seemed to have an ethereal quality to it.

She was still in the room. She had to be.

I sat up. The clasped hot pink bra tumbled to the floor. I leaned to look under the bed and then saw that the box spring lay directly against the carpet. I stood, moved to the dark half-bathroom. My hand crawled along the wallpaper where I thought the switch would be, found it and flipped the light on.

No luck.

I stood there, staring into the dirty sink, when I heard Brenna's moan echo in the recesses of my mind. At first, I figured it memories of the moments we'd just had with each other. Oddly, it was accompanied by an almost exact copy of her voice, but this copy was crying. She lamented in faint words I couldn't understand, words that sounded far away. I stretched my jaw, rubbed my temples, tried popping my ears to get my mind off of whatever it was imagining. But then there was anger, a screeching and shouting. Her voice multiplied and those many copies of her voice seemed to fill my mind, seeming external of my own psyche, yet somehow encased inside my skull. A part of me still thought her voice might've been coming from out in the living room. I opened the door to the room and Badger shot in like a bullet. He leapt up onto the bed, sniffed at a wet spot of cum soaked into the sheets, and then jumped back to the floor barking at me.

At some point during the twenty minutes I spent searching her apartment—through the closets and the pantry cupboards, in the other bathroom, out on the balcony overlooking the parking lot—the copies of her voice had gone from my mind. As I cleaned the cum off my gut, I realized the sensations of my skin were my own again. I decided to leave, thinking that she'd played a ridiculous joke on me or, frankly, had been so unimpressed by my lovemaking that she'd left without saying anything, assuming I'd see my own way out. And yet, I noticed her keys, phone, purse and shoes were still on the carpet near the door where she'd left them when we'd arrived from the bar earlier.

I took my things and left the door knob unlocked on the way out. I could hear the dog still yapping from inside the apartment as I descended the stairs to the ground floor below.

*

The explanation I'd managed to convince myself of at the time was that I'd fallen out of consciousness, passed out because of the alcohol or something, and she'd left me at her place to go do something else, or some*one* else. Strange as the idea was, I thought it at least somewhat plausible. I imagined her bored and awake, beginning to sober up, down at one of the 24-hour diners across the block, irritated or at least less-than-thrilled at the sleeping Casanova in her bed. I wondered at my performance, if I'd kept going after the memories had stopped cataloging. I wondered if I'd said something stupid or asinine in my orgasmic stupor. There had to be a reason for her leaving me, albeit someone she knew but not *that* well, alone in her apartment in the early hours of the morning.

On my way out of the neighborhood, I checked through the windows of the diner on the corner. At fifteen miles an hour, in my tired haze, the profiles of those few people eating inside went by in blurs. I was fairly certain I hadn't seen her as the place passed by. As bizarre as the events had been, with whatever had actually happened still evading my thought rationale, something in me felt good, felt *right* and powerful, as if I'd crossed some great benchmark or obstacle. With her smells still in my nostrils and the grey gloom of the oncoming sunrise creeping up from the east, I rolled down the window and let the cold early air flow into my sinuses.

There was a moment that occurred during that drive, as I sat at the stoplight before the onramp to I-5, a moment that seemed to define the very beginnings of all that I would become, a moment that I would never forget: my vision was saturated by the red glow of the stoplight through my windshield. I was breathing deeply of the cold open window when a tingling sensation started just below my sternum. It was small at first, and then it grew and rode slowly through my stomach, down into my groin and the pit of my balls. A heavy ecstasy came so quickly then, so abruptly, that my foot lifted off the brake momentarily, hiccupping the car forward a few inches into the crosswalk. This feeling thrummed within me as a low thing, something I attributed at the time to aftershocks of the blue pill I'd consumed back at Brenna's place. The sensation then waned to a muted level and the light turned green.

Once I'd merged into the sparse early morning traffic of the freeway, I tried to focus on the lanes ahead of me, tried to keep distracted by the chilly air blowing in from the window. The sensation, however, was building at an ever-increasing rate. By the time I got home and parked in my spot, marked by a faded number forty-nine, I didn't even exit the car. Instead, I turned the ignition off, leaned the seat back, pulled my shirt off and unbelted my jeans, pulling them down to my ankles. I then reasoned again that this had to be after-effects of the enhancement pill, but those thoughts were lost in a lack of caring once I began to touch myself. My hands, again as if moving of their own accord, slid over my body. I moaned as the heat of my own touch against my skin, in some strange alchemy, seemed to mutate the way I perceived my flesh, the hair on my chest, my nipples. For brief moments, I could feel a pair of pert breasts in place of my usual fleshy chest, a soft stomach in place of a hairy gut. As my fingers traced down my stomach and to my sides, my hips tapered in a way I hadn't recognized.

Excited beyond explanation, lost in my own libido, I slid my fingers down to where my cock was but, instead of a cock, I felt a mound and the slit I'd often dreamed of, imagined and obsessed over for so long. It was slick and salivated over my fingertips. I felt the arousal shiver through my organs, to coalesce and come to a point in my groin. I could still feel my actual erection, a spike of granite, and yet, like some overlay of an alternate reality, there was carnal desire deep in me to be exacted, a canal that needed to be filled. Outlandish possibilities played over my thoughts, like I wanted to plunge my own tongue into myself somehow, or expand that throbbing need out to engulf the world inside of it, if only I could find the means to contort myself into a shape to allow such an otherworldly act. And then, as I thought it, so it happened that I lost track of my proportions, could no longer feel the separateness of my limbs gripped by my hands, and felt then as if my body had begun to cave in on itself. The cognitive qualia immediately following was the taste of cunt on my tongue and the feeling of my fingers up inside of me.

Lost in the oblivion of that moment, though I didn't know it then, I was experiencing the arrival of my ultimate nature, the first awareness of my abilities and my true carnate self.

*

I hadn't heard from Brenna after our night together, nor had anyone else, apparently. When she'd gone days without posting to social media or returning calls, someone had reported her missing. Within hours, there were posts online and emails chain-forwarded. Within days, the hollow hashtag #FindBrenna bullshit circulated amongst the coworker social groups, as if posting a hashtag would do anything to help finding a missing person other than satisfy that urge to 'contribute'. I was never approached about my time with her the night of the company party, save for a few messages from fellow employees that I was able to derail by simply stating that we'd parted ways after the party had shut down for the night. Either no one had noticed our mingling beyond that or the authorities hadn't nailed that specific night down as the night of her disappearance.

I'd continued to work at the company for another few months and, once the dust settled, left to pursue another position at a rival studio on the other side of the city. Meanwhile, I was beginning to understand the truth of what had happened to Brenna that night and where she'd gone.

It first happened maybe once a week but, after a couple months, it began to occur almost every night: I'd lay down to sleep in my bed and, sooner or later, an auditory numbness would creep over me. Shortly after, a latent essence or memory of that night with Brenna would come into existence within my mind and drifting focus. And then there would be a chorus of emotional simulations, all of *her* emotions—anger, unmitigated terror, anguish, a harrowing sadness—manifesting like aspects of my own thoughts. The amalgam of the different facets of her, of Brenna, molding together in some kind of mental alchemy, was more than an act of my imagination, I knew. I *had* her somehow, encaged in some part of me.

These occurrences started happening outside of sleep, in my

daily life. On one occasion, while I was on the bus, traffic crawling by outside the window, I'd heard her pleading to let her go. I couldn't help but look to the others sitting on the bus, to make certain none of them could hear her. When she'd then screamed like a shrieking ghost, haunting me, and no one else noticed, I knew that she was either a symptom of an oncoming madness, or that she was truly locked away somewhere from which only I could hear her.

For the sake of argument, if I had wanted to let her go, I had no idea how that would be done. The truth, though, was that I didn't want to let her go. No, I wanted her to stay right where she was.

From this position of power over her essence, I learned I could summon a reaction from her at will, stoke the fires of her suffering just by mentally prodding at the space where she stayed imprisoned in me, like agitating a pet in an aquarium by profusely tapping on the glass, or licking an exposed tooth nerve. Anytime I felt the need for to, whether for release or entertainment, I would find somewhere to lay down, would spend a minute or two allowing those cries and whimpering to come to fruition and saturate everything I was. And with this summoning, arisen from my own flesh would be her under my hands, soft and lush, a feminine layer of meat over my own bones. I could stick my fingers inside of the orifice that arose from the will of my thoughts, and I could taste the images of that black chasm that bloomed in my psyche like latent salt on sweated labia. I no longer desired the effects of those little blue pills for this new-found control, this power, seemed to reignite my body's ability to maintain erectile rigidity. It left me in elation. I would cum to the ebbing waves of lustful mental abuse I found myself drowning in. I would choke on the viscosity of that domination I enacted for, when I put it upon her, it in turn was put upon me. I was my own master. I was *her* master.

Brenna...

That name, itself, means almost nothing to me now. The memories of the actual woman became diluted by the repetition of using her essence again and again, the weight behind her name lost in a kind of semantic satiation. She, instead, ended up replaced by a nebulous feminine energy, one that I milked from its purgatory any time I deemed it necessary.

And that is where she has stayed.

*

It'd been about a year since Brenna when I met another woman with whom I'd had the chance to be intimate.

For some background, I'd tried my hand at poetry as a teenager but it never panned out beyond some melodramatic song lyrics with songs were never written. I didn't play an instrument and no one I knew played any instruments. With the changes that had overcome my mundane life in the last year, though, with everything that had happened with Brenna, a new surge of inspiration had awoken within me, seemingly outside of my own control. With this new creative production, I decided to use the internet to find a group of writers to meet up with one night a week, hoping that I'd be able, with enough editing and adherence to criticism, to get something of mine published somewhere.

I'd been drinking with said writers group one evening, on a night that we called "pub night". This second lover of mine was a newcomer, her first night with the group happening just the week prior. She was shy to speak at the start but, when she opened up a bit, it was her laugh I noticed, a laugh that I immediately fell for. Clarification is in order. When I say *fell for*, I am not speaking of love or any of that preteen romantic bullshit. No, there was something different in my desires, for my capacity to covet had grown along with my understanding of what had happened with my first sexual encounter. I *wanted* this new laugh. I wanted it to lull me to sleep at night. I wanted to own it. If I'm being honest, it's been so long that I don't even remember this one's name, even though her voice has been one of my favorite over the years, even if, when summoned, it has been flavored with a sentiment of hatred at me, her keeper.

She didn't write poetry. She wrote stories, and the story she wrote and shared with the group her first week was horror fiction with a dash of medieval fantasy. I felt it a breath of fresh air in the stagnant literary state the rest of the group seemed to be stuck in. The story had a good deal of body horror in it, guts and evisceration, and the vivid product of her imagination only furthered my desire to have and to keep her.

Possession is what I wanted.

By the end of the night in question, I'd already put on my best charms and convinced her to chill at the bar a while longer after the rest of the group had left. She wasn't the most attractive woman I'd seen but, whether it was the beer-goggles or this almost insatiable desire to somehow *consume* that laugh of hers, I was in it to win it. A nature beyond that which I'd grown up thinking was my own seemed to direct my words and flirting ability, bringing me ever closer to the 'prize' of obtaining her in perpetual matrimony. Since it happened with Brenna, I was convinced it was going to happen with this new one or, at least, I wanted it to happen to her. I'd also grown bored of using the element of Brenna's torture to get off, and the prospect of experiencing someone new had me by the motives, and I was riding that possibility forward.

When we'd gotten back to my place, it was a while before we'd started touching and 'heavy petting' as my friends liked to call it. I'd made us some drinks, put on reruns of *It's Always Sunny in Philadelphia* and we talked late into the night. I made moves to get closer to her on my couch, and she made her own micromovements in my direction. Sometime during a particular few moments, in which I was listening to her tell me about a particular story idea she'd been mulling over and was moving to slide my hand over hers, Brenna's voice screamed in my mind:

Don't let him touch you!

I was so struck by this very clear phrase that it forced an instinctual glance out of me to the one sitting next to me on the couch, thinking at first that it was her that had said the phrase or that, at least, she'd also been able to hear it during her speaking. She didn't stop talking, nor did she change the topic, so I figured she hadn't noticed. Instead, she continued on about her story idea, one in which a woman has a stillbirth and falls into some paranormal nightmare of existentialism. Though I did my best to appear like I was paying attention, I wasn't. The voice had been real, very much in the forefront of my mind. My face must've betrayed me because she stopped and asked if I was alright, to which I responded, "Of course" and urged her to continue.

Whenever she laughed, it pulled me from the distraction of

my thoughts on that strange outburst I'd heard, pulled me back into the lizard mind, and so I wanted to hasten things. We kissed shortly after our third or fourth episode of *It's Always Sunny* had finished. The situation escalated pretty quickly afterward, spurred by a savage lust that roiled and grew within me. By the time we'd entered my room, fell onto the bed together, I'd already forgotten about the voice that'd shouted in my mind. This woman on top of me lifted my shirt, traced her fingers through my chest hair and over my nipples. As she began to kiss down my stomach, the voice came again, reverberating like a lost echo in a deep mineshaft:

No!

The woman whose face was gently mauling my gut, whose mouth occasionally moved back up to suck the saliva from my mouth, didn't seem to notice.

Don't let him do it!

Run, Goddamnit!

She kissed again down my chest, over my stomach, down to my hips. She bit my inner thigh before sliding her mouth around the head of my cock. The slurping sounds and slick salivation she employed brought me close to the edge of orgasm much quicker than I had anticipate. As I then saw in my mind that gaping bloody chasm that accompanied all of my sexual experiences, the pit of indulgence with its almost sentient darkness, beckoning for me as I reached the ultimate moment, my world shifted and mutated, warbled and arched. I felt my body molt, shape itself accordingly to melt into hers. No matter how many times I'd witnessed it, fear and ecstasy were what I felt as I reached the brink, no longer seeing my room around us, staring down into the vastness within my inner eye.

With the last ounce of consciousness, that dark abyss embraced me as it would a lost son and soon after, as the sensations came to a climax inside, existence blinked out and all was left in the greyness of nothing.

*

Again, as was the case with my first time of lovemaking, I awoke and my partner was gone. Her clothes were still scattered around the bedroom like corpses after a battle. I cleaned up any trace of her from the apartment, including her shoes, clothes and purse, which I placed into a trash bag and then into the trunk of my car for later disposal. I even called a tow truck to have her car removed, making up a name and apartment number for myself and saying the car had been in the spot it sat in for a few days now, and that it wasn't registered to anyone who lived in the complex. This proved to be a valid enough fabrication for the tow company, so they sent a truck out within an hour. I gazed out of my bedroom window while they chained the thing up, hauled it up onto the bed of the truck, and drove off with it. For a few long moments after, I watched the empty parking spot, expecting something but unsure of what exactly.

When all was said and done, when I'd erased all signs of Little Miss Writer Group's very presence, I sat down on the couch and stared into the black of the dead television screen, listening to the two distinct crying voices within me, and honestly a little terrified at how satiated I felt.

*

It wasn't long after that second occurrence that I started searching for ways to experiment with this condition, for lack of a better phrase. Maybe power or ability would be a more apt description.

There were now two voices within me, outside of my own, two other bodies I could feel and touch and taste and contort myself into when my arousal needed feeding. At the time, I wrestled with the notion that this was a curse of some kind, something given to me by God for my life of mundanity, or a punishment for a slight I'd committed unwittingly against some voodoo-practicing gypsy or soothsayer. Maybe it had always been with me. Perhaps it was in the blood my father spoke so fondly of. I didn't dare tell anyone about what was happening, whether it was an evolving issue or if it was calcified in me in its final stage. I had no desire to spend the rest of my life in prison for the disappearances of the only two women I'd ever touched sexually.

I'd considered a prostitute in the past, before all of this, someone I could simply pay to help me get over that hump of virginity, but ultimately hadn't followed through with it for fear of contracting a disease or the general shame of it all. Now, though, my experiment required subjects and the prospect of using someone less likely to draw the attention of the authorities seemed a potential boon. I had no idea where to look, regardless if I was actually going to go through with it or not. I'd heard something could happen in the International District but downtown Seattle wasn't where I wanted to be during the times that the 'ladies of the night' would be strutting their stuff. A decent bit of money sat in my bank account, saved up originally for a down payment on a house, and, after an embarrassingly extensive internet search, I decided that I could use some of it to try out Vegas. It would be as good a place as any to find someone to have sex with when all I wanted to spend was money instead of time and energy. Plus, prostitution was legal there.

A week later, I was in Sin City. The plane had touched down around 5PM and I'd been driven from the airport to the Red-Light district immediately afterward. The cabbie chuckled when I told him the proposed destination and said that, if I had trouble finding what I wanted, to get a hold of him. He'd slipped me a personal card, unmarked by any mention of his cab services, with a private number on it. Considering how that the cab smelled of garbage and body odor, and the way he kept smiling and winking at me in the rearview mirror, I'd determined there was no fucking way I was getting a hold of him that night or any other night. But I played it off. I said that I appreciated the ride and gave him a decent tip that would get him away from me as quickly as possible.

Only a few moments had passed since I'd stepped out of the cab before panhandlers rushed at me like a pack of rabid zombies, chanting their service pitches and flapping their stacks of cards in front of me, cards adorned with erotic pictures of women in the nude, with the occasional naked man lounging on a brightly lit couch. 'Anything you want' is what they were advertising.

I ended up settling on this place called Corner of Heaven which turned out to be tucked away in an alley off of a side street of the main strip. The card had not been one given to me by the 'clappers' that yattered after me but rather from a card I'd found amidst the myriad littered all over the ground and in the gutters. The woman on the front of the card was Asian, cartoon stars were over her crotch and nipples, and it was haughtily signed by

'Bridget'. I made it by the bald security guard, built like a tree trunk, who was posted at the front door. He asked for ID, I showed him said ID, he patted me down for weapons and then nodded for me to go in.

Music blared loudly. Lights swirled around the place like a kaleidoscope. Women were pole-dancing in different corners of the place. I asked the co-ed duo at the main counter if 'Bridget' was actually available, slipping the card I'd found over the glass counter toward them. The man gave me a greasy smile and said that she was not, but that they had many other ladies available that would satisfy me just as easily. One of the women standing by approached at the man's beckoning, slid her arm through mine, and said, "You ready for a good time, sweetheart?" My eyes followed the V of her gold necklace down into her cleavage. She wasn't Asian but it really didn't matter.

She would do.

I strolled with her down a side aisle of the main room. Men and woman were sat in chairs around the small circular stages, slipping dollar bills into g-strings and groping when given the chance. Busty women in lingerie were placing drinks on tables and taking orders here and there. The one holding my arm said her name was Trixie over the din of the music and clopping high-heels. We rounded a corner into the back of the place, then started down a long hallway of rooms all marked on their doors with the name of animals (Tiger Room, Peacock Room, Rhino, Grizzly, etc.). We stopped in front of a door near the end of the hall that had a plaque on it engraved with the word 'Swordfish'. When the door closed, the music and chatter from the main hall faded to a dull vibration beyond the almost soundproof walls.

It was a dimly lit room. There was a bed made with crimson sheets and a few pillows stacked over each other, with a crimson couch beyond that against the far wall, the colors of which reminded me of seeping blood. A low lamp sat on a nightstand next to the bed, the only light except for a pink glow out of the unseen corners of the room. In the lamp's cone of light, there was a fish jar filled with condoms, tubes of substances and other small things, with a sticker taped onto the glass of the thing describing the prices for each of the little novelties available inside (ten bucks for a foil of lube, thirteen for a condom, thirty for a pair of edible underwear). She took both of my hands and pulled me to the bed, directing me to sit. I did and then she did as well.

"Well, what'll it be, sugar?" She stroked a finger along the line of my jaw and rubbed my leg with her other hand.

The newfound vigor that had accompanied me since my experiences with the other two women, since taking them into me, was something to behold but old habits die hard and I somehow knew, though the truth may have been different, that I wouldn't be able to perform with a condom on. On top of that, the other two experiences were done without any sort of barrier. So, I bluntly said, "I want to fuck you and feel you on my skin. How much to do it without a condom?"

At first, she said it wasn't going to happen, baby. Then I put a wad of cash, nine-hundred dollars, most of what I'd brought with me, down onto the nightstand and told her I'd give her the regular fee on top of that.

She acquiesced.

It was apparent that she was a pro with how quickly she moved me into position on the bed, and by the way she moved her hips once I was inside of her. I'd had no problem getting hard, especially because I could hear the other two crying inside of my mind. Though this whore's smell was musky, a product of reapplying multiple scents throughout a night of work, her flesh felt as real as I needed it to. She said no kissing when I tried, but then I asked if she wouldn't mind drooling onto me while she rocked up and down, which she said was fine. I also asked her to keep her bra on, something that would serve as an impromptu indicator of whether my little experiment worked, recalling Brenna's hot pink bra.

I'd reached climax rather quickly, licking her spit from my lips as she rocked like a rowboat enslaved by a slow but steady current. She moaned with an artificiality, behind which I heard the screaming of the other voices inside. I closed in on my orgasm and, as my mind floated away from reality to the siren songs of my previous partners in their subjugation, my imagination stared down upon that undulating abyss once again. The vividness of it, the colors, made me anxious and I felt momentarily like I was dying.

The voices shouted for me to leave the whore alone but I ignored them and dove headfirst into the black as the intensity of orgasm overtook my everything.

*

When I returned from unconsciousness, it sounded as if I were still hearing the same song I had passed out to, and so I reasoned that a segment of only a minute or two had passed in my absence. Trixie was gone. Her bra, black, not pink, was clasped and resting on my chest. The chain she'd been wearing was coiled on the pillow next to my neck like a lifeless gold snake, its ends still locked together.

And when I heard this whore sobbing in the midst of the other two defeated energies inside of me, the excitement and adrenaline rode like fire through my veins and I was hard again. I stroked myself, gripping and kneading the flesh of my body as it became multi-dimensional. I moved and contorted impossibly in a fever of sexual elation and, tasting myself and letting the juices flow into my mouth, I ejaculated onto my mutating stomach, smearing it over the breasts and hips that shifted in and out of reality and protruded from my body. I *owned* her as I owned the other two and no one else, still walking around this world, was the wiser.

After I cleaned myself with the towels stacked on the dresser in the corner, I recollected my money and walked out of the room as if nothing had happened, even gave a greasy smile back to the man and woman at the front desk on my way out.

*

Years went by. I'd experimented more with other women, prostitutes mostly, and even a man I met at a bar once, all while my lust for domination and collection grew like a black weed, unfurling its roots more and more throughout my very being. The more that I had, the more my impotence diminished, evolving instead into savage virility beyond imagination. I brought myself to orgasm multiple times a day for all those years, this master libido driving me almost beyond the ability to focus on whatever job I had at the time. I'd find ways to escape into back rooms of the places I worked, into storage closets and boiler rooms just to be able to lay back and let those I'd enslaved do with their torment what they will, for it only drove me closer to the face of my god, the beast I'd become. Heroism and chivalry would be left to the rest of the chattel who didn't understand what it was like to truly *have* someone, let alone multiple someones. Hedonism animated me. This was my calling, to subjugate those that let me into them, to own them. And it was my mental fortitude that allowed me to have them any way I pleased once they were within me.

I am no rapist, no murderer, but I am a fiend. I've always known it. I also now know that I was born to be something great, as my father had always told me. My nature, my place in all of this, is one of villainy. I was born to consume what I desire and to make it part of me, to churn this world and the souls within it through a process, a sexual and spiritual digestion beyond the average comprehension.

I shouldn't be surprised at what has ended up happening, though. It only makes sense that, at some point, what is taken in has to inevitably come out.

*

It has been eight years since that first night with Brenna and, since then, I have amassed, if I remember correctly, seventeen women and one man. They are *mine*. Maybe there were more, though I cannot recall and I know that, by now, years after the fact, some of the voices have dwindled to nothingness, their years of imprisonment having stifled their will to cry out or to beg me for release, or they've somehow managed to merge with the others, or perhaps Death has finally removed some of them from my grasp. Either way, the replenishment of such is like feeding an old addiction. I could go months, half a year, lavishing in these bodies I was able to summon onto myself when arousal sparked, and it satiated me to know that I had them within me, to feel their flesh under my own, but every so often, a particular need would mutter from deep in my gut like some rambling schizoid, something that required a new novelty, required another thing to play with. It was in these times that I would seek out another to join the harem within me.

Tonight was one of those nights.

About twenty minutes ago, I found her, dressed in a mini skirt and short fur coat that left her exposed stomach open to the air and the lights of passing traffic, hanging around her pimp on a corner in the International District. Far removed from my old inhibitions about this place, a result of the power I'd felt I now possessed, I pulled my car up to the corner, rolled the window down, switched to my fog lights. The guy had a silver tooth, believe it or not. Oriental tattoos covered his arms and neck. I was sure they covered his entire body under his clothes. He asked what I wanted. I said I wanted to fuck. He gave me the price, a measly two-hundred, so I gave him three-fifty, which elicited a smile from him, and followed the whore into the alleyway, driving slow and steady. The guy gave me his 'rules' through the open driver's side window as he followed us back. He said that he'd be just outside the car if anything should happen to her and that he'd stuck men tougher than me for less than I'd think, flashing a switchblade that caught the light of the streetlamp on the opposite side of the avenue.

She got into the passenger side once we were clear of the view of passing traffic. I told her I wanted to start by watching her suck my cock. She nodded and in a forced sultry voice said, "Sounds good to me, hon". Strangely, as the sensations of her lips on my nipples and chest fueled my lust, I heard none of my opposing partners yelling or screaming in my mind. They'd been pretty consistent up to this point, at crying or berating me during my sexual congress with any potential victim. Not this time, though.

As one might say, all was quiet on the western front.

When the whore's face had reached my belly button, she kissed around it, sending tingles up my stomach to my chest and neck. It was a feeling I used to revel in but now seemed only a means to an end, that end being my possession of her. It was unnecessary foreplay. I rolled my window up, glancing to the pimp standing at the corner of the alley, a dozen feet or so off the rear of the vehicle. He didn't seem to take notice, and I planned to lock the doors and hope he wouldn't come looking during the time I was inevitably going to be passed out. The risk was part of what aroused me about the whole situation, one in which I'd not only make this woman become my own but that her handler would be none the wiser until I was speeding off into the next district over.

I had it all mapped out. This was the plan.

And then she screamed.

I opened my eyes and looked at her, then down to my stomach where she'd been touching me. A shape was pushing through my flesh, surrounded by fingers kneading from within, knuckles rolling over each other just under the skin. And the voices, they'd returned, all of them at once. They screamed and shouted curses and obscenities.

"What the fuck!" the whore yelled, scooting back and falling out of the passenger side door.

The driver's side door opened and, before I could say anything, before I could assess what was happening to me, the pimp had driven his knife handle-deep into my gut. The pain was immediate and immense. I swatted at his face and kicked him back away from the car, shut the door and slammed the lock down. I turned the keys over in the ignition, watching a shape move around the back of the car to the passenger side. The engine revved loudly and I accelerated down the alley, the pimp and his whore left in the wet and grime behind. The open passenger door grated off of the alley wall, knocked over a recycling bin and then plowed into a homeless man just getting up from a cardboard shanty.

I emerged from the end of the alley and swung a wide right onto the street. Under the orange glow of the passing streetlamps, the knife stuck out of my belly like a thin headstone. It was only a minute or so before I started feeling lightheaded. I pulled into this here parking garage, just off of Cherry Street underneath the I-5 overpass, and sat, breathing as deeply as I could. The numb sensations of blood-loss were already flittering in my knuckles and ears. I flicked the switch for the dome light. I needed to see what was happening with the wound, how bad it was. The mounting prospect of Death approaching seemed to grow as did my mortal anxiety. I grabbed the hilt of the knife and pulled it out, and it slid from me as if it had been stuck in warm butter. I screamed from the pain. When I lifted my shirt to see the damage, my gaze was met by a three-inch wide smile that drooled dark blood down into the crotch of my pants. I leaned my head back against the headrest and began to cry.

It was then that the voices in unison cursed me and began shouting again. The mocked my weakness, the hypocrisy of the stance I'd taken over them with how I now wept at what was happening. When I felt the first wriggling sensation at the site of the wound, the strange movement just inside the sliced flesh, I ignored it, focusing more on that empty warmth spreading over me, the tingling in my limbs, and how much I didn't want to die. I thought maybe I could make it to the hospital, be saved. I didn't know where a hospital was though. I thought to use the GPS on my cell phone but a part of me needed to fully assess the damage first. I moved my hand to my eviscerated stomach and, rather than simply blood and a frayed loose aperture of skin, I felt something else protruding from the wound. My eyes looked hazily down to my stomach and there, pushing through the opening, stretching its aperture further and sending stinging shocks of agony through my core, was an entire human hand. I didn't have time to understand what was happening when the wound opened like a yawn and a forearm quickly pushed through, and then there was the rest of the arm and a mound of blood-slicked hair bulging out of it as if some sort of birth were happening.

I lost my ability to comprehend what I was seeing, my vision blurred and my focus clouded in its dwindling control. I shook my head, set the seat back so I could lay and move my hands to the wound, maneuvering my body into a fetal position. The jolt of pain that followed stretched me erect, as if I'd been electrocuted, and when I regained sight of my stomach, I saw the face of my most recent partner, gasping for air and screaming as she pushed herself from the bloody crevice in my torso. She was a hooker I'd picked up in Portland a few months back and, as she squeezed her shoulders and her breasts out of me, I was too lost in the bizarre emotions and rending sensations of pain to do anything but lay there and watch.

She fully slipped out of me, crawling over the center console toward the passenger door. And then another set of hands pushed their way through the hole now left open and gaping in my stomach. By the time the first one to exit had opened the damaged car door and leapt out into the night, whimpering hysterically but as full and alive as I'd last seen her, the second head was already on its way out of me.

I'd always wondered what carrying a child would be like, how the growth of my body and the gestation of the thing inside would feel, and then the ultimate moment in which what was inside would come sliding of me. One by one, all of them whom I'd kept within me for these years crawled their way out of me, so then I felt I somewhat finally understood. When the large gay man made his exit, feeling as if he was splitting me in half on his way out, he turned and punched me hard in the face, though I could barely feel it by that point. My senses were overwhelmed in the throes of oncoming Death and the mind-shattering pain. The man jammed his thumb into my right eye before I could lift my hands in feeble protest. I felt the eyeball pop like a grape and I screamed a mewling sound of the likes I'd never heard before, a sound that seemed distant from my perspective.

And then, the last one, who was the first, Brenna, came crawling out, crying with madness. Covered in my fluids, she shrieked into the close space of the car interior and climbed over the center console toward the open passenger door and scrambled out on shaking arms and legs.

For a brief moment, I felt a slight relief knowing that I was going to die alone, away from them, that they wouldn't get to witness the shame that was soaking my very soul. I pulled my hands up to my chest, to let them glide over my skin once more but all I felt was a limp and drained form, only my paling flesh and nothing of those I'd held within me for so long.

In the agony and defeat, it was only me I felt.

The sound of feet scampering back toward the vehicle came through the numbness of my dying and I saw Brenna reach for the knife where I'd thrown it on the floor below the glovebox. I could hardly comprehend her movements before she stuck me in the chest with it. It must've slid between some ribs because it seemed to go in easily and, with what shallow breathes I had left, I felt its razor edge serrating my inner-lung as I inhaled to cry out. The blade slipped out and came again to slide through two other ribs. There was no strength left in my arms to stop her. Her dark glistening shape fully entered back into the car, kneeling on the passenger seat. Though I could not feel them, I saw her hands reach for my neck and there they began to squeeze.

*

And now, here I am.

I am no rapist, no murderer, but I am a fiend. I've always

known it. I've come to know that I was born to be something great, as my father always told me. Yet, as all that has happened flashes before my thoughts, the very specific path that has led me to this moment, and as Brenna's hands pinch tighter around my throat, with rage in her gorgeous eyes, eyes I'd completely forgotten about, I now feel that empty space where she and the others so recently dwelt. It is bloody, it is empty, but it is hungry. It is hungry and waiting to eat me, and it knows it will have me once anoxia takes its toll.

Some things a man will take with him to the grave, things that weren't heard or felt by anyone but himself. In that lonesome space lay the true fears and true reveries of his imagination. There, the real soul waits for the experience of Death to come, and hopes that it can hold onto some semblance of what it once was as it passes on, and that, in judgement, it won't have been found wanting in fulfilling its true nature. The mirrored infinity of Death is pulling in from the outskirts of my vision, though, swallowing all the world as it closes in on my perspective, and I cannot escape that I am left hollow and feeling doubtful, doubtful of what I thought my true nature was, my true purpose. I am no longer powerful, as I had felt I was before. Rather, I am now powerless, impotent and limp, falling into that abyss I've only managed to imagine until now.

In these last seconds of life, I am dross in the face of this void.

I am nothing.

I stare into the bland bulb rooted in the ceiling of the car interior, this place of my final painful exhalation. The light is sailing further and further away, like a star being overtaken by the dark beyond the firmament, and I am being swallowed, suffocating alone in the madness of my own depravity.

Notes

"As You Wade into the River of Vermin" is original to this collection.

"Under and In and So It All Begins" is original to this collection.

"The Gate and the Star" is original to this collection.

"Master" is original to this collection and was my submission to the 'Spring Smut' challenge of my writers group.

"The Midnight Baby" is original to this collection.

"The Lights on the Other Car" is original to this collection.

"A Death to See" is original to this collection.

"Eyes Out" is original to this collection.

"The Harem Within" is original to this collection.

About the Author

Born in 1986 in the Pacific Northwest, Jordan grew up in Puyallup, about 40 miles south of Seattle. If he never saw that town again, it would be too soon. He was raised in the fabled 90's and is simply another mind trying to find meaning in the cosmic. He hopes to die staring up at a halo of evergreens.

Jordan is the author of *The Things That Grow With Us*, his debut collection of stories released in November of 2016.

jordanandersonfiction.com
Email: jordan@jordanandersonfiction.com
Twitter: @JAndersFiction

"He had accepted it. The end was contained in the beginning. But it was frightening; or, more exactly, it was like a foretaste of death, like being a little less alive. Even while he was speaking to O'Brien, when the meaning of the words had sunk in, a chilly shuddering feeling had taken possession of his body. He had the sensation of stepping into the dampness of a grave, and it was not much better because he had always known that the grave was there and waiting for him."

—*1984*, George Orwell